PRAISE FOR *POLAR VORTEX*

"The past isn't even past—and the present is tense
with conflicting desires and untold stories. What brings clarity
to this setting is Shani Mootoo's limpid prose, clean and
bracing. *Polar Vortex* is an honest, but also moving,
exploration of true intimacy."
—Amitava Kumar, author of *Immigrant, Montana*

"How to know the shifting pieces of ourselves,
how to acknowledge contradictory desires, as we are
pulled into the maelstrom of desire and memory?
Shani Mootoo's intimate new novel suspends us in
the vortex between acts of betrayal and acts of love. It is a
powerfully unsettling work from a brilliant artist."
—Madeleine Thien, Scotiabank Giller Prize–winning
author of *Do Not Say We Have Nothing*

"What a gorgeous and thrilling novel.
Beautifully crafted, with perfect form and icy-clear tone—
Shani Mootoo held me under her spell until the
shock and release of the last page!"
—Sarah Selecky, author of *Radiant Shimmering Light*

POLAR VORTEX

SHANI MOOTOO

Book*hug Press

TORONTO

FIRST EDITION

Library and Archives Canada Cataloguing in Publication

Title: Polar vortex : a novel / Shani Mootoo.
Names: Mootoo, Shani, author.
Description: First edition.
Identifiers: Canadiana (print) 20200160141 | Canadiana (ebook) 2020016015X
    ISBN 9781771665643 (softcover) | ISBN 9781771665650 (HTML)
    ISBN 9781771665667 (PDF) | ISBN 9781771665674 (Kindle)
Classification: LCC PS8576.O622 P65 2020 | DDC C813/.54—dc23

Printed in Canada

The production of this book was made possible through the generous assistance
of the Canada Council for the Arts and the Ontario Arts Council. Book*hug
Press also acknowledges the support of the Government of Canada through
the Canada Book Fund and the Government of Ontario through the Ontario
Book Publishing Tax Credit and the Ontario Book Fund.

  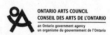

Book*hug Press acknowledges that the land on which we operate is
the traditional territory of many nations, including the Mississaugas
of the Credit, the Anishnabeg, the Chippewa, the Haudenosaunee
and the Wendat peoples. We recognize the enduring presence of many
diverse First Nations, Inuit and Métis peoples and are grateful for the
opportunity to meet and work on this territory.

For:
Jane
Shelagh
Pam
Deborah

I
THE BED

. . .

a cream-coloured kurta, the neck and cuffs of the long silk shirt trimmed in gold thread. a red dhoti. a cream-and-red turban edged in gold, from which a long curtain of pearl-like beads hangs and covers his face. around him red draperies—a ceremonial canopy. behind the canopy, walls decorated in red fabric. my eyes are lowered, focused on his cream silk slipper shoes curled at the toes. he is standing on red flowers strewn on the red carpet. people hover about, their backs to us. they are busy-busy, organizing his life, but they don't pay him, or us, attention. there is a low table inside the canopy. no, not a table, a bed. he takes my hand. we move toward the bed and lower ourselves onto it. we lie side by side, his arm across my chest. i worry people will see us like this. i want him to lie on me. i am thrusting. thrusting my body. i plead, i want him. he is holding his penis, i take hold of it, can hardly breathe, my chest aches for the release of. no, not love, sex.

everything is red. his tongue. his penis. the palms of my hands. red red red.

someone draws back the hanging cloth of the canopy, i pull away just in time and get up off the bed. drums are beaten with fury, cymbals clash, tremble, and chatter, a rhythm red and violent draws near. his soon-to-be-wife approaches, mummy-like, shrouded in flowing red and gold, marigold heads scattered ahead of her steps. i leave through a side door, looking behind me. he remains reclined, no evidence in sight of interrupted pleasure.

. . .

That dream again. In it I always want him so badly. I am shaking from my waist down, like a dog yanked off a human's leg.

I wonder if I moved about in my sleep. If Alex has any idea of the kind of dream I had lying next to her. She's already left the bed. And she's closed the door—that was considerate. She is able to navigate the house soundlessly. How does she do it? Whenever I try to shut that door quietly, the hinges squeak, the handle squawks, the lock hits the jamb loudly.

I must get out of bed. It's 7:56 a.m., much too late to put a stop to him visiting us. I have no choice now but to face him.

But he'll be facing me, too. I'm not the only culprit here. I must remember that. Odd that I'd sleep in on this of all days. But not so odd, I suppose, that I'd have dreamt of him. But this, of all dreams.

It's so quiet with the door closed. Funny, you can't hear a thing from the rest of the house, but you can hear a dog out on the street barking and, from outside the window behind the bed, a bird—at least, I think it's a bird—scurrying along the metal eavestrough. Could be a squirrel. A chipmunk maybe. Or a mouse trying to get in from the cold. We're supposed to be fine with that, supposed to expect that sort of thing living in an old farmhouse on what is technically an island. I doubt I'll ever get used to critters wanting to share space with me.

The desire I felt in the dream lingers in my body. Ripples of pleasure torture me. I'll think of Alex. I'll curl under the covers here for just a few minutes more and imagine her.

But a feeling of regret descends on me, and I take my hands from beneath the covers and pull the top sheet taut up to my chin. I wonder what she's doing. We hadn't ended the night well. Yes, that's right. There'd been all that tension. I wonder how she is this morning.

We'd come to bed, both of us, with heavy hearts. The silence between us crouched on my chest like a small animal breathing in my face. After a while, my e-book held like a wall, I wondered if I should turn and hug her, perhaps say something kind. Instead, I closed the book, and she, closing hers, too, reached up and turned off her bedside lamp. When I heard her gentle sleep-breathing, I relaxed. But for a good while I couldn't sleep. Then, just as I was finally drifting off, her perfectly aware voice ripped apart the veil.

"Was there ever anything between you? Is there anything you should tell me?"

I jolted wide awake. If playful jealousies had been part of our little games of arousal, it was too late—in the night, and in the trajectory that has led us to today—to expect this as a motive for her question. Should I answer with a clearly irritated voice, I wondered, or should I respond kindly? Should I take on a tone of indignation and ask what might she possibly be insinuating by "anything" and by "between"?

"Are you awake?" she persisted.

The pull toward sleep had disarmed me. I was too tired to properly gear myself up for a discussion that could easily deteriorate into argument. "I am now," I said, biding my time. I stared tensely into the blackened room. Another tactic was necessary. "The only thing you need to know about Prakash," I capitulated, my voice low to emphasize I'd been well on my way to sleep, "is that he's loyal. Very loyal. He doesn't drop his friends easily."

She did not respond. This woke me further, and I felt pressured to continue. I added that while I wasn't surprised he'd gotten in touch, I also wasn't worried it meant the beginning of anything—for instance, a connection we'd be obliged to carry on. Again she didn't respond. Fully awake, deciding on kindness, I softened and offered more: that was Prakash, I said—here today, gone tomorrow. Still nothing from her. If she'd picked up on my feeble attempt and the careless contradictions in it to reassure her, she didn't let on. I knew she hadn't just suddenly fallen asleep. She wanted me to speak. So even as I felt worn-out so late at night, and was struggling for the right words, I acquiesced and added gently, "You've been so—suspicious is not the word, nor skeptical, but so—so something regarding him, Alex. As if it's unthinkable that I could have an old friend who'd want to visit me. Am I that unlovable?"

From her came finally a response, and it was one that relaxed me, a soft and breathy cluster of a chortle. I turned on my side and put my arm across her. She drew it tighter, as if it were a seat belt, and grasped my hand. We lay like that for some minutes, and at last, feeling relieved, I closed my eyes. Then, just as I felt again the tug of sleep, her voice, as alert as if we were in the midst of a daytime chat, startled me: "You know, five years ago, when we came here to live, we left so much behind."

What was she getting at, I wondered. I was tempted to beg, *Do you seriously want, at this time of the night, to talk about our move here?* But gratitude for what I imagined was a switch from our previous contentious topic held me back. I gave her hand a light squeeze by way of acknowledging I'd heard her.

"I mean, we're not the same people anymore," she continued.

"Aren't you tired, Alex?" I asked.

"I'm just thinking that one can't really hold on to the past. Not if you want to move forward. We all eventually relieve ourselves of things and people no longer in our lives."

I pulled my hand from hers. Despite the heat beginning to flush my face, I made sure to keep my voice even, and asked, "So what are you saying?"

"Well, just that if we're not in touch with someone for several years, perhaps it's not a friendship worth holding on to, even if it had once been. I mean, you'll find out, won't you? But perhaps these things just take time, and letting go happens naturally. On its own."

I had to bite my lip to prevent my baser self from flaring up and announcing that Prakash was not simply any old friend, and that the history he and I shared—his part in it, my part in it—was more than reason enough for him to want to pay me a visit. But this was approaching truths and subjects I couldn't afford to unbridle.

. . .

That's why I overslept—I'd been awake most of the night stewing about Alex's assumptions and worries, and my own foolishness. Oh, man. If only I could step back in time, I'd undo this mess. Why on earth did I invite him here? Into my home. My sanctuary. Our home, Alex's and mine. But one can also ask: why did he, in the first place, contact me? It should have been clear, at least this time, that I'd meant to cut ties with him. I guess that's what happens when you simply hope people intuit what you're intending. But I couldn't have told him directly, explicitly, to bugger off and leave me alone. Of course I couldn't.

Alex has been testy ever since she learned of his visit. She knows nothing of my connection to Prakash, really, so why this fractiousness? Her discontent about his coming here has been less than playful. It amounts to insinuations, if not accusations, of a dalliance—past or present, who knows what's in her mind?— and, whether or not she's aware of it, casts aspersions on my sexuality.

It's all really unfortunate, and her manner makes me feel guilty. Doubly guilty, in fact. For asking him here, to the home I share with her, *and* for cutting him out of my life.

Alex's unease, given what she knows—and does not know— is unusual and extreme. I ask if something else is bothering her, but it's always that uninviting two-word answer she delivers: "The book." Or: "My work." One and the same, really. Or she just stares at me blankly, unnervingly.

And when Prakash gets here, what will I say to him about why I so obviously tried to snip him out of the picture?

If he is to arrive right at noon, then he's probably just getting in his car for the three-hour drive, if you count rest stops on the highway and all, before he even crosses the bridge onto the island. He doesn't drink coffee. We have black tea in a tin somewhere. It's old, but he didn't used to be fussy. I wonder what he's like today.

. . .

Alex has an unfathomable memory for even the most inconsequential of details. What was it she asked when I told her my friend Prakash had gotten in touch? *The Ugandan guy you met in university?* Something like that. I'd mentioned him briefly, one time, and that was a couple days after she and I first met. One time, that was all, six years ago, and yet she remembered.

We were sitting on the couch, with Elliot, good dog that he was, possessively and conveniently sprawled across a good half of the seat, and Alex and I were obliged to sit against each other at one end. A throw pillow was wedged between her and me. I remember my mind fixed on the small pillow, and how the act of removing it seemed too much of an announcement. We've joked about that since. It turns out that she, too, was focused on removing it but sensed my hesitation and didn't want to "scare" me off.

We were flipping through a photo album she'd pulled off one of my bookshelves. I had one arm on the back of the couch behind her, my body angled toward her, Elliot pressed against me and snoring. I can still feel on the tips of my fingers the slight contact they made with the fine stray wool fibres of her sweater. We came to a group photo of my university table-tennis league teams, about twelve of us. Fiona, my "roommate" at the time (we didn't know others like us; hard to imagine nowadays, but it was true back then), and I were pressed against each other. She and I had relished the idea that, despite facing a camera, the private heat and intensity between us would be known only to us, yet immortalized for all time. This was our secret. Our friend Prakash stood on the other side of me, smiling broadly, giving the photographer his trademark V sign, his two fingers curled just enough to assure that his peace was benign, not militant.

"You look so young. You look like a young boy. How old were you?" Alex asked. This pleased me. The photo was taken in our fourth and final year, I told her. I was twenty-two or so. Alex didn't pay Prakash any attention, but she honed right in on Fiona. "The woman next to you. Who is she?" she asked, her forefinger tracing the seam that joined Fiona and me. I was impressed and, at the same time, made shy by the obvious perceptiveness in the question. There was expectation in her tone. I laughed guiltily and, nevertheless, asked why she was asking. She said I was between two people, a man and a woman, and the woman and I seemed to be leaning into each other. Of course, once she said this, I, too, saw how obvious, how intentional-seeming, such closeness was, and I saw for the first time the looks on our faces. I became in that instant a stranger looking at a found photograph and saw the half-smile and deviousness, a kind of fear and daring at once. And I saw how naive we were, how reckless, in posing so intimately, but more importantly I thought Alex was disarmingly perceptive.

And, Alex continued, it would not have occurred to her that I would have been involved with the man.

Alex and I hadn't yet slept together, but the air in my little living room had become so electric I knew I wasn't the only one with it on the brain. I found myself telling Alex that Fiona and I had met in a first-year class and decided to rent an apartment

21

together, that within days of doing so we became lovers, my first time, her first and only—at least at that time—with a woman. We remained lovers throughout our university years, I said, the wistfulness in my voice hopefully pointing to the unforgotten sensations of first-time love.

"First time?" asked Alex.

"Every time," I remember responding, grinning.

She twisted her lips and smiled at the same time, and said, "Come on. You must have been in your late teens, early twenties? Was she the first person?"

I was too shy to simply tell her yes, Fiona was indeed the first. I quickly explained that when I was growing up on my little island in the Caribbean, women from families like mine remained girls in their family's care until they were married, regardless of their age. You were so sheltered, so watched in my kind of family—an Indian family—that unless you were wayward or just stupidly brave, you didn't get to flirt or experience sexual intimacy with another person until you were married, or, if it was in the cards for you, you left home and went to another country where, in the case of people from families like mine, you attended university—which allowed you more freedom than you'd ever imagined possible. And what do you do with freedom like that? You learn to kiss and you learn to fuck. You learn what's possible, you experiment, and you figure out in the dorms or in your little bachelor apartment off campus what you like to do and to whom, and what you like to have done to you, and by whom, who you are in bed, who you can and can't be. All of that, a vital part of your university education abroad. I laughed coyly when I said this. She didn't think it funny. She nodded soberly. When you went back home, I con-

22

tinued, you went back a different person, with more than one degree under your belt. Still, she wasn't amused. If you weren't so stupid as to marry while you were away, despite the paper degree you had to show off when you returned home, they'd still call you a girl, and you wouldn't be considered a woman until you married—but what a girl you'd become! She smiled.

So, yes, first time, first person. And it was magic—frighteningly magical, I repeated in a quiet, pensive voice. Alex had angled her body slightly to face me. "You?" I asked.

"Elementary school, in Montreal." The throw pillow was definitely an intrusion. "There was a girl, from a very rich and powerful family. She instructed us to touch her and each other. I think about that now," Alex told me, "and I have to wonder how she knew."

I feigned a nervous chuckle and said, "But you don't really count that, do you?"

"So the real first time, then," she answered, "was when I was fifteen. A boy, my age, from my high school. We did it on a couch in the basement of his parents' home."

There *we* were on a couch, and I stopped myself from the tempting crudeness of drawing a parallel. Alex examined the photograph more carefully, and I imagined she was trying to picture Fiona and me, our mouths pressed together, tongues touching, the heat of our bodies against one another. As I was whipping up something between Alex and me, I was aware that we were being stared at by a broadly grinning Prakash waving his weak V-shaped fingers. I decided not to mention anything about him, but elaborated that it was with Fiona I'd experienced that first-time sensation of ascending, ascending, and ascending yet further, and then, that sudden dive-bombing feeling, your body shattering into a trillion shards of twinkling, long-dying light.

In a whisper, Alex asked if I'd remained friends with Fiona, or with any of the other team members, and although I didn't want to get into a conversation about Prakash, I said, "Him," landing my forefinger on his face, and, for some reason, unable to leave it at that, as if it were the most important thing about him, I answered that he was our friend, a refugee from Idi Amin's Uganda.

"You're still friends? What's his name?" she asked.

"Sort of. Prakash," I said, and she left it there.

I didn't tell her that in the last months of our university years, Fiona had begun to have an affair. With a man. A student named Stan. Had I embarked on this story, I might have told her then that it was the man in the photo who'd helped me through that wretched period and many others, but I did not want to derail the moment with tales of woe and disappointments.

· · ·

Yes, Fiona, Prakash, and me, this odd threesome, as he liked to joke about us. We were, for a while, a team. But despite what she and I thought of as a definable intensity in our closeness, he seemed oblivious, and there was never a reason to explicitly explain ourselves. When the relationship ended because of her involvement with Stan, Fiona spent very little time in our apartment. Those were dark days for me, days I felt I could die. The phone would ring, and I'd listen as a message was being left on the answering machine, hoping it was Fiona. But, broken-hearted and desolate if it was anyone else, including Prakash, I couldn't bring myself to pick up the phone.

One afternoon, an insistent knocking on the door tore me from sleep. "I know you're in there. Please open, Priya," he pleaded. He wouldn't leave. I had no choice but to let him in. He leaned against the shut door and looked at me still in my pyjamas. "What's happening to you?" he asked, his brows creased with concern. "I phoned yesterday from the booth out-side. I could see you moving about, but you wouldn't pick up the phone. Were you sleeping? Are you ill?" He bypassed me and walked to the kitchen, where he put the kettle on. He stayed until late into the evening, me lying on the couch as if I had the flu, my feet in his lap, neither of us speaking much. He ordered a pizza over the phone and had it delivered. I nibbled the pointed end of a single wedge, more to satisfy him than any hunger. To get him to leave, I had to promise that I'd eat more of the remaining pizza, and that I'd get up the following morning and attend classes, which I'd been missing.

He knew by then that Fiona was spending time elsewhere, but since nothing more had ever been explained to him, he put down my sudden depression to a natural kind of loneliness, to not having family nearby, or a good substitute for family, which he said Fiona had once been to me. It was he, then, who, more than a few times, came around and comforted me as I cried, he who encouraged me to get out of bed and out of the apartment. He who came and prepared meals for me and tried to get me to eat. It was as if he had decided to be the family he thought I needed. He seemed to want nothing in return, and I began to look forward to his visits. Throughout this time I never even hinted to him about Fiona and me.

. . .

I'm certain it wouldn't have been wise to have told Alex during these last days that yes, he had at one time, but only briefly, been interested. She knows little about the years that immediately followed my emigration to Canada once my university tenure had been completed. There's just never been any reason to get into the details with her of those early days in this country.

I'd found lodging in city-subsidized housing in Toronto. Prakash and I had not lost touch but we weren't as close as before. I had embarked on a practice of artmaking as diligently as anyone pursuing any other kind of career but was, of course, making no money at it, always running out of paint and canvas, and often couldn't pay the bills. My kitchen cupboards tended to be empty, save for cans of ravioli and packages of ramen. Prakash arrived at my apartment one day, unannounced, just after I'd hung up from a phone call with a family member back home who responded to my appeals for financial help—perhaps one too many—advising that I get an ordinary job like normal people, or return at once and marry a man who could take care of me while I pursued my "hobby," as they called it.

Seeing the state I was in, Prakash held my face in his hands and whispered earnestly, "Your greatness as an artist is being heralded in this very moment. Others can't see it, but I can. Do you trust me? Let me help you. We can do this together." I was curious, and my protests were weak, and he easily brushed them away as he carried on with his mission. He tore a sheet of paper from the drawing pad on my dining table, pulled a pen from his shirt pocket, and, handing it to me, directed me to itemize the sums of my rent, utilities, groceries, paints, canvas, and everything else I needed to see me through a month's living. Then he asked me to write down my income. I drew an egg and, while I shaded it in, crosshatching with his blue ink pen, he went to one of the several stacks of paintings leaning against a wall and flipped through it. He pulled out a small canvas board on which I'd made a study in oil of two green glass bottles and a clear one on a tabletop in front of a window through which blue skies topped an emerald-green field. He didn't ask, but announced he was taking it in exchange for the sum of that month's needs, which, he said, would one day—probably after I'd died, he added, laughing—be seen to have been a bargain. That was the first painting I ever sold, and I made it through that month.

After that, I sort of fell, little by little, into him for comfort and support. Yes, there were moments over the course of our continuing friendship he acted as if I were his girlfriend, and although I didn't exactly push him away, I didn't cave either. If I'd long ago told Alex any of this, surely she'd have understood the predicament I had often found myself in as an artist trying to make a go of it on so many fronts and all on my own. Surely she'd have sympathized and seen that I couldn't, after all, have made it in this country entirely alone. Or perhaps she'd have seen something more sinister.

The point is, I hadn't let her in on any of this, and to do so now would be nothing short of foolish.

. . .

It's true, there were times I did feel something for him—love, you could say. But this word *love*, it is a lightning rod that seems, especially in this instance, to have only one meaning. It is so much less nuanced than it should be. I did love him, how could I not have? It is true he had stronger feelings toward me, but mine for him were only ever sisterly.

Well, I suppose one could say my actions were not *always* sisterly. In a situation such as he and I were in, both for the first time in our lives away from home and trying to make it on our own, it surely isn't unreasonable that I would have wondered whether or not my feelings for him were this romantic love I could see he felt for me. There were times, naturally, I had to try and see. For me those times were clarifying, but I guess for him they were confusing.

Alex tells people it was my confidence, my unwavering sense of self, that attracted her to me. In the early days I'd tell her it was nothing but well-practised posturing. Calm on the surface but paddling like hell beneath, I'd say, laughing. But she'd think I was being modest and this, too, she found attractive. And today, if I reveal that this man was so very much a part of my life, what would she think? Discretions and half-truths were par for the course in those early days when she and I were courting each other. But how would they be perceived now?

With her I indulged in the fantasy of having always been fierce enough to stand firm against the norms of society and expectations of family. She liked this. And so I went along with the uncontested assumption that I'd never actually been interested in being with a man. I can't, therefore, admit to her there were times I played the Indian woman to Prakash's Indian man.

If I did reveal any of this to Alex, it would never be the same between us. I can't risk that. We've built a comfortable life together. I don't want to up-end it.

But I'm risking something, aren't I, by hosting him here?

. . .

The dream was just that: a dream. In waking hours I haven't had that kind of desire for him. Not for a long time, anyway. And now, this past night, messing with my head, my body.

Okay, I guess I'm really awake. I should get up.

But it's cold. And there's enough time before he comes. I don't really have to hurry just yet.

. . .

That night on the sofa, when Alex first saw the photo of Fiona and Prakash and me, I told her I'd been on a student visa, and when the term ended, I had to return home—but having experienced that kind of love and the physical expression of it, not permitted back there on that Caribbean island, in my family's home, I knew I could not stay. When, a year later, I emigrated to Canada, the man in the photo and I reconnected; he, a more practical type than I, became a guiding light as I tried to figure out how to live on my own, how to survive on the income from temporary, low-paying jobs while I amassed a portfolio of paintings in the hope of carving out a niche for myself in the city's art scene. I did not add that, yes, he had continued to hope for more than friendship, and that every so often I had to remind him that anything more than platonic was unlikely between us.

Staring at him in the photo, I felt like a traitor downplaying to Alex his presence in my life, and I believe this made me careless—and my mouth runneth over. I found myself adding a thing or two more, albeit in a self-deprecating tone, as if it were slightly funny and preposterous: he used to be "sort of interested" in me, but I set him straight. We used to be in touch occasionally, I told her, but it had been a while since I'd heard from him. Discretions and half-truths, pirouetting on a dime even as I feared my caginess was much too apparent. But Alex didn't seem to notice.

. . .

People have long and complicated lives, and it behooves every one of us to understand and accept that the older we are when we meet our life partner, the more likely that each of us will be dragging baggage, and that we've only been able to grow into the person we became because of that baggage—by having fucked up and learned, fucked up and learned, again and again, and the graver the mistakes we made and the heavier the loads we carried, the bigger the leaps we would have been forced to perform, and it was those very leaps that made us today into better, stronger, more resilient people. Therefore, to go announcing one's mistakes long after they'd been made and lessons had been learned is counterproductive to the ongoing project of creating a better or grander person out of oneself.

Alex wasn't at all curious about the man standing on the other side of me. She shifted her body on the couch, a little movement that caused her to lean ever so slightly against me. It took my breath away—the feel of her, the communication of desire in such a slight rearrangement. She drew the throw pillow out from between us. Elliot, as if he knew, rose up, did his little yoga dog pose, and let himself down off the couch.

Recalling what followed the dance of Alex's shift and pillow removal—and Elliot's theatrical approval—waves of new desire arouse me again. I'd very much like to remain here under the bedsheets and relive that first time with Alex.

But instead, images, unsolicited, of Prakash inside the red canopy, the low bed, the red petals, flood my mind. My heart races, but only with fear.

What oh what on earth was I thinking? Why did I ask him here?

. . .

The day I told Alex that Prakash would be coming to spend a night with us in our house, she was perplexed. She hadn't realized, she said, that the man in the photo and I had all the while been communicating. We hadn't, I told her. Just after I opened my Twitter account, he saw I was active on it and wrote me. She was instantly incensed. "You expect me to be happy that a strange man will come and spend a night here with us?"

I was taken aback, of course, and protested, perhaps too much, which then set the tone for all interactions between her and me regarding him. "What do you mean? He's one of my oldest friends," I said, then corrected myself: "Not one of. He *is* my oldest friend. I've known him longer than anyone else in this country. Longer than anyone I'm still in touch with."

She lobbed back, "Maybe so, but you never talk about him. As far as I can tell, he's not part of your life. And he is a stranger to me. He can stay at a bed and breakfast. You can find one for him."

"Oh, come on. He was once one of my closest friends; when he asked, I couldn't say no. We really were very close. I *didn't* want to say no. In any case, it's only for one night."

"And what do you mean by that—*really very close*?"

"Oh, good God. As close as a lesbian and a straight man could be." I rolled my eyes and laughed. I looked to the ceiling, then added dramatically, "Don't be ridiculous."

"You should've asked me first, Priya," she said.

The truth is, when I invited him it was an impulsive gesture and I didn't expect he'd come all the way down here. When he accepted, I was taken aback. I recognized at once that I'd gotten on a train that was travelling at breakneck speed and I found myself unable to uninvite him.

"It would never have occurred to me you'd mind," I said. "You know, I'd never tell you that one of your friends couldn't stay with us, especially if it's just for one night." She didn't answer, so I continued. "If you're really asking me to cancel with him, you're asking me to make a fool of myself."

I stormed past her, out of the main part of the house and to my studio. At once I remembered the installation—three altar-pieces made for a gallery exhibition that had taken place years before I knew Alex—based on that old recurring dream, the one I awoke to just a short while ago. Pieces of it—three dark brown beer bottles—are stored on a shelf, there for all to see. I'd removed the original labels from the bottles and made my own for each. Alex had once, a good while ago, held up one of the bottles and examined the label, but didn't pay it more than cursory attention. I had observed this but offered no explanation. The label on the bottle she held is a composite photograph of a bride and groom standing around a Hindu-like altar, a square box filled with dirt low on the ground. At the centre of the altar a fire burns brightly. The bride wears a red wedding sari. Behind them is a wall of red paper decorated with gold paisley. The marrying couple is arranged so they seem to be praying together, their eyes fixed on the fire in the altar. Prakash is the man in the photo. I dressed up and posed for the photo of the woman, but my face is hidden behind a veil.

Had Alex forgotten she'd seen this, I wondered. Had she not made the connections? What on earth was I thinking? Then, and now? My heart beat fast as I gathered the bottles and stuffed them quickly into a box, taped it, and shoved it under a table.

I decided then to try to immerse myself in work. But the tension between us had exhausted me. I kept trying to recall how many times she'd come into the studio lately and if I'd noticed her paying those bottles attention. I could not bring myself to focus, to uncap a jar, to lift a brush. Instead, worn out, I turned my easel so the canvas on it faced the couch into which I slumped. I stared at my half-finished painting of two willow trees bent to meet each other and contemplated it. Where their limbs arced, they were gnarled and required a palette of many shades of brown, from ochres and green browns to deep umbers. And where the two met in the centre, there was a profusion of lemon-like greens. The task was to keep the trees separate and yet in the middle create some new life out of the two. But I was too jangled to concentrate. All I did was mull over the unpleasantness between Alex and me. After some time, I heard her approach. I don't know why I didn't want her to see me half-sitting, half-lying on the couch, but I hastened toward a shelf—well away from the table under which I'd pushed the box—on which are stored paint jars and buckets of knives and brushes. She came through the doors, ignoring, I noted, the work on the easel, and without missing a beat she said, "Is he still interested in you?"

A tickle in my cheeks threatened me. It was as if I'd been waiting for her to come in after me. I was dizzy with relief that I'd had the mind to hide the installation bottles. I turned and faced her directly, but then burst out laughing. This seemed to anger her, and she snapped, "Are you interested in him?"

I tried hard to control the chuckling coming involuntarily out of my mouth, the self-consciousness in it, but it was difficult, and I had to angle away from her. I turned my back and fiddled with jars of paint. I reminded her that he and I had a very long friendship, which would not have been possible in the face of such a complication, and I asked if she could honestly imagine, knowing me as well as she did, that I might be interested in anyone but her. In typical fashion, she persisted.

"Priya, I want to talk to you," she snapped. She didn't, for what felt like an eternity, say any more. I could feel her eyes on my back as I culled jars of similar colours in pyramid-shaped piles. All the while I held my breath. Then she said, "Look at me, Priya."

I faced her, my shoulders slumped and my mouth twisted in a show of fatigue.

"We're becoming strangers, Priya. We're growing apart. What's happened to us? We're not communicating anymore. It's as if I don't know you. As if you hide things from me, don't always tell me what's going on."

Well, who doesn't hide things? I wanted to ask. I didn't, of course. But *strangers*? What did she mean by that? Well, she's a fine one to bark. She's the one who's always preoccupied by her work. *The book. My work. The book. My work.* Long before all this commotion about Prakash. She's the one who goes by herself on weekends—weekends when she and I could be together—to our friends' cottage on the Shield to work on the bloody book. When she comes back, there's always a distance between us. Her head still in the work, I guess, and me peeved she prefers to go up to such a beautiful part of the province without me. I distract her when I'm there, she says. Well, it's true: there are walks to be had among the white pines, kayaking along the shore among the trumpeter and mute swans, et cetera, and I am not a loner—cultural difference, I suppose—so I prefer to share these things with someone, and yes, I guess I can be a nuisance when she's trying to think and write. And that's the point. We're not on the same page about the kinds of things we want to do, about doing "extracurricular" things together. Maybe more like roommates than strangers. I suppose that's just splitting hairs.

But *strangers*? Perhaps she was suggesting she saw some sort of bigger problem between us. I glared at her, a look of incredulity on my face, then half turned and picked up a crusty old palette. With a palette knife I began to frantically scrape it clean, flecks of plasticized paint curling, flying, sticking with static to my clothing. I wanted to yell that there wasn't any problem and to stop creating one. And that once he'd come and gone, she'd see we were good. Yes, she'd see that. We're fine. We're good.

Unable to find my voice, I dropped the two items on the table in immense irritation. As if that were an admission from me, she, relentless, carried on. "So is there something you're not saying? If you haven't been in touch with him in all this time, why do *you* want to start back up a friendship with him? Out of the blue. Tell me what you're not telling me, Priya."

It was as if she wanted me to say that I had indeed had an intimate relationship with him, or that I had been interested in him, or that he was coming down here so he and I could begin something illicit. As if she wanted me to destroy all that she

39

and I had, right there and then. I went to the easel and dragged it back to the painting station, then walked past her to the doorway, where I turned and answered, "Out of the blue, yes. It's called social media, Alex. It makes people go in search of their past lives. Of their past selves. Prakash and I never stopped being friends. Our lives got busy and we faded away from one another. Leaving the city to move here, we—you and I—gave up a great deal, including certain connections, and his was one of the friendships I ended up neglecting. I'd always expected he and I would somehow, sometime, somewhere reconnect. I mean, it's a small world. And indeed, we've reconnected, for better or for worse, and there's nothing to be done about it. It doesn't have to be like this between us, you know. You're the one creating all this distance. You used to admire, you'd say, my attention to friends and to family relationships. What's happened? Why have you become so cold, so distant? Strangers? Yes, perhaps, but why? Is there something *you're* not saying?"

I wanted to add that if she was so peeved she should just leave for the weekend, go up to the cottage on the lake and work there. Stay out of our way. But I would have hated it if she were actually to have left me here with him. Anyway, the cottage had been closed for the winter ever since Thanksgiving weekend.

I left her in my studio and waited for her to follow me back into the house, and I waited for the comeback, but there was none. Nevertheless, I held my breath.

. . .

Days later, she and I, in the TV room. The TV was on but the volume was off. The TV's light and colour emissions were disconcertingly erratic. I held my laptop on my lap and was reading an article, and she, sitting next to me, seemed engrossed in something on her electronic reader. Suddenly, apropos of nothing (well, that's not exactly true, is it? It's more like apropos of an elephant named Prakash in the room), she broke the silence to ask what work he did. I didn't know about the present, I muttered as I tried to keep focused on the laptop screen, but last I knew he was designing software for one of the big banks. "Great," she answered. "Scintillating weekend that'll be."

I inhaled loudly, exhaled loudly, and shook my head in irritation, but I didn't say anything. I could almost hear her staring at the silent TV screen. I closed my laptop and, aiming the remote at the television, began to scroll through the channels. I stopped on a travelogue about Prague and increased the volume.

But Alex doesn't give up easily. She said, "Can we talk for a moment?"

I emphatically aimed the remote, made a show of pressing the Mute button, and dropped it on the couch between us with just enough intention to suggest irritation, but not enough to be hostile.

"Seriously," she said. "Is he single?"

"Why are you so threatened by him?" I didn't mean to raise my voice.

"Threatened? Should I be? And don't raise your voice at me."

Raising it a bit more, I said, "I didn't raise my voice." I lowered it, but the words that followed sounded harsh. "This island is in all the Ontario destination magazines. He found out I live down here. Two birds, one stone. I'm sure it's as simple as that. Look, it's not strange or weird or odd. At least, not to me, and I should know."

She ignored my tone and reworded the unanswered part of her question: "Is he married?"

"Last I knew, he was," I allowed. I couldn't imagine Prakash leaving his wife. Perhaps I should have simply said yes. That might have tamed the topic. But I actually and really didn't know for sure, and it was one of those times when I was—as I can be—perversely drawn to the taunting inherent in vagueness.

"Does he have children?" she asked.

"Yes. Three." It was a trap, a ridiculously small trap I'd nevertheless fallen into.

"As you said, the island is a holiday destination. Everyone knows that," she responded. "So why isn't he coming with his family?"

I glared at her. "How on earth am I supposed to know?"

Has she detected something in my responses, in my behaviour, I wondered, that might have caused her to question me in such a manner? It is unusual for her. She's never even expressed jealousy when I've been just a little flirty with a woman. She might have curled her mouth, but not shown actual worry. Why on earth would she be worried about a man? Is there something about me that I myself can't see that makes her think I'm not as committed to my sexuality as I profess to be? It unsettles me. It makes me angry. Sometimes I feel as if she doesn't know me. Doesn't understand me. Doesn't trust me. And in other moments I feel as if she wants to push me away. It really had not occurred to me that asking him down here would drive such a wedge between us. Or is there a wedge I haven't noticed?

We've been living together almost half a dozen years, but there are times I look at Alex's face in repose and realize I have no idea what goes on in her head unless she actually tells me. And if I were to ask her what is on her mind, how do I know if what she'd tell me is the truth? I can't know. And vice versa. We just have to trust. Or believe. There's a difference between these two, isn't there? I wonder what she really sees of me that she doesn't say out loud.

Do I speak in my dreams?

Last night, did my body shudder in sleep? When I go out of the room this morning, what exactly awaits me, pray?

. . .

I wonder what Prakash will see of me when he gets here? People used to think, when we were youngsters, that we were sister and brother—no doubt because of our race. We certainly didn't look alike. I wonder what relationship people would imagine there was between us if they saw us walking side by side on the street. How I wish things were simpler between him and me; I do miss the times we had that were good, and there were many of those. He was always doing things to prove to me he wasn't as conventional as I used to tell him—in a teasing way—he was. I remember we once took an extra-large pizza, always vegetarian for him, of course, to the beach in the east end of the city. We sat on the sand on a straw mat and ate two slices each. After, while we watched a group of people play volleyball, he broke the remainder of the pizza into bite-sized pieces, which he dropped in a plastic bag he'd pulled from his pocket. I showed some feigned disgust that he was destroying more than two-thirds of a good pizza, and with his bare hands, too, but he ignored me. When he was finished, he wiped his hands in a white handkerchief from his back pocket and suggested we take a walk at the water's edge. Every few steps, he took a handful of pieces of pizza from the bag and dropped them on the sand behind us, and in no time a fluctuating line of screaming gulls were dive-bombing around us and nipping at our heels. The gulls realized the food was in the bag and some actually began to attack it in his hand held high above his head. It was quite hair-raising, and eventually we had to run to try and get away from them, but we were near tears with laughter, too, even as I knew better than to feed birds such food. If Alex knew we'd done such a thing, she would likely not see the silliness or the fun in it. She'd probably wonder how I could have condoned feeding pizza to gulls. I wonder if he does such silly things still.

. . .

The day Alex and I sat in front of the muted television, I decided after some prickly silence between us to retreat to my studio and build stretchers. I could barely concentrate on what I was doing, my mind fixed on what I might have, could have, or should have said to her, analyzing every nuance in the words she spoke to me. Distracted to the point of making mistakes in my measurement with the stretchers, I decided to return to the main part of the house and speak with her again. She had not moved from the sofa—which I understood to mean she was not finished with the conversation and was waiting right there for me. I sat next to her and put my hand on her knee. I grabbed the kneecap firmly. "Alex, you can't possibly imagine there'd be anything to worry about. I mean, look at me. Am I the type? Seriously. We're *not* strangers, Alex. Even if someone were interested in me, I'd have to be available, and I'm not."

She stared at my hand on her knee. For some painful moments she said—and did—nothing. Then she put one forefinger on my hand and tapped it once. She got up and said she needed to get some coffee. That was that. At least my assurances changed the mood.

. . .

"I guess that's the thing about getting older, isn't it?" Alex said. We'd been chatting, just days ago, pleasantly at last, as if all was well between us, and then she came at it from what she might have thought of as slightly higher ground: "We start searching for anyone and everyone we used to know in our younger days. That's what social media has done to us. It makes us imagine we can create this expansive story, this full picture, of our lives, stitch every single recorded moment of our pasts and presents together seamlessly. Everyone's an artist these days, creating self-portraits, portraits via social media of their world."

Now what, I thought. But I didn't bite, and so she just came right out with it.

"We're different, Priya. You and I. In regards to our pasts, we only know what we tell each another. You have more in common with this man than you have with me. Isn't that so? You have history with him. You and I, we don't share a past. I'm impressed that he, a straight married man, the father of three children, would come all the way down here to seek you out after so many years, and he intends to spend a night. What doesn't make sense is that he'd come on his own, without his family. This is unusual for an Indian man, isn't it? What does his wife think of all of this, I wonder. And I have to ask—I'm just saying—why you've encouraged, or allowed, this. I think it's a bit much, don't you?"

This did not deserve my defensiveness, but I couldn't stop myself. "For God's sake, Alex. What? Yes, I had a life before you.

So had you before me. A good part of it in different countries. There's a lot we can't know about each other. Am I supposed to just chop off my past? Is this a prison I'm in? Are we so tied to each other that we can't have any thoughts or feelings or ideas or friendships that aren't shared? Why won't you accept that an enduring and platonic relationship between a straight man, a straight Indian man, and a lesbian, as unconventional as it might be, might simply be refreshing? And how do you expect me to know what his wife thinks? I can't imagine he'd come down here if it weren't fine with her. Enough now. Seriously. Leave it alone."

But she wouldn't. "One of the differences between us, Priya, is that your boundaries are far more fluid than mine." I let her continue as she launched into her elaborate explanation. "You come from a place where family and friends are in each other's lives every day. You miss your family in Trinidad, your friends in Toronto, your food from back home, the constant closeness, the ceaseless chatter between people. I left my family because I wanted independence. I don't need to hold on to the past. I left Toronto for peace and quiet and to be left alone to think. Where you come from, no one's an acquaintance—everyone's a friend. And you're bringing this into our home. You should have asked me. You should have asked. You're in a relationship. You're not the only one living in this house. You can't simply do whatever you want."

What I heard loud and clear was the insinuation that I had to ask permission to invite someone to my own home. "So, this *is* a prison," I said. Then I added, "We live as equals in this house, and I don't need permission from anyone to have my friends here. We might be different, but room has to be made to allow for *both* our differences."

That night she slept in the guest room upstairs, and I in our bed on the ground floor. I listened as she moved about restlessly. I thought I heard her speaking, and imagined she'd called her sister in Florida looking for sympathy. I tried to hear and though I was sure she'd been speaking, after a couple minutes there was no more such sound, and I assumed it was crying I'd heard. I wanted to go upstairs and comfort her, ask her to come back down and sleep with me, but I didn't. It was not a good sleep for either of us.

An incident surfaces that I thought I'd put out of my mind for good: our last year of university. Why must I be reminded, now of all times? We were youngsters, him and me, just getting to know ourselves. Fiona had begun her thing with Stan, I was falling apart, and Prakash was trying to gather up and put together my broken pieces. A long weekend was approaching. Our classmates were all preparing to travel to their parents, or taking group trips here or there, and he and I were on our own, with no plans. Days before the holiday, he showed up with airplane tickets that would take us to his parents' house on the Atlantic coast. As he described the various places we'd visit, the beaches and coves, the lighthouses, my spirits rose. An adventure was just the antidote I needed. I flew with him, lighter than I had been in weeks, to visit his parents on the coast.

Our first evening there, they invited two other couples who lived in a nearby town to have dinner with us, older people who had travelled on the same plane with them from Uganda. Prakash's mother had made samosas and pakoras, and the smells of the meal cooking in the kitchen reminded me of my parents' home. Although they all, including Prakash, launched frequently into Gujarati, which I could not understand, the talking and excited shouting over each other, the slapping of their palms on their thighs when they burst into laughter, made me homesick. The guests fussed over Prakash, hailing him throughout the evening as a brilliant and talented young man. They wanted to hear about the university and about the students in his classes. They seemed genuinely impressed by him, and I felt they were eager to let me know how well they thought of him. He was delightedly embarrassed to be so cajoled in front of me. At the table, we ate an endless meal of curries and Indian breads that were different than Trinidad-style Indian foods. They ate Indian-style, and I didn't mind being the brunt of teasing as one of the guests repeatedly tried to instruct me to use the tips of the fingers of one hand to corral my food and lift it to my mouth. We were from different cultures, different countries, and they spoke their language half the time—but how comfortable I felt with them.

Then, later, after the guests had left and we were cleaning up, to my surprise and, at first, amusement, Prakash's parents treated me like their future daughter-in-law. His mother kept hugging me, telling me how glad she was to finally meet this friend her son always spoke of. She wanted to know about my parents, how long their families had been in Trinidad, and was surprised and disappointed that I didn't know exactly from where in India my ancestors had come. She sat me down at the dining table and showed me photographs of older family members in India and friends from their Uganda days, and his father kept looking at Prakash and me, nodding and grinning. I decided to play along and imagined that later Prakash and I would share a good laugh about it.

That night, after his parents had gone to bed, he invited me to see his room. I had spent a great deal of time alone with him in my apartment, and being in his bedroom should not have felt any different, but it did. I imagined his parents, old-world people I recognized from my own background, would not have been pleased if they knew he and I—regardless of their hopes— were alone in his room, and so it felt as if we were children doing something we weren't supposed to. No more than five minutes had passed when he became distracted, unlike the man I knew at university. He went over to his bed and lay on it, leaving me standing by his desk. I remember him calling me to sit on his bed. I felt unsure, but I went over. After some unpleasant fumbling on his part, I, appalled, left his room swiftly and went to the one in which his father had put my suitcase. I knew then that I had to tell him about my sexuality. The following morning, after a sleepless night, I rose early, dressed, and went out into the hall- way of the house. No one seemed to be moving about. I tiptoed in the still, dark house to the door of his room and tapped. I could hear him rush from his bed to the door. He opened it, shirtless and half-hidden behind it, and held his hand out for mine. I backed away and said, "No. We need to talk."

He opened the door wider, beckoning me still to enter.

"No, not here," I said. "Let's go somewhere. Let's go for a drive. I'll wait on the verandah for you."

I did not want to say what was on my mind while he was driving, and the silence between us in his father's car was unpleasant. As we drove, no destination having been decided on, I kept wanting to say something, anything, to quell the tension between us. I thought to comment on how beautiful the early- morning light was. At university, to get around the town we tended to use public transportation or to walk, and I had never been driven by him before, so I thought to commend him on his good driving skills. Or to ask about birds of the region. But anything that came to mind seemed false, like a pretense.

Not too soon, we came upon a provincial park. A sign pointed to a viewpoint on a protrusion overlooking a picturesque bay. He pulled into a parking space, and we got out. From the top there seemed to be a straight drop to the water, but closer to the edge a path came into view, and once we were on it, what had seemed like a cliff turned out to be a slope of wide, well-groomed switchbacks that led down to a bay and a beach. I took the lead almost at a canter, and he kept pace, but a little behind. There was no one else on the beach, and as the sun rose, the seawater turned from sharp braiding threads of gold to glistening silver, the cold wind settled down, and the air warmed. We headed to the lone picnic table. I sat on the bench so I faced the water, and he took the opposite one, the table between us. I could not look at him. Staring out to the horizon, I felt his eyes on me. I had never before told anyone I was gay. I was trembling. I wanted to go to his side of the table, sit next to him and rest my head on his shoulder, hold on to him and cry. I wanted to tell him how much I loved Fiona, and how much I cherished his friendship. I felt fatigued as my entire future flashed before me and I decided I should simply curl my body into his and give myself over to him. I looked from the distant horizon to his eyes, to his lips, and I imagined his mouth on mine, and then in my mind I saw Fiona's face, her lips, her grey-blue eyes, and it was this that broke me—or perhaps strengthened me. As if taking a running plunge into the cold waves ahead, I blurted out in a shaking voice, "I am not interested in being with a man."

"I know," he said.

Had he already suspected? How, when I thought I'd been so careful, did he know, and if so, then why had he tried to be intimate with me the night before?

He answered my unspoken questions when he said, with sudden confidence, "In time. Don't worry about it. I should have let you come to me first."

I stopped him and said, "No, you don't understand. I mean, I don't want to be with a man. Any man. Ever. It's not just you. It's not just at this time."

He stared blankly at me. I could read nothing on his face nor in his posture.

"I am gay," I whispered.

After some prickly moments of nothing but the sound of waves crashing and wind rolling into the trees on shore, he shook his head and asked, "How do you know?"

I felt my face flush. "What do you mean? I know myself."

"But have you ever been with a man?" he asked hesitantly.

I knew if I answered that I hadn't, I'd subject myself to a certain line of logic and reasoning, but I was too flustered to respond otherwise. I said, "No. But that's because I don't want to. Look, I have always known."

"But if you haven't tried being with a man, then how would you know?"

I wanted to come right out with the unequivocal words *Because I have been with a woman*. But I couldn't bring myself to draw his mind to Fiona and me, especially since it could be said that she had "tried" me—and had in fact given me up. "Prakash, you have to accept what I'm telling you. I am quite sure I'll never be interested in a man, at least not as a lover."

He sat immobile for long, cruel minutes. I wondered how much more I should tell him, and just as I was about to confess about Fiona and me, he lifted his legs over the bench and turned his back to me. He stood slowly and said, "We better get back, my mother is making roti for you." He led the way to the car, and on the path I had to stop myself several times from turning and running down to the beach again to escape the embarrassment that bore down on me like a wet coat. We did not talk on the return trip to the house, and the rest of the weekend seemed like an eternity in purgatory.

Once we'd gotten back to Ontario, he argued with me about it, as if my sexuality were something he understood better than I, something about which, under the right circumstances, my mind could be changed. When he asked me, as if it were the most reasonable request, if I could just please "try" him and "see," an experiment at least, I told him it was best we part ways. As if at gunpoint, he at once put a stop to his persistence. He said my friendship was more important to him than anything else, and he would end any romantic interest in me.

. . .

I'd decided to say to Alex that Prakash had invited himself. But no sooner, I thought it would be better to say nothing to her and simply wait until a day or two before his visit and then write and tell him something unexpected had happened, something to do with her sister in Florida, perhaps, and that we had to fly there immediately, or she had to come here, or some such thing.

But even as I foresaw the possibility of a rift between her and me, as the days wore on, I realized how much I wanted him to come, and it startled me.

. . .

Surging in me is this urgency to explain myself to Prakash. And lately, I've been experiencing a certain feeling of nobility in grabbing this opportunity to explain why, so late in our friendship, I needed to cut ties with him, to explain all the pushing and pulling of the past. During the decades when our friendship ebbed and flowed in the natural, uncontrived way that it did, I'd not really bothered myself too much about the whys and whereofs of it. But in the last few years, after the intentionality of the distancing, whenever he'd come to mind, something welled up, making me a little ill, remorseful. I noticed at some point that I have a tendency to hum a single note whenever I think of him. It is not exactly a pleasant sound but more like a sound meant to hide a groan. This strange, sudden, and involuntary emission is a chord made up of the notes of regret, remorse, and guilt. So perhaps my need to get on with a visit with him is not really out of the blue. What is out of the blue is the recognition of this pending visit as a chance to clean up an aspect of my life—a chance to scrub karma, or something like that.

The days following that initially unmeant invitation and its at first terrifying acceptance, I experienced convincing moments of confidence that, because Alex and I are solid, a breach between us could be easily overcome. I felt strong and virtuous, and there was comfort in such certainty. I was convinced in those moments that I could juggle three balls in the air: my desire to see Prakash, my relationship with Alex, and Prakash's presence in our house.

I went back and forth between experiencing such confidence and the fear of what might happen between him and me, between her and me. So for several days I did not tell her, or ask, or whatever it was I was supposed to do.

. . .

It's possible, at least in the very grand scheme of things, that thoughts are more material than they are ephemeral, like radio or energy waves, and must necessarily leave our brains, and when they do they float out into the universe. If so, then a googolplexian of thoughts—oh, way more than that, a googolplexian times a googolplexian of one-word thoughts, novel-length thoughts, unfinished thoughts, all, this minute, are criss-crossing the universe, each carried in a microscopic elastic bubble of something like an invisible gas or whatever medium might surround and preserve it. The bubbles are so small, smaller than a proton, that no invented microscope could see them as they slam into each other, and although they do so, no bubble is ever punctured because the gas or oil that preserves them is also slippery. They float bump slip slide float and bump again until they arrive at the head of the person or persons to whom they pertain. Perhaps they buzz—without an actual buzz sound, of course, perhaps more like a vibration—waiting for their intended receptor to tune in, to undo the latch, open the mind, and catch them. I should probably get up and out of this room right away, but I want to finish this thought. Whenever I dream of someone, particularly someone I have not seen or been in touch with in many years, I wonder if that person has also just dreamt of me, or if not "just," then if that person dreams occasionally of me.

Surely we're lurking in the darkened auditoriums of each other's consciousness, and when—according to the whims of the universe—it matters, a spotlight snaps on, and there we are, appearing in each other's dreams simultaneously. I have dreamt—no, I *dream,* occasionally—of past lovers with whom I am no longer in touch. The be all and end all of our actions in those dreams is lovemaking, thwarted sometimes, successfully accomplished at others, that leaves me, when I awaken, spent and as breathless and aching as if it were real and true. I surprise myself sometimes, too, by dreaming of sweet, intense intimacies with people with whom I have had no such interactions, nor for which I have consciously wished. Surely this happens—whatever the case, and with whomsoever—because I am merely responding to their dreams of me. Or, haggling over the possible chicken-or-egg nature of the situation, one could say they had caught my subconscious dreams of them and were reciprocating. Surely.

And if so, a similar logic might well pertain now: either Prakash's reappearance in my life is at the whim of the universe or unconsciously I've been calling to him. Perhaps this is one and the same. We are supposedly microcosms of the universe. By the same token, it could be that *I* opened a Twitter account because it was Prakash who was, intentionally or unconsciously, calling out.

. . .

It was early one morning and Alex was, as usual, up before me and at work in her office upstairs. I didn't want to disturb her when I awoke, so, rather than going to her, from the bottom of the stairs I called to let her know I was up and heading to the studio. She called back that she'd soon be down. My task in the studio that morning was to gesso two canvases. As the gesso needed to dry before another coat was applied, I wanted to get that out of the way before attending to business on the computer. Alex shouted from the kitchen to ask if I wanted a cup of coffee. I suggested we have our coffees in the studio. I finished the gessoing, washed up, went to the computer, and switched it on. Just as I typed in my password on the keyboard, Alex appeared with our coffees. I stood for our usual hug and little snuggly kisses. I rested my mug on the desk to better engage in this tenderness, during which I shifted us both so I could glimpse the screen over her shoulder. My mailbox was open, and in the lineup of bolded names, there was Prakash's. I felt a jolt in my heart, and as careful as I was not to react in an obvious way, Alex pulled back, looked me in my eyes, and asked if I was all right. I said yes, just a kink in my neck from gessoing the canvasses, that's all. She moved in toward me again, cupped my neck with both hands, and began to massage.

The time, since then, has flown too fast, and it has, too, been an eternity.

. . .

The universe—or whatever—being or not being in control, the fact is, Prakash, for some reason or other, has gotten in touch. I, for some reason or other, invited him here. He, for some reason, is on his way here this very minute. And all we can do is trust in the wisdom of the bloody chaos and patterns and symmetries of—of what? Well, might as well be the universe.

Look, it's not as if we've never run into any of Alex's past lovers. Take the one at a restaurant in Little Italy on College Street in Toronto. I could have made comments after, asked questions, wondered why on earth, et cetera, had silly insecurities for a few hours, but I didn't. And that other one we ran into while walking on Queen Street. I knew of her, but we'd never before met. Alex introduced us—she did not introduce me as her partner, I noticed, but that made sense: why rub it in? And at first it all seemed fine. I stood there as they chatted about this mutual friend and that one and the dog they once shared. It was still alive but on medication for arthritis. I remember being happy there didn't seem to be any animosity between her and Alex. This spoke well of Alex, I thought. I could see I was being inspected.

But then, out there on Queen Street, after talk of the dog, it was clear that the strain of an old torn-up intimacy had crept in between them. There was something unresolved. I wasn't upset. I was with Alex and she with me. There was nothing to fret about. Somebody had to do something, and it looked as if I were the only grown-up on the pavement. I glanced across the street and pretended to be suddenly interested in something over there, then excused myself with great lightness and, ignoring their protests, leapt in between the slowed traffic, shouting back to them that I'd just be a couple minutes. Alex came across to meet me after about fifteen minutes. She was broody and distracted for a good half-hour after. Did I get all bent out of shape about their very visible unfinished business? Did I ask all kinds of questions and make a fuss about her being so shaken? No, I just hugged her. She let me. I knew and felt secure that she was with me, and not with that person.

Why can't she be like that now, for Christ's sake?

. . .

Tall dark evergreens loom in my mind. Driving toward them on a lonely highway. A drive Prakash and I took to Tobermory. We were young then. It would have been before he got married. I don't know why that time and this particular image comes to mind—it hadn't, as far as I can remember, been eventful. It had been a pleasant day. At that time, he was truly my family of choice.

The day in the city had begun so hot you felt you couldn't breathe. A drive, then, north, to a resort town, a landscape new to us both, was an escape. A little adventure. But the sun, I recall, beat down on the shimmering highway ahead all the way north. I had brought apples and sliced them with a pocket knife and handed them to him while he drove. I don't think we stayed long in Tobermory, I don't remember getting out of the car. We must have, but all I remember is the dripping dark and heavy green, despite the heat and the sharp, cutting light. Perhaps that trip comes to mind to say that all is okay, that he and I had indeed had good, ordinary, uneventful times together. Perhaps this is precisely why, as I lie here, as I await his arrival, this memory presents itself: because nothing had happened. We used to do together the kinds of things friends, or siblings or cousins, do.

. . .

The day I met Alex, strange tingles ran up and down my body, little seizures of certainty flashed in my brain, a never-before-experienced confidence that *this is it*. It was shocking. We'd both attended the after-party of the opening of a much anticipated group-art exhibition at a warehouse space. I'd gone with a couple friends who knew everyone, it seemed, including this woman who, when they introduced us to one another, never took her eyes off me while we raised our voices to try to chat above the music. We discovered we had several friends in common, including Trinidadians involved in the arts and in activism. Prompted by the relentless *thump thump thump* of the electronic dance music, we commented on how seductive and yet boring it was. She contrasted it with Caribbean music styles, and I was surprised to learn she knew the difference between calypso, chutney, and soca. I was enthralled and made abundantly curious, particularly because knowing these things appeared to be of no consequence to her. She seemed interested and knowledgeable about many things unrelated to her personal life. We suddenly noticed that we were shouting even louder and having to repeat ourselves above truly deafening music and that the space had become crammed to capacity with people. There was a press toward the edges of the room as throngs of people pranced frenziedly in the centre. I suggested we leave and find something to eat. Restaurants in the vicinity were closing by this time, but we knew we'd find ones in Chinatown still open.

I walked several blocks in the warm night beside this stranger with whom I felt a beguiling familiarity, and the air bristled with expectancy. We were soon sitting in the blaring cold light of a noodle house, Lotus Land, at Dundas and Spadina, drinking green tea and picking at spicy cold noodles, spare ribs, Chinese broccoli, and taro cakes. There, against the trills and meandering notes of a guzheng zither, she sang verses, to my amusement and pleasure, of old calypsos. I learned that she was six years older than I—not much, in truth, but those few extra years she had over me gave her, to my mind, an edge of reliability and trustworthiness, a concrete sense of self, that I felt I lacked. It was—she was—immensely attractive. I did not want the evening to end, and I could tell neither did she. Hours passed without either of us having consumed any alcohol, and yet I felt drunkenly brave and uncensored, as if there was nothing in this world I couldn't accomplish. It seemed as if every sentence either of us spoke begged a segue into a new topic, and time passed unkindly swiftly. We left the restaurant at 3:00 a.m. because it was closing. Outside, a cool, refreshing wind gusted down Dundas Street as garbage and recycling trucks cleared the sidewalks, and produce trucks beeped backwards or lurched out of alleyways. There was a feeling of business as usual on the street, an intensity that suited our sense that we'd only just begun to chat. After we'd exchanged phone numbers and email addresses, I watched her get into a cab that would take her to her home, and I took the half-hour route to my apartment on foot. The following day—well, that day, actually—I stopped myself several times from calling her. I later learned that she had done the same thing. Two days later we went to a repertory cinema to see *Fitzcarraldo*, which we had both seen ages before but thought would be interesting to see again together. There was already in such an act a kind of intimacy. Afterwards, she came to my apartment. And it was there, sitting on the couch in my living room, with Elliot on one side of me and she on the other, flipping through the photo album, that a window opened wide in my mind, through which I saw the future, a beautiful view of rows and rows of sun-facing sunflowers that reached all the way to the horizon, and in the bluest cloudless sky a pair of Cooper's hawks elegantly glided, dipping and rising, like kites on strings. And then, in a flash, the window closed. It banged shut tight. Somehow, I knew she was the person with whom I would work to accomplish the bliss I'd so clearly glimpsed when the window had been open.

And on a different day—not today, I suppose—Alex would say it was the same for her. It was instantly a no-brainer, is actually how she put it.

. . .

It has not, of course, been quite so smooth a ride for Alex and me as the term *no-brainer* might suggest. I remember the first fracture, two months after we met, the way one remembers a first kiss. She'd wanted me to move in with her as much as I had. We behaved well through the strain of packing and transporting my belongings, Elliot prancing excitedly one minute, then cowering and trembling the next. Our laughter and incessant, impulsive intimacies belied the nervousness beneath the making of such a commitment. But finding a home for the contents of my many years' worth of possessions was less easy. It was a small house, one half of a duplex, and making space was a challenge. Alex wasn't actually prepared for her home to be encroached on roughly by half. One day, in frustration, she kicked one of my unpacked boxes that, with several others, towered up one of the walls of the living room, and shouted, "Goddammit, Priya, you have too much stuff! It's too much. It's just much too much. Get rid of things, or..." She stumbled in her speech, and repeated *or* again, then stopped.

I quietly said, "Or what?" anticipating a hurtful choice. "Or leave?" I added. As I thought, *So this is what* her *anger,* her *temper, looks like,* I also felt terrified I'd be in an instant thrown with my dog onto the street.

In the first few years, we took turns being the one on the verge of storming out, leaving forever. In between, little drafts would come through the seam of the window and remind us of the refreshingly cool air and the magical sunflowers and birds on its other side. I'm not saying we don't squabble still—naturally we do, like any two bonded birds in a cage.

And up until three weeks ago, until the resurfacing of Prakash, that is, a squabble was just that: a little disagreement that would settle down in no time, and might even leave us laughing at ourselves. The window-vision, I felt, and still do now, to some extent—or at least, I did until—well, until you know when—wasn't a lie.

. . .

What is it that makes family out of two people who have not known each other from birth? Having children together is the most convenient answer. Alex and I don't have children. Elliot was the closest thing, I suppose. He was my child, so to speak, and her adopted child. He was the centre of our lives, and when we had to have him put down just before we moved here, she grieved as much as I. His loss bonded us even more. She and I *are* family. I'm certain of that. We bought this house together, and most of what is in it. There's land enough for her to garden. And I have my studio. We have everything we need to be settled and happy. We take holidays together, have friends we made together, dreams for the future. We know each other's intolerances and needs, and for the most part we cater to one another. I am more carefree than she, but I think it is a quality she likes in me, as I appreciate and need the opposite that is in her. We have memories of shared moments—but, it's true, our memories do not always match. Nor our interpretations of things said, things meant, things unsaid and unmeant. But that's a relationship, isn't it? That's what it is to live in a family. Constant negotiation. Perhaps it's true that all good things are bound to come to an end. Entropy. The law of physics. All things fall apart. But things also go in cycles, of course. Gravity. Decline. Disintegration. And then renewal. The process toward disintegration beginning always in renewal, and renewal preceding *and* following disintegration.

I take solace in the fact that she and I are no longer young-sters in search of ourselves. We're old enough not to truly disrupt our lives together—and I wish Alex would recognize this. I may be bringing a bit of chaos into our home, but it will be short-lived. Alex is, as I am, comfortable in this home we've made. Neither of us will completely tear this down over a dis-agreement about the one-night visit of an old friend. We just have to get through the next few hours and all will be well again.

We'll figure this out.

. . .

When the larger world around you does not support your kind of love, it can be hard to nurture and sustain a relationship. It's hard to stay in when things get rough and tough; you don't see your problems as common ones that any relationship might come up against. You can't talk to your mother and get advice or comfort or stories from her. You see your failure as a result of who or what you are, of you as a person—you begin to chew on leathery words like *normal*, and when that happens, when you question your own worth, it's impossible to embrace someone else who reflects to you what you are. Well, at least that's how it was for me in my younger days. It's different now, but I do wonder how different it really is. Anyway, it's not something you can talk to other people "like yourself" about because even if they have privately experienced the same set of feelings, they want the actions you take, the things you say, to reflect a kind of politics that says that, no matter what, we're out and we're proud and we're happy, very happy, to be the way we are, and you'd better get used to us.

. . .

Alex and I have always been pleased that neither of us had to be chased by the other, that we knew there was potential here without any of the craziness or need for hurt or pain associated with falling in love. We both knew from the start we'd found partnership and companionship, and we felt the potential for love between us. As if in a fortuitous arranged marriage. Without having been subjected to a single whirlpool in the sea of limerence. Or, as we say back home, we had not gone *tootoolbay*. We did not, when we were not together, walk about in a lovesick daze, bumping into things, seeing each other in everything around us, unable to eat, living only for our next encounter, pursuing that encounter ad nauseum. We did not suffer insatiable hunger. Hover about the phone hoping and waiting. Say no to invitations from friends because we worried we might give up opportunities with one another. And I believe for this we were both thankful and, in short order, we decided to give it a go.

. . .

Alex is fierce and won't be taken advantage of, and yet, when she decides to trust you, hers is the trust of a child or a hand-fed bird; she can be as gutted as either if she is deceived or her trust betrayed. To be trusted by someone so strong and yet so vulnerable is irresistible. But it makes you susceptible, too. You can so easily be found wanting.

I knew, then, that if I wanted this relationship with Alex to last, we were going to need a clean slate on which to map our journey forward.

It was I who suggested, therefore, we leave the city, where our individual past foibles and achievements had been recorded and were played back in just about every one of our present-day social interactions—in other words, where much baggage, good and bad, had come to identify us and was aired interminably. How could she, too, not also have wanted to leave the place in which we had both spent most of our years, and go somewhere neutral where we could remake ourselves and also create a new life together, where we could develop a circle of friends and acquaintances that were not mine or hers, but ours? It seemed only logical, and I'm sure, if prodded to rummage beneath the surface, she'd say she felt the same way.

But the fact is, we did not delve into each other's reasons then. For my part, it had felt mature not to do that; it was a nod of respect for what I thought of as a Westernized notion of individual "boundaries."

I wish I could go outside, or Alex come and lie here with me, and we could look at this entire situation and marvel at how it came to be, rather than fight about it.

Among the areas Alex and I searched for a place to make a home outside of the city was this area that stuck out into Lake Ontario, joined to the mainland by an isthmus through which a channel had been cut to make boat travel easier. In effect, an island had been created. On the island, we discovered this hamlet of just a couple hundred residents nestled in a bucolic landscape of farmland. When we found this old house we live in, we felt as if the universe were anointing us with a future together. And so we let go of the house in the city, bought this one, and embarked on the clean slate on which our intention was to truly discover ourselves and each other and to fall in love—the latter, we felt, best experienced slowly.

The week we moved, I deleted my Facebook account and ditched my cellphone, explaining to Alex that a land line was all I wanted or needed. Alex was more admiring than curious. I also gave up my email account and created a new one on a new server, selecting which contacts to transfer from the old address to the new one. If I had not been in touch with someone in the last five years, I deleted them. If I'd been in touch only a handful of times with someone who could be categorized as a social contact, I deleted them, too. And then there were those with whom I'd been in touch more often, but with whom I really had nothing in common, and was fine letting go of them in this new life I was creating. As a consequence, I lost touch, naturally, with many people. It was as if I were a landscape architect embarked on a new opportunity, clearing, pruning and weeding, preparing to move the earth, to build retaining walls, put in streams, a maze here, an herb garden there, a field of bluebells, poppies, and gayfeather to attract butterflies. A row of sunflowers stretching all the way back. An orchard. The development of a sightline from foreground to something worth seeing in the distance, a new landscape in which the right ecosystem, although cultivated, would eventually naturalize. The view through the window.

It was during that time that the opportunity presented itself—even though it was not the first time I'd imagined or wished it—to disappear from Prakash's sight. In this new life with Alex, it was clear: he, more than anyone, had no place. And yet, when it came time to highlight his name and address and press the Delete key, it was not easy. It was as if I were applying a Rototiller to my history. To my heart.

Alex, however, remained on Facebook and was on it and other social media sites, including Twitter, more than once a day. I often sat at her side while she scrolled down the screen, show-ing me who had posted what recently, what was trending, what had gone viral, and opening links to one thing or another that was in that very moment making news and about which, out here in the country, we wouldn't have otherwise known. Like this, we remained knowledgeable about what people in the city—our city friends—were doing and thinking about, mobi-lizing around, and wearing, and I found myself wanting her to connect at times that were inconvenient for her. And then, when sitting beside me she did go online, I myself began to want her computer set on my lap rather than hers, so I could decide what links to click on, and when and how fast to scroll up or down on a page.

That was five years ago, and so began the longest period, by far, during which Prakash and I had no contact. Even on a fake island such as this one, one can imagine oneself to be cut off from old concerns and problems of the mainland, and so, eventually, I decided it was safe to assume that ties with Prakash had been effectively severed, that he had surely gotten the message that I did not want to be in touch. The time had come when I could safely emerge again, I thought, and so I opened a Twitter account in order to send my own two cents out into the ether.

I'd been on Twitter three months, mostly reading other people's tweets, seldom tweeting and not even retweeting much, when that message in my email inbox informed me of a private tweet from Prakash Acharya. It is not overstatement to say that, even before I saw the actual message he'd sent, the appearance of his name in my inbox was enough to cause me to feel as if the sky had crashed down on my head. He'd found me. Barely three months on the site, and he'd found me. It was only then I realized that not a day had passed since I opened the account that I had not, somewhere in the back of my brain, expected a message from him. Therefore, there was even, I might say, a kind of relief.

Hi. Write me. was all the message said.

It was not likely he'd have come across my presence on Twitter by chance. We had no friends in common; the people or organizations I followed and those few following me would have been of no interest to him. He'd have had to enter my name in the search window. I wondered how often he'd done this over the last five years, and what he felt when a profile for me finally came up. I was immediately unsettled.

He's surely still a married man, I thought. His children are likely still at home. And yet he always finds me.

Hi. Write me.

Such assertiveness.

At once I checked my home page and tried to imagine myself as Prakash, reading how I described myself in my profile. I read the few things I had ever tweeted and retweeted until then, and imagined him having gone through them, taking part in my life without me knowing it, imagining who I'd become. I resigned myself to the idea that it was best to turn myself in, as it were. To not put off what, there in the recesses of my mind, I now realize, I always knew was inevitable.

. . .

In hindsight, I can say that when I was with lovers BA—Before Alex—I saw not them per se, but my own reflection. I related my life to them in stories and I recounted past personal dramas in detail. I have no memory if any of them ever told me theirs. If they did, I might well not have been listening. They provided me with opportunities to hear my story every so often as I related to them how I'd grown in life and how each new experience gave me a finer understanding of how I became the person I now was. Lovers BA provided me, in other words, the chance to give form to myself.

With Alex, on the other hand, the old tendency to command space and time with stories about myself dissipated. When she would ask about my past, I found myself newly bored by my own tales, the same ones I'd repeated elsewhere, wording and structures honed for desired responses; I wanted instead to be regaled by *her*. Such a thing hadn't happened before. It unsettled me. This drive to know every detail of her past seemed more powerful than sex, and I knew instinctively it was a sign that she was the person for me, for life.

But that morning when Prakash's message arrived, the old shape-shifting that was once required of me to survive resurfaced. Even if I no longer need him, his reappearance, coming at a time when Alex and I have tended to be off in our own worlds, had the effect of igniting in me that old feeling that I could not let him get too far from me, for one cannot ever be certain about what one's future may hold.

Although I didn't respond to him immediately, it wasn't long after his name lit up my inbox that I began to wonder if the calm in which Alex and I lived was possibly a veneer, beneath which lurked a disquieting incompatibility. And in other moments I had an indestructible conviction that she and I were solid enough to endure the harshest of storms. There were moments, then, that I imagined showing her off to him and him to her.

. . .

Hi. Write me.

I mulled over how and if to respond. A long-shelved memory from the time before I knew of his pending marriage bubbled up like gas escaping from something decaying on the ocean floor. He and I both lived in the city but had not been in touch for several months, during which time I was engaged in a torrid but short-lived romance. When it ended, I was depressed and lonely. Characteristically, as if he had an eye trained on me, he resurfaced just in time and invited me to accompany him on a business trip to San Francisco. He knew what I needed, he said: "Come with me. It'll be a little getaway. We can commiserate about how women break our hearts." He guffawed, saying that was something we had in common. "We'll go to galleries, to Fisherman's Wharf, a gay bar, anything you want, just name it." Nothing denied, all expenses paid, he added.

Neither of us mentioned the only other trip we'd taken together, in the last semester of our final year at university, to his parents' home on the East Coast, but I certainly thought about it and accepted this offer of a holiday with him only after I was sure he understood I'd tag along as his good friend, his buddy, nothing more, and that we'd have separate rooms.

He agreed heartily. "But of course. What are friends for?" he said.

I remember San Francisco of that visit as a city awash in rust reds and golden light. After checking in at the hotel and depositing our luggage in our respective rooms, we headed out onto the street. My post-relationship gloom disappeared at once, a shadow hit by sunlight, and I felt a sudden shock of hope and lightness. I hadn't heard myself laugh in weeks, and there I was grinning and ready to guffaw at his silly stereotypical comments about West Coast fads and fashions. Over a bowl of soup at a Tibetan Buddhist restaurant a few doors down from the hotel, we studied a map of the downtown area and drew up a tourism plan of attack. We hopped on a tram and playfully jostled against each other as it rumbled downhill. We hopped off at the Railway Museum and browsed souvenir shops. At one, I helped him choose a royal blue hoodie with an image of a tram and the Golden Gate Bridge. He had the shop embroider on the sleeve of the sweater *P & P, BFF*. Prakash and Priya, Best Friends Forever. It was as if I were with a brother I hadn't seen in ages.

Hours later, back at the hotel, we parted outside of the elevators on the sixth floor, and I went to my room to freshen up and change into appropriate clothing for dinner at a dressy restaurant reserved for us by the hotel's concierge. We had agreed to meet a half-hour later, but before fifteen minutes had passed, he was at the door knocking. I had him wait while I pulled on my clothing, and, imagining we'd head out at once, I threw my bag over my shoulder, opened the door, and stepped into the hallway. As the door was swinging shut behind me, he stepped aside me, pushed it open, and entered, saying, "Wait a minute. What view did they give you?" And he walked across the room to the window. As I waited at the door, he said, "Just a minute. Come here, come see this."

The door shut as I joined him and looked where he was pointing.

"It's a very different feel this high up. Just look at that," he said, as he put an arm around me, onto my shoulder. He continued pointing to the busy corner way below, to billboards that were almost eye level with us, and to rooftop gardens, and tried to figure out down which street and in which direction we'd walked earlier.

Blood rushed to my brain, and I felt as if I couldn't breathe. There was something new in his voice and manner. I'd heard and seen it before, but I couldn't remember where or what had happened. My brain seemed to slow. He pointed things out and spoke, but he seemed distracted, and I, too, had become distracted and couldn't make out what he was saying. His voice gradually became hoarse, and he cleared his throat several times. He moved behind me, and with one arm already on my shoulder, he rested his other hand on my elbow—in effect, embracing me. And it was this particular weight, this tender, trembling touch that brought me back to myself.

"And we're wasting precious time. Let's get out of here," I said, angling from him.

He caught my hand and stopped me from moving away. Then he placed his hands on my shoulders, turned me to face him, and drew me closer. "A little hug, come on," he said.

I looked up at the ceiling, I shook my head, I sucked my teeth in a show of mock irritation, all the while smiling, and threw my arms around him for a quick and muscular bear hug, drawing back at once.

"Oh, come on," he said. "Give me a proper hug."

I felt a kind of defeat, but the smile remained on my face. Contradicting thoughts raced through my mind, the first of which was, *Priya, you damn fool, nothing is free, didn't you learn that at least once already? Was helping him choose a hoodie an intimate gesture, an indication of something I didn't mean to suggest?* And then, *You've known him for years, there's no harm in a small hug.* And, *You've known him for years, which is exactly why you should have known better.* And, *Why are you accusing him when nothing has taken place of which to accuse him?* I became unsure of myself, worried that were I to push him away or chastise him for asking for what might really be a harmless hug, I'd cast a pall on our little holiday. I jutted my chin toward the door.

He was looking at me, but I felt he was not seeing me, and the muscles of his face had gone slack. He said, "Yes, yes. We'll go in a sec. A proper hug. Come on."

I relented, and I remember it was as if, in that instance, I shrank in size, in strength, in my understanding of who I was. In my mind flashed images of past girlfriends. Of my lesbian friends in general. Of the compliments meant when they called me "boy." And I felt diminished. He pressed his body against mine in the cold room, tightening his arms around me, his breathing close to my face. The pressure, I told myself, was not exactly menacing, but it was enough to make me rest both palms on his chest to keep some space between us.

And then I watched myself, in mere seconds, come undone by the scent of cologne and the warmth of a strong, firm body meeting mine, and a thousand thoughts ricocheted in my brain, my body wanting and terrified at once. We were both grown-up, so to speak, experienced in ways we hadn't been in our university days, when I had spent that long weekend with him at his parents' house, for instance. And we were anonymous in San Francisco, I reasoned. I'd always felt a kind of love for him, and here in this hotel room I could try it out. No one need ever know. I could use this as an opportunity to see if I felt anything deeper for him than the love of a brother, a buddy. And as I entertained the whys, the hows, and the how muches, my body raced ahead of me and answered yes, yes, do it, just do it. It's okay to be—no, it's good to be, fine to be, necessary even—to know, to see. Here and now. If anyone, him. Yes, with this very person.

He walked me to the foot of the bed. With the bed behind me, he held me, and I relaxed, perhaps even tilted my pelvis toward him. I felt his hardness even though no clothing had been shed, and I believe I moved in to accommodate him, to grant myself the pleasure my body now insisted on. I parted my lips when he put his mouth to mine. The bristle of his moustache delivered electric waves of desire and I wanted to explore his mouth with my tongue. But before I could, he'd taken over and it was his filling mine; I was to let go and receive him, I understood. I was forced into an unrecognizable and unpleasant passivity, but my mind and my wanting body were too confused to bring a halt to any of this.

He began to tremble, and it was the strangeness of the trembling body, his sudden weird intensity, the animal smell that emanated now from his face, that tongue not in conversation with mine but seeming to want only what it wanted, that awoke me from the bargaining in my head. I'd wanted warmth, a back and forth, the push and also the pull, the hard and the soft, the fear and pleasure, the dangers and the playfulness that were my experiences of having sex, but there was none of this. It was as if I abruptly awoke, and I pushed him hard. He stood for a moment, confused, and then his face became contorted by a mix of anger and hurt. Neither of us spoke. I turned my back to him and covered my face with my hands. He picked up his jacket and left the room. Dinner out had been, of course, derailed.

I ordered dinner through room service and, with the television on, picked at the food on the plate. I could not pay attention to what was on the screen, but it was enough of a distraction to temper my distress. A couple hours later he telephoned to ask if I'd please go with him to an Indian restaurant in the Castro. If we were to rescue the next few days spent in a foreign city, I knew we had to talk, so I agreed. Seated at the table there, he began to apologize, but I stopped him, saying only, "Please, don't do that again. How many times must we go through this? I won't continue this thing—this whatever—with you if you won't take 'no' for an answer. You said buddies. That's why I came with you."

He said, "I know," and after an awkward silence, he stumbled with words as he added, "Priya, you almost—you seemed— why did . . ."

Before he could say more, I said tersely, "You should know. Our own bodies so easily betray us. I'm sorry. I'm sorry to you, and I'm sorry to me. It's not what I want. I thought you understood this."

Remembering what had happened on that trip, I considered not only not writing him back, but also blocking him from access to my account.

But—and there are always buts with Prakash—there was another side to the man behind the words in the Twitter message. A couple months passed after that trip, and he turned up again, as if no breach between us had ever occurred, and treated me as if we were precious family or the closest of friends. I felt small-minded, petty, a prude, to have banished him from my life. And I let him in; at the time I was jostling a constellation of rebukes—I'd lost a part-time job, I'd been turned down by a gallery for an exhibition, and by an arts-funding agency to which I had applied for a grant—and I sorely needed a little kindness from someone who wasn't going to judge me for these failures. He was an unusual friend. A soft drug. He had a way of healing me, making me strong again.

It seemed ungrateful, callous, to delete his message.

. . .

Hi. Write me.

. . .

I am with Alex now. This is both reason to be okay with seeing him again and reason I probably should have kept far away from him. But if he'd found me on Twitter, it was only a matter of time before he learned where I lived—perhaps I'd have gotten lazy or too comfortable and unthinkingly posted a picture of some recognizable place or thing in the area, like one of the many farmers' markets or craft fairs, or the popular "Taste" events or our Christmas parade.

The days before I responded to his tweet, I avoided Alex. When I did engage with her, I was distracted, unnecessarily gruff, or it was from the position of feeling "weirdly" ill, of having a "strange" headache. Hence the long showers, the long solo drives across the bridge to the town on the other side, the sleepless nights I lay staring into the darkness. I thought about the meaning of friendship and the meaning of commitment, about expectations in both, about trustworthiness, loyalty, honour, and dishonour. I thought about what it means to be human—that humans are social animals, and we are supposed to be cognizant of and care about consequences, we have the capacity to feel sympathy, empathy, and gratitude. And, on the other hand, we are a random formation of far less consequence than we imagine. An accident of molecular attraction and repulsion. That consciousness, and having a conscience, might define us as humans, but they are, too, our downfall—because, in the end, living is indeed a matter of the survival of the fittest—

you take care of yourself first, put on your oxygen mask before you try to help anyone else—and at times a matter of each for herself, himself, themselves—everyone else be damned.

I couldn't go on like this. I felt I had no choice. The time had come.

Hello! Long time. So happy to hear from you. Where are you? I finally wrote back. Enthusiastic yet innocuous. As if it were nothing at all.

I barely pressed the Return key, and his response sprang back: *You've moved. You changed your email.* DM *it to me.*

I instantly felt I'd done the wrong thing. What had I thought? That he'd just write back and say, *Oh, there you are, I just wanted to say hello. Hello! I'll leave you alone now*?

I should not have responded. I should either have deleted the Twitter account or just ignored his message, and if another came, I should have ignored that one, too. Before I knew it, I was giving it all up: this is my email address; here's where I moved— *more space to think in the country, more room to work, quiet, less expensive for a still-struggling artist.* And perhaps it was an automatic reaction, the kind of pleasantry one engages in without actually meaning it, that I added, *Come visit us sometime; I want you to meet my partner.*

It was meant to be the same *Come visit us sometime* I have said repeatedly to friends from the city and to certain family members. I meant it to suggest I was so unaware of any reason I should be nervous about having been tracked down that I would not only happily and easily give my contact details, but might actually want to entertain him in the house I shared with my partner. And that *us* bit—an announcement upfront that I'd set myself up with another person. Something he'd never seen me do before. And, if that were not enough, that phrase, *my partner*. Two words that expressed an idea he'd never heard me utter before, with its inherent notion of commitment. And of exclusivity.

I hadn't expected he'd take up the invitation, and I especially hadn't imagined he'd act on it, precisely because I'd thrown in the fact of my partner.

· · ·

There isn't an actual thing, a specific thing, I can go to Alex with and, in a sentence or two, explain, or for which I might apologize. Is it reasonable—more to the point, is it *fair*—to have to defend actions taken, a life lived, before we met?

I don't want her to see how powerless and frightened and alone I had often felt. That there were times I allowed this man a kind of closeness because of it, and he was there, willing to give me what I needed. That when I was on my feet again and didn't need him, I pushed him away. I don't want her to know that I engaged in such a push and pull. Would she scorn me for this? I couldn't bear scorn from her, or even an ounce of her love for me to be predicated on pity. Surely all people have a little lockbox, if not a full closet, that contains shards of shame.

So who will I be when Prakash gets here? The person he once knew, or the one Alex lives with?

. . .

Every time I have that dream it's almost pure repetition. The groom, and me. All that red. It keeps grabbing hold of me, pulling me under. The altar, the tassels. And his penis, fleshy and firm at once, in my hand. The feel of him, hard and directed, urgent, pressed against me. The desire so intense, even well after I've awakened.

I mustn't. Not today. Not this day. Who was it who said the chariot comes out of the mouth? Life should be simpler. Our big brains don't really serve us well. That's what's wrong—our brains. Our minds. All this consciousness, and for what? I wish I could just go back to sleep, stay right here for the rest of the day.

. . .

If I took from him, it is because he gave willingly. It takes two to carry on the way we did. I needed, he gave. He needed, and— well, I tried my best.

When I was okay, when I didn't have to reach out for him, I didn't. Doesn't that say something positive, too, or must it only say the negative?

What place does he expect to have in my life now that I no longer need him?

He will have spent a day here, and a night, and tomorrow morning will soon come. And before he leaves, I will have cleared the air with him.

. . .

I really should get up this minute, roll up my sleeves, go out, and prepare a proper breakfast—eggs and toast, or pancakes. A little lemon and a dusting of sugar on them. There's time to construct a leisurely morning with Alex. I can make time for such a gesture. A gesture of appreciation for her. Might as well begin the future now. I will set the table nicely, but not too elaborately to bring it notice. We'll sit at it and eat breakfast and chat. I've been meaning to ask her about her work.

Christ, I must truly be off my mark today—Alex seldom eats breakfast, but more than this, she hates eggs. It is Prakash who loves his breakfast of eggs. Eggs and potatoes. Which I dare not make tomorrow morning, for he'll surely see it as a sign of something or other. I will make Alex and me toast, I'll butter it lavishly. That, she'll like.

I'll just wash my face, brush my teeth, go out as I am. I'll remain in my pyjamas. It mustn't seem that I'm trying hard to—well, I was about to say, to appear guilty of nothing. I *am* guilty of nothing. Or, if not, surely it is possible to be at the same time blameless?

It's much too cold to go traipsing about the house in thin cotton. I'll get sick if I go out like this. But no, going out dressed as I am is an announcement. Today is not a normal day. Whatever out of the usual comes later, it will seem to have been foreshadowed from the very beginning of the day by my late waking, and then this manner of presenting myself.

That's right, let the day begin, then.

2
COLD

. . .

The house is quiet. Alex is probably already upstairs in her office, ensconced in her writing. The most successful art forgeries of all time. How she comes up with these topics for her books amazes me. There isn't a subject she isn't interested in. But I can't tell if she's up there unless I call out to her or go up, and I won't do that just yet. When she's working, a bomb could go off next door and she wouldn't notice.

Forgeries. A paradox, isn't it—successful art forgeries—the artistry of the forger being an incidental sidebar. The real story is the length of time and the many hands through which it passed before fraud was discovered—how and by whom, all those fooled people.

How unpleasant the still air is, achingly cold when it settles on my upper arm and around my elbows, or at the back of my neck.

Alex and I need softness between us. No tension. Just a little softness. Tenderness begets tenderness.

As if the presence of a human moving about the house triggers it, the furnace kicks in, and a grumble, and then a prolonged hum, barrel through the house.

I hardly reach the kitchen and there is that smell again. For several days, ever since the pest-control man set poison throughout our country house for mice that come inside to shelter from the cold, we've been plagued by the odour of decomposition in the kitchen. We smelled it first in one corner, where a wall of cupboards abuts a wall of drawers. But the odour migrates—one day it seems to come up from under the Afghan rug in front of the wine fridge, and the next, to jump nearer to the sink at the end of the counter, then later, halfway across the room to where the microwave is housed. The smell this morning is worse, as if we'd dumped shrimp shells behind the fridge. A few days ago Alex went into the basement to see if there were any dead mice rotting down there, or some other animal that could be the source of this smell. She saw nothing. There wasn't even the faintest whiff of decay there. Now it fills the kitchen again.

Coffee has already been made. The milk carton, half full, sits on the counter. I won't make anything of this today. I round the central counter and glance past the TV room, to the sunroom. She is there, on the couch. I can see her through the haze of pale blue cigarette smoke that swirls lazily up to the room's high ceiling, sitting in her corner reading, the wide hood of her long black coat pulled up around her head. The second to last finger of the hand that holds her cigarette alights with a dramatic staccato tap on the screen of her electronic reader. She reads fast. I have accused her of skimming, but she swears she reads every word on a page. I count seven seconds, and as usual, sure enough, there's her finger, a little hammer, coming down again, a perfect rhythm. And again: One. Two. Three. Four. Five. Six. And exactly on seven: tap. Which comes first: does she actually finish reading the page in—no more, no less—seven seconds, or is it the rhythm that dictates the drop of her finger, whether or not she has read every word?

I wonder how long she's been there. Under the "smoking jacket," she wears her pyjamas, a red plaid long-sleeved flannel shirt and matching pants, which she puts on when she gets out of bed. Perhaps she hasn't been to her study to work at all this morning. That's not a good sign. We may have ended last night with a semblance of kindness between us, but that was last night, and today is not just any ordinary day. The sliding door that separates the insulated part of the house from that room is shut, so she can't hear me. She looks like a monk. A hermit. She doesn't care that wearing the hood indoors makes her seem a little odd. Her rationale when I once teased her about it was that she tucks her hair into the hood—summer or winter—to keep cigarette smoke from getting into it, into her thick, wiry mass of unruly hair that otherwise rises like a halo around her head, hugs her face, and cascades about her shoulders.

She is so absorbed in her reading that she doesn't see my movements in the kitchen. This is probably not her first cigarette of the day. I so need to keep peace with her, but there is that little flicker of irritation, anger even, inside me, and I want to march out there and ask how many she's already smoked for the morning.

One. Two. Three. Four. Five. Six. Tap.

I remain as much out of sight as possible and pour myself a cup of the tepid coffee, but it is impossible to hide entirely. How can she be so absorbed that she isn't aware of any movement inside her own home? Does she feel so safe in this house that she isn't bothered by movement in her peripheral vision?

If I take the time to make a fresh cup, she'll soon enough see me and come inside, and I'd rather go out there, greet her in the sunroom. It will be easier to begin the day, to confront it, looking out at the land and the trees, at the lake ahead, than inside, facing each other. It's good she isn't yet aware that I'm up and about.

But the sunroom is the coldest room in the house in wintertime. Perhaps I should go back to the bedroom and change my clothing. Except I want to greet her out there, and she might come inside before I finish changing. I won't waste time; I'll carry on as I am.

Even as I approach the sliding door, she still isn't aware of my movements, and I grin now, as I know she'll look up as soon as I begin to slide the door open.

And, indeed, I finally have her attention. She is solemn. Last night's conversation no doubt still weighs on her, too. She closes the reader and sets it on the couch beside her. Her phone is partially tucked between her legs. I wave a hand at the thick blue air and laugh.

"You slept long," she says, pulling the hood off her head.

"I must have needed it," I answer, my voice bold and cheerful.

Because she has been smoking, the door that leads to the patio is ajar. The room faces the lake and a cool wind off it comes in. Shivering in pyjamas too thin for even such a mild morning, I set my cup down on a window ledge and cross my arms in front of me. I rub my shoulders briskly. Even so, I pull the door open wider. I lift the pair of binoculars hanging on a hook next to the door and look out at the lake.

"Fuck, it's cold," I exclaim.

"It's not all that cold. It's nine degrees outside. Why are you standing in the doorway like that? You're in your pyjamas. Are you okay?"

I shrug.

She shifts and extracts from under her the fleece jacket she wears while gardening in the fall. I shake it, and twigs and leaves and a cloud of dust—or it may be dirt—fall out.

"Whoa! That's going to have to be vacuumed up," I say, catching and attempting to alter my irritated tone mid-sentence. I arrange the jacket around my shoulders and pick up the binoculars again, aiming them at the trees on the far side of the neighbour's land. She asks again why I am in my pyjamas. They've caused more of an impression than I'd intended. I finally answer, "Well, you're in yours, aren't you?"

She pulls out her phone and looks at it, and says, "Yes, but that's not strange for me." Her face seems drawn, pale. There was a time when she derided anyone who was tied to their "devices," as she called them. Lately, she's constantly checking email, Facebook, Twitter, and looking at the various news sites on her phone. I am old-fashioned. It irritates me. But I mustn't take notice of it this morning.

I didn't really expect her to be in a grand mood but I hadn't thought she'd be quite so sombre either. I am already on the defensive, despite my good intentions. Tenderness, I must remember, begets tenderness.

People are ambling on the beach that runs along the edge of our property, lazily tossing Frisbees for their dogs. They wear windbreakers and running shoes, strange for wintertime.

The phone on her lap buzzes. She looks down at it, concentrates. "Do you need to get it?" I ask. She doesn't recognize the number, probably phone soliciting, she says. My parents are aged now, and I always imagine that one day soon she'll likely be the one to receive a message from back home telling her to break it to me gently that I need to go back immediately. And it is in the middle of the night when it seems like the appropriate time for death to come, or early in the morning—like now, particularly on a weekend morning—before the time friends or telephone solicitors actually dare call, that the ringing of the land line or the buzzing of the cellphone can make my heart stop.

Prakash doesn't have her cellphone number so it couldn't have been him—whose number she would not have recognized—calling from the road to ask or say this or that. I am relieved on two counts.

I am clearly jumpy—at least on the inside. I must steady myself.

Her own unease is not hidden. I decide, however, not to ask what is bothering her. I know, after all, and it's too late to have that kind of conversation. I don't want Prakash to arrive and find us cool with one another, and her to be unfriendly toward him. It will cause me to be so, too, or at least to pick sides, and I don't want to be put in such a situation.

Her phone buzzes again. She looks down, depresses the power button, and shuts it off. I want to say thank you, but if I do I'm sure to say it with sarcasm in my tone, and that isn't advisable, is it?

At the beginning of this year there had been massive craggy hills of ice created by waves of lake water freezing upon previously frozen waves of lake water that were snow-covered in time along the shore. Those hills were so high you couldn't see behind them. It was thrilling and frightening at once, just metres from our back door. They called to you, made you want to climb them to see what was on the other side, but I imagine that would have been foolish. Nevertheless, some days through the binoculars I saw tracks on them that might have been some foolish person's footsteps, or perhaps a deer's or a coyote's. Alex and I are not the type to attempt any such thing.

Today the sky is so clear, the air so crisp, that there is a slight quiver of light on the horizon, a shimmer on the water nearer, gulls skimming, soaring, diving, and dogs and people passing by on the shore.

I want to ask her where she thinks I might take Prakash, but I don't want the question of her accompanying us, or not, to come up, and the mere mention of his name presents the opportunity for more questions to be asked about him, about him and me.

I say, "Christ. I wonder what this winter will be like for us. Do you remember the last one, those big craggy mountains of ice just out there?"

"Um-hm. That was just this January past," she says. She's making an effort, and it's as good a topic as any with which to try to communicate lightly.

"We're just weeks away from another January," I continue, "and just look at it; there's hardly any sign of winter—save for how cold it is."

"It's not yet cold, Priya. It's nine out."

"I guess. It's cold to me. Remember? You can take the girl out of the tropics but not the tropics out of the girl? That's what you say about me." She twists her mouth.

I ignore this. The tropics. There will be two people from the tropics in this house in a few hours. Two brown people in this town where, when I see one on the street, it's cause for excitement. Prakash used to love to tell people when he first met them that the equator runs through Uganda, and that he used to be able to stand on the ground with the equator running between his legs. If things were different between her and me this morning, I'd tell her this and we'd chuckle.

"Eleven months ago—ten, even nine months ago," I say, "the words *polar vortex* were on everyone's lips. Doesn't that freak you out?"

"Um-hm. Cold is what it was this time last year," she says. "The body is always in the moment. It doesn't care if it was warmer or colder any other time. It's concerned—a matter of survival, naturally—only with how it is in the present." She's finally more engaged. How grateful I am. "But the polar vortex phenomenon didn't really begin until January. And yes, it is odd, January of this very year," she says, blowing smoke up into the high ceiling. Getting things right always animates her. Even so, she still sounds worn down. Burrowing into one neutral issue helps to skirt others, I guess.

The binoculars still at my eyes, moving them about our yard, I notice that the birdfeeders at the edge of the patio are empty. Empty birdfeeders are a sign of neglect. I must refill them before Prakash arrives. Last year, there was that day I noticed the feeders were low in seed, but the temperature outside was already in the minus double digits, and I was loath to have to dress up to go out there in the even colder wind. I reasoned that since the feeders weren't actually empty I would wait until the following day to replenish them. But the next day, even though the temperature remained far below zero, freezing rain began to fall. It was so strange. Frozen dagger-like pellets came stabbing down on the land for days on end, and we watched amazed and frightened, as sheets of ice formed a sleek, thick, impenetrable sheath around us, and just when we thought enough was enough, more ice rained down, a carapace resolutely preserving what had already been laid down. Then the temperatures dove further and remained like that, fixed for weeks. The ice that covered everything wouldn't melt. I wasn't able to reach the feeders for the rest of the winter.

By the time the ice had stopped falling, I remember, Alex and I had had enough of being cooped up in the house. Once the roads were salted, we dressed warmly, packed an extra blanket in the car, and a knapsack with a thermos of hot choco-late, a container of crackers and cheese, apples, some local biltong, and the fully charged cellphone—a survival kit, in other words—and we drove to a park in which the sole road, plowed and salted, runs parallel, metres away from the edge of the lake.

I pulled the car to the side and turned off the engine, and we sat there, terrified and full of chutzpah at the same time. I can still see it all clearly in my mind. The wave-rocks glistening like sharpened steel. Stabs of light glancing off them, an indication that the boulders were not stable.

I ask brightly, "When did we go for that drive through the park to the lake? I think we were mad to have done that."

The cigarette has dropped from between Alex's fingers, scat-tering ashes on her clothing and the couch before it hit the rug. Although she mutters, "Damn," she gets up and dusts off around her as if nothing much has happened. I stare at the lit cigarette on the rug that was made somewhere in Africa of recycled plastics. A thin curl of dark smoke floats upward. She picks up the cigarette and flicks its head toward the ashtray on the side table next to the couch. I stare at the spot on the rug, expecting to see a pursed black lip of burnt plastic. I can't see it from where I am, but I think better of stooping to inspect it at this stage of interactions between us. The glass on the table next to the couch is already covered in ash, as if she had been flicking the cigarette on the table rather than in the ashtray. She doesn't use the opportunity to clean off the tabletop. After years of being together, I still can't tell if this, and many of her other idiosyncrasies, like that habit of leaving the milk out or the cutlery drawer and cupboard doors open, are the marks of a forgetful genius or of a person who can't be bothered. I am determined not to say a word.

"Oh, I don't know. It was sometime after the ice had stopped coming down. Nothing happened. We were safe enough," Alex suddenly responds, and for a moment I've forgotten I'd asked when it was we'd gone for the drive.

Were we really safe enough, though? I still wonder about that sometimes. Sitting in the car, the only people on that road, facing an expanse of frozen water as far as one could see. Metres from us, massive iceberg-like formations, frozen waves piled one atop the other. Knife-edged cliffs jutted out of the ice boulders into the sky and then dropped off into gemlike blue-and-green canyons. I had brought my window down a fraction, and we listened. A heaving, thumping rebellion came from beneath the surface. It wasn't a stretch to imagine water undulating, restless, captive, wanting an escape from all that ice. It felt as if the force of the moving water beneath might actually, any second, wrench the boulders above from whatever anchored them and send them skidding toward the road, shoving us into trees or, more mercifully, simply crushing us flat. What seemed like a choreographed row of geysers, seven powerful spouts, one after the other in quick succession, rose every few minutes into the air.

"I'll never forget the tinkling, one minute, like a crystal chandelier in an earthquake, and that insistent thumping," I say, then laugh. "And you told me then that Lake Ontario was the smallest of the Great Lakes, and the thirteenth largest in the world."

She nods. "It sounded alive. As if it were breathing. The music from the blowholes—it was like a strange tune played on an oboe," she says, and although she remains glum, I feel grateful.

"And do you remember, you quoted Hardy?" I ask.

She takes a puff and nods. After her long exhalation she says, "'The sun was white, as though chidden of God.'"

I was not surprised that she knew Hardy's poem, but I was impressed that out of her brain she was able to pick an appropriate literary phrase to describe the scene in front of us. Impressed, but not surprised. On the way home, in another more sheltered section of the lake, where swans are known to gather for the winter, I brought the car to a crawl so we could see how they were faring. On the glass surface we counted thirteen swans, frozen stiff, some as if in full swim, some off-kilter, some sprawled on the surface, their wings unnaturally bent, stuck in parts to the ice while tips of feathers flapped in the wind. That was this same year, just eleven months ago. The feeders in our yard had remained empty until the middle of what was supposedly spring but still felt like winter. The moment I was able to, I went out and filled them up. But for weeks on end, no birds came. The seeds in the feeders stayed untouched and mosses flared up the sides of the clear plastic tubes. The songbird population—particularly the little chickadees, juncos, and finches—had suffered because ice had encased their food supplies, and we humans hadn't been able to provide for them. I would not have experienced any of this had we not moved from the city. It has felt like some kind of privilege, albeit, at that time, a sad one.

I lift the coffee mug to my mouth and its lip is unpleasantly cold. "Gads," I say. "The coffee is like ice."

Alex stands, and as she walks toward the sliding door, she says, as if resigned, "I'll make a pot."

"I'll make it," I say, bypassing her, ignoring her tone. "I'm making myself some toast. Want some?"

She doesn't. She'll have a banana later, she says.

In the kitchen she has stopped at the counter. I grind the beans, and we both stand there and wait for the water to boil. I wet a cloth and wipe the counter. She has leaned against it, her back to me, and she scrolls the screen of her phone.

While pouring our coffees, I see her in my peripheral vision, feel her eyes on me. The air in the room is prickly again. She wants to say something. I can feel it. But perhaps she is, rather, waiting for me to ask her what is wrong. That's what it is: she wants me to bring it up.

A bubble of irritation swells. My jaw tightens. It is inconsiderate and foolish of her, I think, to be so withdrawn mere hours before a house guest is to arrive. Doesn't she see—or does she— that this is a kind of sabotage?

It is as if an earth-moving tractor, ready to tear up the field of sunflowers I continue to wait for, is idling in the kitchen. I will not be drawn in, I tell myself. And yet I feel as if I am rolling up my sleeves, readying myself.

I pour milk into the coffees and can't help but make a grand gesture of putting the carton back in the fridge. The fridge door closes, and the muffled *snap* it makes is all that is needed to flip the switch of emotions competing inside me again. I really do want to be calm. I know today is a difficult day for her, that she has not wanted Prakash to come here, so it's natural she's agitated. It wouldn't hurt me to show some consideration. Perhaps, after all, I should say something about him. Something conspiratorial with her. But I don't know what exactly. Should I mention that he is fond of statistics and carries in his brain an armoury of facts and figures about the most obscure things, and that she must watch for this quirk of his? Isn't this love of trivia something they share? Or that I've never known him to hold a grudge, or to say an unkind thing about anyone. Perhaps I could tell her a thing or two of what he's told me of his family's escape from Uganda. How young he was, and how much responsibility he'd taken on when they arrived here in Canada. He'd had to quickly improve his high school English— Swahili and Gujarati being his main languages—and interpret for his parents at their medical appointments, and when they went to a store to buy, say, a television or a fridge. Or should I tell her something with less potential to endear him, something that shows her I can be critical of him and I am not in the least attached to him? Such as, he enjoys being coy, thinks it's playful and amusing to goad women with statements about their inferiority to men. I can imagine her rolling her eyes at this, and that alone might be enough to temper this impasse. I can tell her I'm willing to bet that when he gets here he'll try to make them quick pals by getting her to join him in teasing me. Or shall I tell her that I never really meant to lead him on, that he's the kindest, gentlest man I've ever known? Or that I fear he's coming here to make sure I'm being treated well? Or to disrupt the peace and quiet of life here with her?

I open the fridge again, but my mind is not on what I am doing. I stand there, staring in.

"You seem rattled," she says. I remain as I am, and she says, "Are you?"

And then, that switch again. A heat begins to rise in me. I can feel it travelling upward from the heels of my feet, fast, and this time it is uncontrollable. It makes me want to stomp, to slam my fists at the walls. Why should I be the one to have to break the stalemate?

"You're the one who seems rattled." I'm not sure it's what I should say, but I can't stop myself. "It's a beautiful day. Are you just going to remain serious and glum? You're not helping things, you know."

I want to throw the mug that is on the counter, the one I love, at the wall so hard it smashes. It is one thing to want to, and quite another to actually engage in so violent an act. It would, I'm certain, be the kind of statement from which there would be no retracting.

Just breathe. Do not do it. I rest the mug on the counter and move away from it.

I have to wonder if something else is the matter. The matter with her, that is. She's been trying these last few weeks to control me, and I won't let her. This is the problem with living with someone. Suddenly, just so, just because you live together, you lose your independence. You're expected to halve yourself, merge with the other person. But *I* don't try to stop her from doing what she wants. I don't even ask her for details of her day. It's not that I don't care, but rather that small harmless mysteries stoke the fire of my interests and attractions. The feeling of jealousy, as long as its causes are not wounding, affect a delightful flame in me. This provocation and playfulness of feigned jealousies was a shared trait, a sensibility, that attracted us to each other. She'd not truly been a jealous person before. Why now? Am I misreading something here? I'm not doing anything wrong by having Prakash visit. I need to see him to clear up some misunderstandings between him and me. Why doesn't she just trust me? There is nothing sinister about this. It should be a noble thing. Just let me have some freedom here.

How I wish I were on my own.

Okay. That's not true. I wouldn't want her to go away, or us to be apart. I just want her to be more understanding. If she were to leave, if we were to be separated, I think I would go mad. I do love her. I love her. I don't want her to hurt. We shouldn't be hurting each other like this. Not today.

She doesn't move; her hand is fixed on the handle of her coffee cup where it sits on the counter. She says nothing. She is not a weak person. Far from it. I feel she wants a fight. But she won't initiate it. She wants me to start it.

I am tempted to tell her everything about Prakash and me. I want to hurt her, to let her see how she is making me want to hurt her.

But this is not me. I am not a cruel person. I love her, can't she see that?

Why doesn't she just come out with whatever it is she wants to say? It's in the air, so why don't we just get on with it? It's what we do, she and I. We get on with it.

I can't bear this. I walk around the counter swiftly, taking a wide berth as I march past her on my way out of there, toward the bedroom shower.

The hard spray of hot water hits my head and the back of my neck. Memories of Prakash wash across my mind. Fiona, him, and I in the apartment she and I shared. How young we were then. How he loved being the man in our lives. When we walked on the road together, he'd place himself between us, linking his arms through ours. When she and I were on our own, we'd marvel one day at his naïveté and presumptuousness, while on another we'd talk of him as one of the sweetest people we'd ever known.

I should—

There I go again: should should should. But I really should shower up quickly and get back outside. I could be washing dishes in the sink, straightening books on shelves. There are papers to gather and put away someplace they won't be seen. It wouldn't hurt to plump the cushions in the living room. None of this has been done yet. Alex began yesterday what she would have considered her share, but I stopped her, saying he's a guy, he won't notice a thing, and in any case, I'll do whatever needs to be done. Relax, I told her, and I was grateful she backed off.

His long slim fingers come to mind. His nails were—probably still are—smooth, shiny, a pale pink shade, like the inside of a seashell. I remember walking a couple times with him in the Don Valley. Arm in arm, because there I was unlikely to run into anyone I knew. No ex-lovers, no potential ones. We could walk for hours and not come upon anyone: bicyclists or the lone walker, runners, yes, but we never met anyone we knew. What an amazing thing it had been then to link arms in public with another human being, to be able to declare to the trees and the grasses, to the sky, to the river, the closeness we shared— to not have to worry, like I would have had we been two women—about the lash of strangers' eyes or tongues and acts of scorn. Even as I cherished walking with him like that, I was made sad, too, by it.

He'll arrive around lunchtime. We'll have bagels and hummus here, and then we'll go out for a cup of tea or to the pub for a drink. The three of us, perhaps, but more likely—I hope—just him and me. People who know me will probably assume he's my brother, or some other relative. But I am recalling, too, that he loves—or loved—to engage in conversation with strangers, and he would always implicate me, when I was at his side, as his girlfriend. Come to think of it, I'd rather not run into anyone I know with him. This is a small town. Everyone knows everyone—even if you don't know people by name, you know them to say hello to, and you recognize couples, and families, and friends of friends. People here are less tolerant of infidelity than they are of same-sex relationships. I'd hate it if, when talking to someone—a waiter, perhaps—who is a stranger to him but not to me, he were to refer to me as his "lovely woman" as, to my horror, he once did at a pub in Toronto. When I chastised him out of earshot of the waiter, he apologized, insisting that he was simply meeting the man on his terms and having a little fun. He might not repeat that mistake now, but who knows? The only café on the island that remains open after Thanksgiving is Madame Bovary's. It's smack in the middle of town. Perhaps we can start there, go for a drive, and then finish with a drink at the pub.

Surely he has, as I have, changed.

Will what I do, what I say today, be interpreted by him as signs of my present-day feelings about him? How careful do I need to be? I don't want to mislead him. But I also don't want to be too calculatingly, obviously resistant to him.

Tonight we'll eat supper here, at home. I'll have to orchestrate the flow so as not to make too lengthy of an evening with him and Alex at the same table. And there's breakfast tomorrow. We have apples, there's a carton of half-and-half, a loaf of bread in the freezer. I'll make a custardy apple bread pudding. There's no history there, and it'll satisfy his sweet tooth. I must remember to take out the bread. After showering I'll quickly prepare tomorrow's breakfast and put it in the fridge overnight. I can bake it in the morning before anyone else awakens. And hopefully he'll leave before lunch.

But maybe that's too much of a fuss. Alex likes granola. That's what I'll make. That won't be too hard to pull together. I'll do that while we await his arrival. She likes it with roasted almonds and chocolate chips. I don't think I ever had granola with Prakash. It won't have any association with him, and Alex will be pleased. She'll feel I made it for her. And regardless of how I arrived at this decision, it ends up being true, doesn't it?

I crank up the hot water and lift my arms. The hot spray hits my sides. I turn and it cascades down the middle of my back. A delicious heat spreads over me every time I shift position. The steam fills the stall, and I'm hidden from the world. Alone, like an incubating egg. This is my home. And yet, sometimes I long for home. The old, the first, original home.

I had had to return home, to Trinidad that is, on graduating from university, but I wasn't there a month before I decided to leave again. I sent in an application to the Canadian High Commission in Port of Spain, for emigration to Canada. Within two years I was approved and, losing no time, l returned and set myself up in a small apartment in downtown Toronto. But it isn't easy to replace one home with another simply by wishing it to be so. And city living presented bigger—sometimes more overwhelming—challenges than I'd had at the university. Prakash was also living in Toronto by then, and in no time we reconnected and he became my ever-ready guide. We spent a great deal of time together at first. We'd shop for groceries, cook together, go to movies, for walks on the waterfront. There was that time we went to Point Pelee, he and I, for an afternoon outing. He picked me up at my apartment in an old car he'd recently bought and was proud to own outright. How great it was to be seated with him in his own car. I could imagine myself being courted, on a path that could lead to acceptance from so many quarters of life. There was no one around to watch me try this out, to see me fumble or to witness whatever pleasures might surprise me. At the seaside, we shared an ice cream, with big frozen chunks of meaty black cherries in it, walking on the beach, seagulls dive-bombing everywhere, squawking as if they were being murdered, the metallic smell of the sand, and the weird, silly intimacy of one ice-cream cone between him and me. It seemed playfully provocative then, and all the laughter we shared that day. As we neared the city on our return, the fantasy dissipated. I wouldn't let him come up with me when we arrived at my apartment. He was visibly crushed, and I detected a hint of anger. Had I led him on? A little, I suppose.

There were times, before Alex and I began living together, when I would have that dream, and in the dream I would be wracked with desire for him, my body opening like a pulsing tulip, but always, just as I felt him hard against me, just as he was about to penetrate me, something or someone would interrupt us, and I would awaken. I would awaken to thoughts of telephoning him, of insisting he come over at once, my intention being to have sex with him that very day. I was convinced, in those first few waking moments, that that was what I must do. But once I arose, the moment my body left the bed and I was exposed to the reality of the day, the desire turned to torment and confusion and depression that I could have had such a dream. And I was further appalled that even in my waking state—though it would have been for no more than, say, fifteen or twenty minutes at most—I'd been convinced I should have sex with him. I'd shake the dream off, like a dog just out of water, and put him out of my mind.

But, goodness, the memories come like rain. Walking into a lesbian bar on Church Street with him, feeling his mix of excitement and fear, my simultaneous discomfort with his presence at my side, embarrassment even, and gratitude that when I left the bar there was someone to walk home with. Late-night walking, together, while he gaily nattered on about something or other, every so often throwing his arm around me when he laughed at something he said, leaving his arm there until the awkwardness of my not drawing closer made him drop it.

But it wasn't all gratitude: walking back to my apartment knowing I had not had the courage to go to the bar on my own, to flirt there with some vivacious woman, buy her a drink, dance holding her lightly at first, as we sculpted the imminent possibility of a night spent together. Time had passed since I'd emigrated, and yet I had long remained terrified there'd be a Trinidadian lurking somewhere who'd see me and report back home to the entire country. The idea that another Trinidadian in that situation would likely have had the same concerns about me, and that our secret identities might have been safe with each other, could not be fully trusted. And so Prakash was my willing foil.

I close my eyes and rub my face with a gritty cleanser Alex says makes a remarkable difference on my skin, smoothing, brightening it. It's been more than six years. I'll have aged visibly, I'm sure. Will he see that I have? I'll put rose cream on my face, tidy my eyebrows. I'm trying to remember the last time I saw him, but it is him dressed in a cream sherwani, the collar and cuffs embroidered in heavy gold thread and pearl-like beads, that comes to mind. The dhoti he wore. And the ceremonial canopy, the Mandap from which the beaded curtains hung. Those pearls and all that red and gold. And his joota chupai, like fancy boats in Asian waters, pointed and curled at the toes. With my eyes closed, and the wet and the heat gushing on my breasts and on my stomach, I see him standing on the petals of red flowers. I remember it all, as clearly as if I'd been there.

But I hadn't, of course. Some months after the wedding—I hadn't yet met his wife—he and I met for tea—well, he for tea and I for coffee—and he showed me a photograph he kept in his wallet. I asked if I could keep it and he obliged. His wife had been in it, obviously, but I don't recall what she looked like then. After cutting him neatly out of the photo—I discarded the rest—I pasted him on one of the beer bottles for my installation. I invited him to the opening of the exhibition that included the piece, and he came, alone. I remember him stooping low, looking at the cutout of himself in his wedding attire standing next to the pasted-in image of me in a wedding sari. He stared at this for a long time. I worried he was upset that I'd used his photograph this way. He moved to the second part of the installation, another beer bottle on which there was a label made to look like a classified ad in which a lesbian seeks a gay man to marry, and then to the third staged photo of me and a woman who resembles me, French kissing.

When he stood, he put his hand on my shoulder and said, "I would have let you do whatever you wanted, you know."

I twisted my mouth even as I smiled broadly in that room full of people, and said, "Don't be ridiculous," as I walked off to speak with other attendees.

Alex's voice outside the shower stall jolts me. It's as if I've been caught. I wipe steam from the glass door, and she waves at me. She's holding up her phone. It's our friend Skye, one half of the couple with the cottage to which she goes to write. Skye wants to walk from her house in Macaulay to ours in Crescent Bay. She'll do it if I agree to give her a ride back. I calculate and imagine Skye would get to our house by ten. If she visits for an hour or so, I could drive her back to her house and return before Prakash's arrival. I am finding it difficult to feel warm toward Alex; she's making unnecessary waves—or rather, the timing of whatever waves are cresting in her is causing us an inopportune problem. Skye would be a good distraction. I tell her, sure, I'll drive Skye back.

I turn off the shower and dry myself. I bend down and aim the blow-dryer at my upside-down head. I recall the telephone conversation I'd had with Prakash before he left Canada for a visit to India. I knew he would be away for some weeks; he'd told me he and his parents were going in order to visit an aged and ailing family member, and because it was such a costly and time-consuming venture for the three of them to fly all the way to India, they'd stay a few weeks extra and do some touring. Then, days before their departure, he telephoned, and I could at once hear uncertainty in his voice. His parents, he slowly revealed, had arranged a marriage for him in Jaipur. I misunderstood and said, with humour and a tinge of ridicule in my voice, that finding a wife who would put up with him would be an impossible task. He said, feebly, no, a woman had actually been found. I was shocked. I felt as if I'd been hit on the jaw with a fist, but I did everything I could to not express any consternation. "How long have you known about this," I asked, thinking of all the times we'd spent together over the last year, the last months, the weeks before, of his attentions to me that had been sometimes confusingly tender, of the trip to San Francisco we'd taken just about a year before. Not even a year ago, actually.

He found out on his thirty-third birthday. His parents had asked him to return to New Brunswick for his birthday, he explained, and so he went for a few days.

I had forgotten his birthday. I didn't know he had gone to New Brunswick and hadn't noticed his absence.

At a party held for him, in front of family and friends from Uganda, they announced that a woman from a very nice family had been found. He thought they were playing a prank on him, but when everyone began to congratulate him, he realized it was not a joke.

I quickly calculated and was relieved that our trip to San Francisco had taken place almost six months before his birthday. "Don't you have any choice?" I asked.

"I didn't know if I had other options. I mean, I don't know."

He seemed to be waiting for me to say something. When I didn't, he said that over the previous weeks plans had been solidified with the family in India, mostly without his involvement. There was some urgency to the arrangement, he explained, because the woman's father was ill, and they wanted the ceremony to take place while he was still able to attend. He said he was calling to ask me if he should go ahead with this arranged marriage. I shocked myself by how flustered and deeply saddened this strange turn made me. I asked him to hang on a second while I turned off the stove, which was only a way of taking time to compose myself, to regain strength in my voice, for there was nothing on the stove, and when I returned after some long seconds I told him as dispassionately as possible that I couldn't tell him what to do.

"So you won't tell me not to go ahead. And you can't say I should either? I am to leave soon. Six weeks from now, when I return, I will be married. Please tell me. Should I do this? Does it mean anything to you?" he asked. He spoke so softly, his voice flat—almost without emotion, it seemed—that a few beats passed before the sounds would take the shape of words in my brain.

"You've not spoken of her before. I know nothing of her," I eventually responded, ignoring his last question. "I don't know what you feel about her, what she feels for you."

"You know that's not what I'm asking you." There was a murky silence. I didn't fill it, and finally he said, as if resigned, "I've only seen photos of her. We've spoken on the phone."

"So you're going to marry someone you've never met. You'll marry someone because you've been told to do so."

It was a statement rather than a question, and the critique in it was loud and clear. Oddly, I felt, he defended the situation: "It's tradition."

My impulse was to remind him that he was living in Canada, and this was the place where we could question traditions and the blind following of old ways. I felt myself, too, on the verge of dissuading him from leaving Canada. But as much as I did not want him to marry, I also knew it would have been wrong of me to discourage him.

He carried on. "She's young, Priya. She's twenty-four, but she doesn't know anything about the world. She's been sheltered—you know what it's like for women like her—she's never left the subcontinent, nor has she ever had a boyfriend. She's had crushes on movie stars." I wanted to say to him he was in trouble if he was already complaining about her, but I kept my mouth shut. He spoke again, and this time a little more directly. "But I'm not asking you about *my* feelings. Those you should know. What I want to know is about yours. I want to know what my options are." Even though I would surely have said no, I felt ridicule toward him for what I thought was a lack of courage for not coming straight out and asking me to marry him. With as clear a voice as I could muster, I said it was best for both of us if he married this woman.

No beat was then skipped when he said, almost as if we'd been having an entirely different conversation, that he'd bought a house. I hadn't known he'd been house-hunting. Huge changes in his life were taking place and clearly had been for some time, and I felt betrayed that they'd been put in motion without my knowledge.

My feelings confused me. I certainly could not have expressed them to him. To what end? I was not about to say, *Stop! I'll do it. I'll marry you.*

I at once attempted to lighten our moods, and I gave an edge of excitement to my voice when I asked him about the house. As if his mouth were filled with cotton, he answered that there was nothing to tell. I persisted, "What kind of house? Where is it?"

It was in a new development, a new suburb that was being built, half an hour outside of Toronto, he said, sounding as if he were confessing. The house was almost finished being built, one of the first in the development, but there weren't even paved roads yet. By the time he returned from India, his section would be finished, he'd been promised. I didn't respond right away, and he said, "It doesn't look like anything much at this stage; it's in the middle of nowhere, but not for long."

When I did speak, I asked why on earth he'd chosen to live so far away—why hadn't he bought something in the city, an old house, something with a bit of character and stories in its walls, in a neighbourhood with old trees with fat trunks, over-hanging branches.

He said, with frustration in his voice and disappointment at my response, "I'm an immigrant, Priya. And Aruna, she will be one, too. We like our homes new." I reminded him that I was an immigrant, too, and to that he answered, "Yes, but you're different. Everything about you is different. You're not like us."

I continued to try to make things light. "Well, see? That should answer all your questions. That should warn you off." He was quiet. We were both quiet.

Then he said, under his breath, "It's what I like about you, Priya. That's exactly what I've always liked." He abruptly said goodbye, his voice papery, choked, and he hung up.

There was no part of me that wished to dissuade him, but from somewhere tears filled my eyes and rolled down my face. I felt ill. He would not now, I knew, step off this train he, his family, she and hers, had embarked on, and that I had not known about even as it was being arranged. That had been my last chance. But I felt relief, too. Tears of sadness and relief, at once. Next I heard from him, the marriage had taken place, and he'd brought Aruna to Canada. We met without her, and I took the photograph of them from him. This odd, amorphous thing between us would, I had thought back then, stop.

Stepping out of the suffocating heat of the shower, I dry myself and choose my clothing for the day, imagining myself as Prakash will soon see me: deep blue jeans, a navy V-neck cashmere sweater over a white T-shirt, and brown leather shoes. My style of dress hasn't changed much since the early days when we were inseparable at university. The shoes are different; they used to be simple runners.

Alex returns and dresses. She wears a black turtleneck and black jeans, and a chunky silver Moroccan necklace. She looks particularly good. Is she, too, dressing to make an impression? I have to smile. She slides a matching bracelet up her arm. She once told me that jewellery is armour. I guess she thinks she needs this today.

I say, "You're dressing up."

She says, "Skye will be here soon." She leaves the room without having looked at me once.

In truth, why is Prakash coming here alone? Has his marriage ended? Knowing I'm settled with a partner, why isn't he bringing Aruna, or at least his children? He wouldn't stay with us if they were also coming, but we would have had them over for dinner or lunch, or maybe just tea. We would all have been perfectly awkward with each other, and more than likely she'd be uncomfortable with us—two women living together, sleeping in the same bed in the house in which they sat sipping tea, eating cookies—but perhaps I misjudge her. I don't really know her, only what he has told me about her, and should I trust this? But after—what, twenty-five years?—living in this country, surely people like Alex and me would not be novelties to her. Being with us could be a lesson to their children in acceptance, open-mindedness, new kinds of difference and of love. They'd go off on their own to the beaches, to the tourist shops, the food vendors, a winery or two, speaking about us the instant they got in the car, deciding that in the end, as kind as we were to them, we weren't really their type of people—not because of our sexuality, but our vastly different interests, and we wouldn't have to worry about any sort of ongoing relationship with him and his family. And he and I could then put all that had happened between us truly in the distant past. Yes, just like that. Like magic.

But the fact is, he's coming on his own.

I check myself one last time in the mirror. I want him, when he gets here, to take one look at me and think, *Yes, she is no longer the person I once knew. I wouldn't have made her happy.* And if he thinks, too, that I wouldn't have made him happy, that will be fine.

Open the bedroom door boldly, Priya, head out confidently. The day is yours.

. . .

Alex is removing dishes from the dishwasher and shelving them. "It stinks in here," I say before I can censor myself. My tone is accusing, as if the smell has been caused by some sort of neglect for which she is to blame. I don't mean to come across like this, of course, but I know I do. Over the clatter of stacking plates, she answers, "Yeah. Too bad. Especially when we have people coming by." I can't fathom her. Is she accepting of the fact now?

Remember, tenderness begets tenderness.

But I don't want to catch her eye. It seems like I don't have to worry, for as calm as she appears, as accepting as she sounds, I can see she won't look this way either.

What and how much has she intuited, I wonder, and yet chooses to remain quiet about? This unease is painful. At the very least, it is an indication that this thing with Prakash and me must be sorted out this weekend, once and for all. Obviously, not in her presence.

She looks, even so beautifully attired, as if she is drowning. I want to reach out and calm her. All I have to do is take two steps closer to her, put my arms around her. Draw her toward me. Press my cheek to hers and say into her ear, "There's nothing to worry about. I love you." But I can't move. My heart doesn't even feel as if it's beating. This may all seem like stoniness, callousness, but rather, I feel like the visceral mass of a mollusc stripped of its shell. If I reach out to touch her, it is my flesh that will wither or tear.

Skye mustn't arrive and see such static between us. We need to shift this mood fast; I suppose I should say or do something to break the iciness.

I go by the fridge—we avoid each other—and sniff the air. She lifts the dishwasher door and shuts it. The effort makes it seem heavier than usual. She is about to walk away but notices a cupboard door left open, and she reaches back and flicks it shut. Unusual for her, and therefore noticeable. Such a small place, yet she sidles past me, managing not to brush against me. I want to laugh out loud. I turn my head to hide the strange spread across my face that resembles a grin. So odd, this heightened tickle in my cheeks—yet, if I were to let out the thing that corresponds to the spreading, thinning out of lips, the resultant bulge of cheek muscles and slitting of eyes, rather than a laugh its sound would be that of a fierce and terrifying growl.

If I betray Alex's trust, there will be no second chance. That thought strips the contortion of grin off my face. As if it needs underlining, this tension makes crystal clear the impossibility of a continued friendship with Prakash, and that I must use this weekend to end the expectation that it would continue. The paradox in trying to orchestrate such a severing is wicked—the gamut that will inevitably be run of memories, the multifaceted emotions that will be wrought, the stirring up of explanations for then and convictions about now, about how things must presently be.

I stoop and sniff the floor in front of the fridge. Where is the hell from which this smell emanates?

It's plausible, of course, that Prakash simply wants nothing more than to reconnect and say hi and see how I'm doing. But I know that I took and took and took from him. How could someone not want a little bit returned, or at least explanations for why I went into a sort of hiding? Not *sort of*. Plain old hiding, really. Explanations, apologies. Is this how I will forever live my life, owing explanations and apologies? When did this manner of making my way through the world start?

Someone who doesn't know or understand the circumstances that once glued us together might say I led him on, but I didn't. I guess, though, it could be said I did little to deter his attentions—until shortly after Alex and I got together. A couple days before my birthday, while I was shopping with her at Kensington Market for the special meal we planned, he telephoned. She had gone to the deli for buffalo mozzarella, and I was next door at the butcher's waiting for a rack of lamb to be frenched for me. My cellphone rang, and I swiped the answer bar before I looked to see who it was.

"Priya! Finally!" the voice I knew so well shouted excitedly. I positioned myself quickly so I could see through the large glass window to the shop next door. Determining I had privacy, I spoke with him for a couple minutes, promising to call him when I had a free moment, which, I told him, I didn't then have. He said, "What are you doing for your birthday?"

"I can't talk, I told you. Let me call you back."

"Just tell me, do you have plans for your birthday?"

My eyes had been glued to the door of the deli. Alex was approaching. "Yes, I've got plans, but let me call you later." I didn't hear his response as I shoved the phone in my pocket and turned it off in there.

I put off calling him and, when I was with Alex, simply kept the phone off. Eventually, about a week after my birthday, feeling guilty, I called him back. He had had tickets to a play put on by the Desi Entertainment Society and had wanted to invite me, he said, but it was too late, the show had come and gone. I asked why he didn't go with Aruna. It was, he said, not the kind of thing she would have enjoyed. He hadn't even bothered to tell her about it, he explained, but thought it was something I would appreciate and he wanted to share the experience with me. I told him I was seeing someone but didn't reveal that I'd actually already moved out of my apartment and into her house.

"So who is this lucky person?" he asked.

"Let's just hope she is lucky," I joked.

"What's her name?" he asked.

"Look, Prakash, let's not do this," I said.

"Do what? You're being cagey. I went by your apartment. I knew you'd moved out. I could have helped you move. So does that mean you're serious about this one?"

"I am serious. Yes," I said. There was quiet, and then very jovially he said he needed, then, to meet this person, that, in effect, she was like his family, too. I said, "In time, not now. I need time to nurture this on my own, Prakash. I just want to keep this one to myself for now." I knew I was hurting him.

"Priya," he said, and I heard the tremble in his voice that made me want to put the phone down. But, as usual, I listened. "I haven't stopped caring about you. Do you know how often I think of you? I've tried not to bother you, but I've felt lately that you are the only person with whom I can relate and confide. You will understand. I need to see you."

"You know, Prakash, if I were to have given myself over to you, you'd have run. You don't want me. You only want me because you can't have me. You just don't want to be rejected. You should figure that out and get on with your life. Aruna won't like you speaking like this with me," I blurted out.

He carried on as if I'd said nothing. "Aruna and I have an unspoken agreement. What she doesn't know doesn't hurt her. Let's go for a drive, we can go to Niagara Falls for the day. Just for a few hours. I need to speak with you. I need to see you. Don't do this to me, please."

I didn't discuss Aruna and his "unspoken agreement," didn't ask what he wanted to chat about, and I didn't want to hear, or think about, what I was doing to him. I simply said I didn't want any complications.

He said, "You're happy now. What about later? When she dumps you, or you get bored? It'll happen, you know. And then you will want me around. There'll come a day when I might not be there for you, Priya." There was an edge to his voice I had not heard before. Then he said, softly, "No, no, that's not true. I'll always be there for you."

I felt so irrationally pulled toward him that I knew I had to end the conversation. When he called from then on, I simply didn't answer my phone. That had been the last time I spoke with him. When Alex and I moved out here, I knew I couldn't simply not answer my phone when I saw his name on its screen, so I gave it up and relied only on our land line, which wasn't convenient—but it was necessary.

He and I were together—ah, there I go, so carelessly using this colloquialism that, unless I immediately clarify its usage, will suggest I have not exactly been forthright. *Together* is not the right word, for as I say, we weren't a couple—it would never have matched up to what Alex and I have. What I meant was he and I knew each other for decades longer than Alex and I, and we were close for much of that time. He does not, however, know me now. I am a book Alex has read numerous times, and I'd like, this time, to give her the ending she hopes for. Oh, but who knows, really, what *she* hopes for? I do feel at a loss.

It must be remembered, my intentions from the start—the start being when he accepted my invitation here—have been clean and noble. Who knows, I may end this weekend with the strength to tell Alex everything, and to face whatever comes of that.

Or the wisdom to simply put it quietly behind me.

Alex's back is to me as she fiddles with something on the corner of the counter where she keeps bills, notebooks, and scraps of papers with reminder notes scribbled on them. I decide to ask if she'd managed to get any work done earlier, but I am unable to lighten my voice completely. At least it is not as dark as when I mentioned the stink. She doesn't turn to face me, but she manages to answer as if we are suddenly in a different time, a time when things between us are lighter. She says she got up at five and had been working in her office until just before I came out to the sunroom.

"Writing?" I ask.

"Revising a chapter," she says.

So I am wrong. She wasn't sitting in the sunroom all that time squirming about her and me.

Her work is not something I can focus on at this time, but still I ask which one.

She looks directly at me, but says nothing. I shake my head by way of saying I don't understand why she isn't answering. She says, "You don't usually ask about my work. Why do you want to know now?"

"What do you mean? I just asked."

There is a long pause, and I wonder if she'll veer away to another subject. To Prakash, or to something about her and me, something that indicates there's trouble that needs to be addressed.

"The one," she relents, "on forgeries that, had they been successful, could have changed the history of the world."

I soften. I stop and look at her back. I decide I will follow my desire of a moment ago: I will go to her, hug her from behind. I will gently kiss the back of her neck. I will tell her I love her.

But the moment passes in a flash when she continues, "I've had an email exchange with a forger in England. A man who's been in prison for his work, and who is called upon by the police to help with authentications." I must concentrate, I must engage with her on the subject. I ask if she thinks meeting with him in person would be of any use. She says she is not interested in meeting him, there isn't any need to, and adds, "I feel so impatient. I just want to finish this chapter. The whole damn book. I've been working on it for such a long time."

She is either compartmentalizing again or she is truly focused on the book. Her answer provides me with an opportunity. "If you need to work," I say, "I don't expect you to come and hang out today. I'll just be showing Prakash around the countryside." She says nothing, and it is becoming awkward again. Making sure I sound as if this is all about practicalities, I add, "Yeah, that's probably not a bad idea at all. That way he and I can catch up and not bore you to death with talk of people from the old days, and you'll get a good two, three hours to yourself, perhaps a little more, before we return. And then we can have supper together."

Long, messily quiet seconds go by again and then, turning to face me, she asks, "Would you rather I didn't come?"

Is now a good time to embrace her? But I can't move. I feel stuck in this spot. "Of course not. To tell the absolute truth, I'd rather you came, really. I mean, that would be great, but in all honesty, I suppose I don't know how scintillating"—I bat my eyes playfully to emphasize the word, knowing she'd remember having used it days ago—"it would be for you. He tends to talk incessantly about himself. As I think about it, I recall that when he and I are together, we don't really engage much around things that are happening in the larger world. I mean, if you don't mind that sort of thing, hearing every detail about each of his children, about his home life, about his parents, you should come, definitely. Anyway, it's only for a weekend that he'll be here, I suppose, and I am looking forward to hearing what he's been up to. I wonder if his children are still at home. The youngest, she must still be with him and his wife." Too much? Am I protesting too much?

"You're right. It might be better if I stay and work."

"Sure, whatever. Do what you need to do," I toss off nonchalantly.

"You were going to make dinner. Are you still thinking of making pasta and a sauce? Vegetarian, you said?" she asks, and I am grateful for the normalcy that this talk of dinner promises. I'm about to say I'll be back in time to do it, but she carries on, "Just go with him, don't worry about dinner. I'll make it."

"To tell the truth, I think you're oil and water," I say unnecessarily. I wish I could just tell her that I do actually care about this man, that I feel with him a kinship, the kind of love one feels for a good brother. And that I love her more than anything.

She looks at me again, and I smile quickly, sheepishly. I get down on my knees and sniff the area rug that lies in front of the wine fridge and coffee machine. The smell really does seem stronger here. I peek under it, but there's nothing, no mouse droppings, not even a telltale stain on the rug or the floor beneath.

I imagine Alex watching Prakash, listening to him speak, wondering why I'd chosen someone like him as a friend, and Prakash doing the same with her, it dawning on him, for the hundredth time, or for the first, why I might not have wanted a life with him.

When I stand up, she is facing me. She catches my eyes and says, "You keep hinting at that, but I've more or less liked all your friends so far."

"Look, if he and I were to meet for the first time, today, we wouldn't be friends. It's the circumstances in which we met that made us friends. We were both like fish at the university, both out of our element. We were oddities, misfits, and the instant our eyes met we recognized this in each other. We might have run from our reflections—others might have. But *we* didn't. We gravitated, like magnets, toward one another. It was years later, once I'd found my feet in this country, once I began to think of this place as home, that my eyes opened to how different he and I actually are, how conventional he is. Left up to me, we wouldn't have stayed friends. But he's a better person than I: it was he who made the effort again and again. It's his best trait and his worst: he's incredibly loyal."

"Incredibly loyal? The same Prakash you said, just last night, was here today, gone tomorrow? Which is it? Why all the inconsistencies? Time is short, Priya."

I mustn't turn her off him entirely. What does she mean by "time is short"? Thank God Skye is coming over. I answer lightly, "You know what I think will happen this weekend? I think he'll see me for who I am. He'll see what has become of me. You and me

133

together, the kind of people we are. And he'll realize that he and I—that *we* and him—have little in common. He'll appreciate that what brought us together in the first place was circumstantial and therefore flimsy, and what kept us in touch was his own kindness, his own insistent blindness. He'll see that you and I are solid, more than he could have imagined I'd ever be. This is good, this visit here." I repeat the thing about her and me, that he'll see us together, and see that we're one, that there's no room for him in our lives.

She gives her head a little jerk to say I should follow her out to the sunroom, the cigarette already hanging in the corner of her mouth. Her words are slightly garbled: "You say he's conventional. Conventional is about following norms, doing what the majority does, conducting yourself for the approval of your peers, of society in general. Conventional people like it when everything runs in the ways they believe are 'normal.'" She makes quotation marks with her fingers.

"He isn't homophobic. That's what you're asking, isn't it? He isn't."

She stares at me in expectation of more.

"He's known about me from day one. Well, for the longest time, anyway. He's even known a couple of my previous girlfriends. He became friends with them." Am I boasting? I want to add, *Sort of,* but I don't.

She doesn't miss a beat: "Yes, but you told me you weren't serious about any of those women. If he'd been interested in you, as you said he was, he'd have known this, instinctively."

I wish I had not said he was once interested in me. I wish her memory was less sharp.

"He went out, on a few occasions, with me and whoever I was seeing at the time. He actually asked to go to a club with us." Why did I use the word *actually*? As if to suggest how amazing he was for making such an amazing request! Alex sees through walls. This is exhausting. Nevertheless, I carry on. "We went dancing together. I mean, we danced, he didn't. He just watched. But he was totally at ease, totally congenial." The instant I say this last part, I can just hear a possible retort: of course, what straight man, given the opportunity, wouldn't jump at the chance to go with two lesbians to a lesbian club? What straight man wouldn't "watch"? So I take front before front takes me, and say, "Yeah, yeah. I know what you could say to that. But he's never been disrespectful of or to me, or questioned me, or shown a bad face in any way, to me or to any woman I was with."

I also wish I had never used the word *conventional*. I had simply hoped my argument would bring her to her own conclusion that she would rather not spend the day with him and me. I am tempted to ask if it can't be suggested that her own questioning resembles conventionality. But I don't. No need to score points.

I don't want to carry this on, so I say, "Okay, I don't think he's homophobic, but I also don't think he spends a lot of time judging people. Forget conventional. He's the epitome of a computer nerd. Not your type." I point toward the kitchen and say, "Were you tidying the counter or looking for something? It would be nice if you could clean up your mess of papers. Just tidy it up a little?"

She ignores me and says, "So, what I'm getting out of all of this is that you don't want me to tag along."

It has to be better to just own up to it. "Yes," I say. "He'll bore you to tears. And I will worry about you being bored to tears."

"Fine. I hear you. Go. I'll entertain myself here. I hadn't really wanted to come, anyway. I have things to do. Where will you go? Almost everything has closed for the season. The Cider Company, that's closed. The cheese factory, that's closed, too."

"We'll probably go to Madame Bovary's, drink something hot, and talk."

"You could always do that here. I won't mind, I'll just go upstairs and work. But suit yourself. I understand you want to show him around. Makes sense."

"Right. Exactly."

She exhales loudly. I take that to mean we're finished with this conversation.

Just as I turn to go back to the kitchen to start making the granola, she asks if I've told him that she and I are married. I spin back around and shout, "Alex, come on!" She raises her eyebrows, and I lower my voice again. "I've barely had a conversation with him. I called you my partner. He knows I'm lesbian. He knows I live here with you. It never occurred to me to say that. What do you want? Don't you think that might have sounded a little defensive when there's nothing for me to be defensive about with him?"

"Just asking," she says, waving her cigarette at me by way of saying, *Carry on, go do what you will.*

Will I tell him we're married, I wonder. It's a big deal among our gay and lesbian friends. But I'm often uneasy revealing it to someone who's straight. I do, but not easily. And him? Will I tell him?

It had been my idea. After I moved into Alex's home, I wanted to make every effort to make this relationship work, come what may. In the six years since same-sex marriage had been legalized, I had not been with anyone I'd felt so sure about. One day, I said to her, the words falling out of my mouth almost by themselves,

"If we're serious about this thing between us, why don't we get married?" She said, "Yeah. After all, we can. Let's." And so we did. There was a small ceremony in the backyard of friends of hers and a party with finger foods afterwards. When she and I returned to our house that night, a married couple now, we felt deliciously ordinary, and more in love than before. I experienced a sense of responsibility I'd never known. The love we made that night was slow and thoughtful, as if the act were new to us. The strange thing is that it was only after I told my parents that I'd married a woman—not an easy confession to make—that they finally accepted me as lesbian and said they hoped to one day meet my "friend." But I'm not sure I want to tell Prakash that she and I are married. I don't know why not, but, at the moment, I have the sense that this visit is not the time to tell him.

It is with the smell of a dead and rotting-animal thing as a backdrop that I am preparing the granola when Skye arrives. I must watch the syrup on the stove, so Alex, dressed for the day, lets her in. From where I am I cannot see them. I hear Skye say to Alex, "You're looking rather lovely. Nice necklace. Armour?" So she knows of Alex's theory that jewellery is armour. Some minutes pass. I hear their voices, muffled from this distance. Shoes and jacket are no doubt being removed and put away. Then Skye does what all our friends do—makes her way directly to the kitchen, bypassing the living and dining rooms.

In the kitchen she comes around the counter and meets me at the stove and we embrace, squeezing the life out of each other, playfully hard and rough, the cool of her cheek refreshing against mine. It is always so good to see her. Her corn-yellow hair, thick and curly, has recently been cut. She keeps it short, and must cut it every few weeks. I tussle it, tell her it looks good. With her sharp, angular features, her lean athletic body—although her main physical activity is no more than these long walks—she must surely have once passed easily for a very handsome boy. How I wish I had her genes. Tall, lean, muscular, and no amount of sugary desserts or quantity of food seems to alter this. She is, indeed, a rather handsome woman. She inspects my pot of bubbling syrup, waves the steam up toward her beautiful aquiline nose, and inhales the cinnamon-and-maple aroma. Then she lifts her head, that nose of hers leading her in the direction of the corner of the room. Her brow furrows but she doesn't say anything. I say it: "We think it's a dead mouse or, judging from the smell this morning, it might well be a person down in the basement, an intruder who came in through the basement window, slipped on a wet mossy spot or tripped on a pipe, fell, hit his head, and died down there a while ago. Smells like that, eh?"

Alex prepares coffee. Skye pulls open drawers and sticks her nose toward the backs of them. I tell her I've already done that. Nevertheless, she carries on. I want to repeat that I've already checked out that area, but no need, I suppose. The walk, she says, took her an hour and twenty minutes. There was a bicyclist on the trail, she says, at this time of the year, can you imagine? Normally, there'd be snow on the trail and it would have already been closed. And the lake, there're ducks still bobbing about on the lake. Don't they know they should be long gone? And the shore, with as many people as on a summer day strolling about.

Prakash might arrive while she's here. I am less concerned about him and Skye meeting, I realize. In fact, I am pleased by this possibility—friends from different ends of my life meeting, one looking through one end of a telescope, seeing traces of my past, the other through the opposite end, my present life in sharp focus. People who grow up and live in their hometowns all their lives, or nearby enough, don't have to think about bridging gaps. It would be wonderful if he arrives while she is here.

Skye asks for and is given a flashlight. She unhinges and pulls out the drawers completely and peers down behind the framework of the cabinet. She puts everything back and tells us that it was so strange, there were buds on some of the trees along the trail, and new springlike tufts of ornamental grasses coming up in gardens that abut the trail. A strong woman, she grabs hold of the wine fridge and shimmies it out of the very tight cranny in which it is housed beneath the counter. I couldn't have done that. Thankfully, I am not the type to feel diminished by the physical strength of other women. Alex gets the hand vacuum and deals with the matted grey dust and mouse excrement that covers the floor like wads of dryer lint while Skye gets down on her elbows, unfazed by the likelihood, at least in my mind, that if there is excrement on the ground, there is likely dried mouse urine, too, and she shines the light all over the back and into the mechanisms of the fridge. As she does this, she tells us about her own fridge at the cottage having been brought to a sudden noisy and messy halt by a mouse that jumped into the fan at the back, a terrible splatter she had to clean up on her own because Liz was in Vancouver at the time.

"Ooooh, that smell, can't you smell that smell? Ooooh, that smell," she says, to which Alex responds, "Lynyrd Skynyrd." Skye raises her hand in the air for a high-five, and Alex lifts hers, but indifferently. Skye grabs Alex's hand, clutches it, and forces Alex to shake hers. They know of what they speak. I don't ask for an explanation, but I do wish Alex weren't so lethargic. Skye's laughing, but Alex seems so reserved. A good slap of her palm against Skye's would have been chummier, funnier. Skye is going to sense that something's wrong. There's not much I can do about that.

No dead thing is found behind the wine fridge, but the smell, that ooooh smell, definitely rises up from behind it. Something must be caught in the walls or in the subfloor beneath the cork flooring. We'll have to live with it. So will Prakash. I have to smile. This must surely be the universe delivering to me a dose of comeuppance for the contempt I felt when one spring day I visited Prakash in the house he shares with his wife. Or shared. Who knows now—new house, no wife, new wife? Anyway, that visit was the only time I ever went to his house, and the second and last time I ever met Aruna.

The first time, several months after he'd come back from India with her, we met outside a café in Little Italy near my home. She clung to his arm. To enter the restaurant, he tried to extricate himself, but she held on and in they went awkwardly. She was slight and shy. She wore a knee-length Indian top in shades of red and pink that was made from a shiny fabric, and low-heeled open-toed sandals. Her waist-length hair, blacker than mine, was braided at her back. Mine was as short as Prakash's, but I had long bangs that fell to one side. I wore a white T-shirt under a vest in a flowery textured upholstery fabric, blue jeans, and tired old red-and-white sneakers. I expected my choice of clothing to do the work of instantly differentiating us one from the other, and to suggest that I was not one to follow rules, I had removed the laces from the sneakers and wore no socks. I wanted to appear "cool." The three of us were in essence foreigners to each other. She was the most authentic Indian of us all, and I imagined she'd find me, from the Caribbean—and despite my sartorial choices—crude. Over the course of a long drip-slow hour, our differences were, in the end, not accentuated by the clothing she and I wore as much as by Prakash's discomfort; he was juggling two different personalities within himself, one of the relentlessly pursuing man and the other of a man caught, a man with traditional responsibilities and who had to be in charge. The booth in which we sat was big enough for three people on one side; even so, she pressed against him. From my side of the table, I could tell that one hand, although kept out of view below the table, made constant contact with his leg. He shifted away from her several times, but each time she adjusted so that contact was made again. I could see his chagrin, but she seemed oblivious, like a child not comprehending being shrugged off. He would have known me well enough, I was sure, to guess I wasn't missing any of this. Perhaps if I hadn't been there, he might have put his arm around her and kept her close.

For a while, I was amused by their dance, but it occurred to me that he might have wanted me to see their discomfort, and so, perversely, I pretended not to notice a thing. She seemed to speak English well enough, yet I'd ask her a question and she'd look to him to answer for her. I can even now recall him saying, in English, surely meaning to be encouraging, "Come on, you can answer for yourself," after which he said something to her in Gujarati or Hindi—I couldn't tell which—perhaps repeating what he'd just said in English. Perhaps it was an admonishment, but if so, it was gentle, for his tone wasn't much different from when he spoke English. I remember her pouting, mumbling something back to him in their language, her free hand cupping her mouth to his ear, like a child. He finally answered on her behalf the questions I had directed to her.

Then, that night, shut away in his study, he phoned me. He apologized. Although I knew what he was apologizing for, I told him I didn't. He explained she was shy. As if I hadn't noticed. He said he was like a teacher, always showing her, instructing, cautioning, cajoling. He said he often thought of me saying to him, *Let's do this, let's go here, let's try that,* and wished she possessed a similar curiosity and verve.

Months later, he invited me to come to his house. For the longest while I found reasons for being unable to go. It eventually dawned on me that to him the hospitality of a man in charge of a household, a man with a wife, was a display of success. He wanted his wife to cook for me, and he wanted me to observe as he sat back at the table with me while she served us. I decided to allow him this dignity, as corrupt as it might have been. It had been a cool, bright day in early May, and outside crocuses were just beginning to push up out of brown earth around their newly built house and you could smell the end of winter in the air. When I arrived, Aruna came to the door, her arms folded across her chest. I stepped forward to engage in an embrace, but she did not move her arms to welcome me. And so an awkwardness with me was exposed.

The air inside their new house smelled of spices, and a nose-singeing scent of curry and cooking oil rose up out of the acrylic wall-to-wall carpeting. We sat in a living room that looked as if it was rarely used. Hanuman figurines stood in a glass-and-oak cupboard. There were two large wedding photographs, printed on canvas, framed and hanging on a wall, and on a glass coffee table were a brass lotah and tarria that I assumed were used in the ceremony. Barely five minutes had passed when Aruna excused herself and went to the kitchen. I called behind her that I'd love to help. She said, "You stay. He wants you to himself."

We all sat at the table for dinner, but again, before long, she got up, cleared her plate, and said she was going to watch her favourite TV program on an Indian station. When I heard the television sounds, I said, "She's not comfortable. Is everything all right?" He did not answer, he just stared at the food on his plate. I asked again, "Are the two of you okay? Or is this about me?"

He launched into an apology and complaint. "See? She makes a point of not being welcoming to any of my friends from here. If they're from India, she'll entertain them."

"But I'm Indian," I said, adding quickly, "Well, sort of. Heritage, ancestry. Do they count for anything? Or is it just me?"

"It's not you. It's her. She won't speak Gujarati with me. I must speak Hindi to her. She is not very sociable, but don't take it on, it's not personal. She's like that. She doesn't mean anything."

I suggested we go to the TV room and watch with her. The furniture was all Indian, carved wood and brass tops, except for three leather sofas, strewn with pillows in embroidered fabrics studded with mirrors, from which rose a sweet and oily fried-dessert fragrance—sugar, oil, rosewater—an odour with arms that pawed at me and wrapped itself around and around me like an affection-craving child. The stinging scent seemed to pose a test; how you took to it marked you as either one of them, who would stay easily, or an outsider who couldn't wait to leave.

Neither Skye nor Alex has noticed I haven't been paying them attention. If I were facing them, they'd see on my face what could be a smile. But it's not a true smile. It's the silly spread of embarrassment, for what I suppose is a kind of shallowness on my part.

Prakash may not want to escape the instant he arrives, but at least the smell of this dead thing might allow *him* to turn up *his* nose.

He and I are both Indians who were born and grew up outside of India, and we're vastly different, one from the other. And he'd say his Indian wife is different from both of us, too. An Indian from the Caribbean. An Indian from Africa. And a real Indian, from the subcontinent. But he and she speak Hindi. I don't. There were—*are*—so many things between him and me, separating us. It would never have worked.

Even if Alex and Skye saw the contortion on my face, I'm safe; another of the many oddities in the design of the human form: the body, a manifestation of some considerable length, with only two tiny slits we call eyes in English, tiny relative to the size of the whole, each slit about one and a half inches wide, with which to apprehend the physical world, and both placed an inch away from one another, give or take the fraction that makes each one of us unique, and way up at the top of the whole length of the person. This time the oddity is an asset rather than a flaw. If Alex and Skye had been looking at me, they would have seen the awkward thing I was doing with my lips and interpreted it as a sign that I was listening and was amused by them, or that I am pleased with my syrup, which I seem preoccupied with, but my eyes are impenetrable—they are a shield. Thankfully, no one can see the pictures and thoughts behind them. At the same time, what is good for one should be good for the other—and there are definitely times I wish I could see behind Alex's eyes.

Skye, still on the ground, makes herself comfortable, crossing her legs. "If we were vultures—and believe it or not, I saw one this morning sitting in the top branches of a naked tree—this smell would intoxicate us. We'd be smacking our great big beaks and clapping our smelly feet in delight." She is a forensic pathologist and never fails to drop ingots of related trivia: "Do you know they defecate on their own feet to keep them cool?" she says. Sometimes it's best to ignore Skye's delight in trivia. Alex and I make sounds of disgust. She carries on, of course: "Talking of vultures, did you know turkey vultures can vomit up their food and use it as a projectile at anything or anyone that bothers them? They can send it flying as far as ten feet! Imagine that!"

"And humans use solid projectiles to get their points across, too," says Alex, as she flicks the towel at Skye, purposely missing her. It's good to see Alex livening up at least a bit. Hopefully her mood will change completely and things will be better for the rest of the day.

Alex is telling Skye she's begun the chapter on forgeries that could have changed history. Skye says, "Have you decided if you'll tackle your theory about Valla's analysis of the Donation of Constantine? You should, Al. It's brilliant."

I guess they discuss her work. Before I can stop myself I say, "What's that?"

She looks to Alex to answer, but Alex remains tight-lipped. It is Skye who enlightens me. "Lorenzo Valla. A fifteenth-century Catholic priest. He did a textual analysis of Emperor Constantine the Great's decree that supposedly gave—that's the donation part—Rome, and much of Western Europe, to the Roman Catholic Church. He is said to have proved the decree was a forgery."

This is why I like Skye. Without judgment, she answers. Even if I am not actually enlightened, I am at least acknowledged. Alex, on the other hand, has looked away, as if she wishes I hadn't exposed myself. Or I suppose that look-away of hers could also mean, *See, this is what I have to deal with, someone who isn't interested in what I do.* Oh, I'm being foolish. I am being unnecessarily defensive. It is just that around Skye I often feel a great warmth, as if I am an actual person, and this lays bare the coolness that has come between Alex and me.

I nod with my chin as Alex responds to Skye, "Well, it's been written about from all angles, ad nauseam. My question about Valla is what exactly were his motives in having taken on such a controversial analysis. Why did *he*, what motivated *him*, a Catholic priest, to place his patron's desires to take on such an analysis above the authority of the Vatican? These are questions not about the supposed gift, not about the forgery, not about Valla's exposé of it, nor about the Church, not even about his patron's motives, but about Valla himself—man of God or not—about the nature of loyalty, self-preservation, patriotism then and now, how this links up to the leaking of documents today. I mean, I'm making a leap here certainly, not an impossible one but an important one. These questions are on my mind. That Valla's assertion that the treatise was a forgery might have been a calculated lie is one of many angles."

To this, no one says anything. The stirring of the ingredients in my pot, the scraping sounds I make, are embarrassing. I let go of the spoon and busy myself more quietly. After some seconds, Alex adds in a low, almost despairing voice, "Is this kind of work of any real importance? Does anyone care? If we, as a species, carry on as we do, will there be any of us left to care?"

I understand her despair about the state of the world today—I even share it. But I have no idea about this Valley man, or whatever his name is, and despite how surprised I am to hear her so vocal today, it irks me that she has carried on so about him and about her work. She doesn't usually talk with me like this about what she's doing. Clearly she has with Skye. I'd listen if she did. But then again, it's true she's invited me to lectures in the city and abroad, given by her and others, and I've chosen not to go along, but only because half of this is all gibberish to me.

It's as if Alex is using the occasion to let me know that Skye—or if not Skye, specifically, then someone who is not me—shares knowledge in common with her. But to what end? I wish she wouldn't use Skye to fight me. Skye and I are alike. I think it's that Skye is Catholic and I am Trinidadian. Not all Trinidadians are Catholic, as I, case in point, am not, but I would wager it could be assessed—perhaps by someone with Alex's brain—that all Trinidadians have Catholic traits. Open, warm-hearted, generous, forgiving. Like Skye, we sense what's going on around us, we want to take care of others, and we tend to blurt out what's in our hearts. Most of the time, at least. Alex might be an atheist, but her background is Protestant, private. Closed. She tends to hold her thoughts and feelings to herself. She too is an observer, but this does not allow her to excuse and forgive, but rather to calculate, analyze, and critique. Nothing is believed by her until it can be seen and proven. It's what makes her a good theoretician, a good critic, I'm sure.

"Well, you can ask such questions of the work we all do," Skye says, looking first at me and then at Alex, meaning, clearly, to include me. "None of it will change the price of corn, or how fast the ice melts. But doing the work affirms our existence, especially now, in the face of an uncertain future," she says, pointing beyond the sunroom, out toward the lake. "And I'll contradict myself by saying: write it all *now*, as if—and in case—there won't be another chance, another book—although your theories about Valla can well fill an entire book."

So Skye, it is clear, knows that Alex has many theories, so many they can fill a book. If Alex talks with Skye about them, and not with me, then I am not to blame. I'd listen, yes, if she were to try. It would, in my case, be as if she were teaching me, so I wouldn't be able to participate as well as someone who already has a depth of knowledge about these things. But at least we'd be sharing conversation about her work. If she invites me to another lecture, given by her or by someone else, here or abroad, it would serve us well for me to go. I hope I soon have such an opportunity.

But is there anything I can teach Alex? Sometimes, facing Alex, I feel as if I've come from a backward place—and a place known to her, too, before she and I even met. Despite all my time in this northern white wonderland, it seems I have picked up nothing with which to impress even a banana slug.

Alex raises her eyebrows and nods, almost resignedly, as if to say Skye has a point. She mentions another topic of her book that is supposedly less known but, as one would have guessed, Skye—and not I—knows that one, too.

I continue to stir the syrup, and consider that Prakash can be to me what Skye appears right now to be to Alex. A kind of foil that validates her. So will he, then, validate me in front of Alex?

And seeing this home I share with her, so different from his, will validate me, and he'll conclude that I've landed on my feet and therefore no longer need him as I used to.

That's true: I don't need him.

Now, that is. I don't need him today. But nothing stays the same forever. One can't actually know the future. Where more than one person is involved, there isn't such a thing, for either, as total knowledge, or control. It isn't over—until it is. It isn't over, and then it is. I suppose it's true I don't exactly want to lose him entirely. Not *exactly*. Not *entirely*.

Skye is watching me. She says, "She's not with us. She's in a world of her own."

She's up, off the ground, and is dusting herself off. "Where have you gone, Pri?" she asks me. Alex watches closely.

Thankfully I am able to say, without missing a beat, "Oh, I was just thinking about the strange weather. About how long we have left. You seeing buds on trees this morning, and vomit-launching vultures. Climate change. Our uncertain future."

Washing her hands, she says, "Climate change? Ah no, no such thing. It's a hoax." She snorts to emphasize she's being ironic. She watches as I pour hot syrup into the bowl of nuts, seeds, and grains. I stir the mixture with a wooden spoon, conscious that I am being watched expectantly, and spread it flat on cookie sheets. I hand the spoon to Skye. She works the entire bowl of the spoon into her mouth and makes garbled flattering sounds around it. I set the alarm for ten minutes—and who knows why, but we all stay right there in the kitchen, I on one side of the granite counter, she and Alex on the other, the smell of the dead thing like a bell clanging behind them.

In the sudden quiet I ask, "How's Liz? Isn't she supposed to be coming sometime soon?"

Alex slides around to the fridge, opens it, but doesn't take anything out of it. Her distractedness is irritating. I wonder if Skye can see it, and I feel a little embarrassed.

Liz, Skye's partner, who teaches at a university on the other side of the continent, is indeed coming for the Christmas holidays, Skye says. She's supposed to be here end of next week, but who knows for sure? She sounds sarcastic when she says this. Everyone has their little troubles, don't they? I tell her they'll have to come for dinner, and ask, "Excited?" dancing my eyebrows up and down to suggest a slight lewdness.

She looks down at the counter, laughs, and says, "You know, Liz and I have been together twenty-one years. No, twenty-two. Eh, twenty—twenty-something. We stopped counting a while ago. We've been doing this back-and-forth thing for nine of those. Not my idea of a good time, but that's the way it is."

Oh dear, sounds like there really is trouble over there, too. But I am not about to start prying. There isn't time. I'll ask when there's enough time to get into it. I do wonder, however, and not for the first time, why she's never gone out to Vancouver. Vancouver! Imagine that. Who doesn't want to go to Vancouver? Liz comes every three weeks for five days, but Skye has never been. One does wonder why. They're very lovey-dovey when you see them during those five days. But I sometimes imagine she has a lover, someone who is there with her at this moment saying, *Oh, Lizzy, just move here, why don't you.* Perhaps she and Skye have some kind of agreement. And Skye, what about her? She's never expressed an interest in anyone else, at least not in front of us, but who knows, really? You can't know everything about a person, can you, even if you think you're close to them?

I say, "I often wish I'd met Alex when we were younger, that we'd been together long enough to forget how long it has been." I look at Alex and, smiling, say, "It would have been nice to have grown up, as it were, together. You know, we'd have the same memories."

Alex, fumbling with opening a package of cheese from the fridge, responds, but the three seconds or so that it takes for her to do so feel like an eternity. "We could fight about details remembered differently, and who's right," she says.

What is she trying to do? This is so unlike her to drag an outsider into our kerfuffle.

Skye does a little chair dance and looks at me and says, "So. Who's the visitor? What's his name?"

"Prakash," I say.

Alex, answering over me, says, "University friend. She hasn't seen him in years."

Skye repeats his name and asks, "What kind of name is that? Sounds, hmm, Indian. Hindu, Muslim? I mean, is it okay to ask a question like that? Don't want to be rude, you know."

I laugh. Alex says, "Hindu. From Uganda."

"I've known him since I was nineteen," I elaborate. "We met in our first year. He's a year younger than I. Which means our friendship is my longest here in Canada. He and his family were refugees from Idi Amin in '72. We haven't seen each other since Alex and I came down here to live."

Skye draws her eyebrows up as she makes the calculations. "Ugandan Indian. I remember that era. Nobody wanted them. Good old Pierre, though. You don't hear much about the Ugandan refugees nowadays," she says.

The alarm goes off, and I remove the two trays from the oven. "He was so much like a boy when I met him, he didn't fit in with the university culture. If he were a girl, you'd have called him slight. The other students used to insist he was from Biafra, not Uganda. People weren't all that kind."

"Well, we're a cruel species," Skye says. "You have to marvel at how people like him learn to fit in at all."

I am eager to reveal something redemptive, something endearing about Prakash for Alex's ears. And the words tumble from my mouth as I think of them, the ideas constructed on the fly. "He didn't make a lot of friends, but he managed. He could make fun of himself, play with the very kinds of things people laughed at. For instance, he pronounces v's the way we pronounce w's, and w's like our v's. Not something, you'd think, that university students would make fun of, but they did." I don't tell her that Fiona and I also teased him about this, trying to teach him where to put his tongue and how to press his teeth to his lips. "So we'd go out for dinner," I carry on, "and he'd make sure whoever was at the table was listening before he asked the waiter what *weggies* were on the daily special. Of course, the waiter would be stumped for a few seconds, then you'd see the dawning and earnest attempt not to react, and you just knew he was wishing his job allowed him to make fun of this customer's pronunciation. Yes, he could laugh at himself and make you laugh with him."

I am the only one laughing at this little story, bemused too that Skye and Alex seem unsure of how to react to someone making fun of his own accent.

"You were his closest friend, then?" Skye asks.

I turn the contents of each tray and return them to the oven, resetting the timer, thinking fast how best to answer this question so that it provides Alex with an answer that would be useful to her, too. "I and my roommate at the time, misfits all." I grin, putting air quotes around the word *roommate*.

She slides her head awkwardly side to side on her shoulders, imitating an Indian dancing doll, as she says, "Oh, yes? And?"

I assume she's asking about the supposed roommate, but Alex answers, "He had a crush on her."

Said in a different tone, she might have been teasing me, but this is more like a complaint. I am beginning to think she actually means to open a discussion in front of Skye. I grab it by its neck and deal with it.

"It might have been in the air, but nothing came of it, naturally. We were both out of our element. He was a nerdy kid, and I was just beginning to understand things about myself, about my sexuality. It was so odd back then, such excitement and terror at once." Skye's elbows dig into the granite counter, her head propped in her cupped hands, and she's batting her eyes at me to continue. I was uncomfortable and guarded around the other Caribbean students, I say, terrified of being shunned in that community, and of news of my depravity— that's how they'd have seen it—travelling back home to my family and their friends. "Prakash didn't know people from the Caribbean. He was safe to hang out with," I add. "We found each other. Two awkward brown kids—I was nerdy in my own way—aware of how different and uncool we both were, and what a friendship between us could do for us both. But, of course, we had different ideas about what we wanted from that friendship."

I am telling this story to Alex, but I look at Skye and add that his parents, the instant they heard about me, considered us, according to what Prakash had relayed to me back then, a couple. My parents, on learning I'd made friends with a man, were pleased. Actually, my mother was more than pleased: she was relieved. She'd ask me every so often if Prakash had "popped the question" yet.

Skye grimaces, and out of the corner of my eye I see Alex has remained stony—but she's listening.

I tell them that it took a while for my mother to finally hear me when I said for the umpteenth time that I was not interested in marrying him. She then, without having met him, began to find her own faults with him, by way, I suppose, of dealing with her great disappointment that there was not soon going to be a wedding in the family. She actually began to warn me, as if I needed to be warned off him: Indians like to think they are better than we are. Alex is used to hearing about these kinds of prejudices among diasporic Indians, but Skye has a look of horror. I am not sure if this look is because I would say such a thing or because of any fact in that assessment. I carry on about my mother, saying that when I reminded her that Prakash was Ugandan, not Indian, she responded that since he and his parents were fluent in Hindi and Gujarati but not in English, they would imagine themselves to be truer Indians than we were, even though they were not from India, and she didn't want to be disrespected by them just because her only language was English and she was born in Trinidad. I laugh as I relate this, but Skye looks uncomfortable, and I imagine she is wondering if there is any racism in all of this. Alex sees her discomfort, too. A reassuring nod passes from Alex to Skye, and Skye relaxes. I appreciate the calm that seems suddenly to be descending on us, even as the source of my story is the pebble in Alex's shoe.

When out of concern for my mother's prejudice I defended Prakash and his family, I conclude, my mother, who one cannot ever really successfully argue with, dug in her heels: he might have been born and brought up in Africa, she said, but he's still an Indian, to which I responded she sounded just like Amin.

To this, Skye says, "Yeah," in a tone that makes the word rhyme with *duh-uh*.

Grateful for this by-the-way opportunity to throw some light on my relationship with Prakash, I elaborate: "I knew all along that marriage and men were not for me. But I didn't at that time—back then, in *those* days—feel I could tell this to Prakash. And so he would try to hold my hand, I'd pull away and slap his shoulder affectionately, and say, *What's that about, come on, moron, you're like my brother,* and he'd shrug, mutter a string of words like *I know, I know, I'm just…it's not a big deal, you should know that.*"

Alex is listening to every word I say. This is all new information. It's easier for me to expound in front of Skye. I get the impression that in front of Skye it's easier, too, for Alex to hear.

"Same here. I know exactly of what you speak," says Skye. "I used to have friends—guys—who knew they didn't have the chance of a snowflake in hell with me, and that was always the way: they treat you, at first, as if you're one of them, respectful, totally accepting, and then, next thing you know, you're fending them off. *Get away, shoo, go away.* It was as if they were deaf and blind."

"So you, too," I say excitedly, and add, "I always used to have the conversation—*But you're like my brother, don't you see?* Every two or three months, the same conversation. And I was so boyish in those days, it was amazing."

Alex says, "It's not amazing. They're guys. They know you're a 'woman.' Everything else about you, to them, is inconsequential. Beneath your tomboyishness, under the boy clothes, the forthrightness, they know what body parts you have, and that's all that matters."

I wish she hadn't said this. Skye and I affirm the boyishness we see in one another, mostly by never contradicting it or making mention of anything that might point in even an askance way to the lie—for want of a kinder word—in it.

I insist on finishing what I want Alex to hear. "But in our last year of university," I continue, "I realized that I really did like him and that if I wanted to keep him as a friend, I'd have to tell him that I wasn't and never would be interested in guys—not just him, but any guy. He didn't understand at first. But he too wanted the friendship, so he backed off. It's been almost thirty-nine years, you know, that he and I have known each other."

The timer goes off again. I feel exposed and a little ticked off with Alex, but I mustn't show it. I remove the trays and set them on wire racks to cool. Alex comes around and pulls some of the hot granola off. She blows on the chunk and pops it in her mouth. The aroma of the toasted nuts and oats hasn't tempered the stench of dead something or other. I suggest we go into the living room.

After we've settled there, Skye wants to know, "So, Pri, what happened? Did he ever get married? Or is he still pining?"

I wish she'd leave the subject alone. "He married," I say, adding quick on the heels of that, "So, what plans do you and Liz have for her time down here?"

But Alex is already saying, over my words, "It was an arranged marriage."

If only Skye would answer my question, but she says to Alex, "Is his wife coming, too?"

"Nope. He's coming on his own. Apparently, it's an unhappy marriage. They live in the same house, but they don't speak to one another, except about the children," Alex says, recounting things I recently told her as if she'd acquired knowledge of it on her own, and as if I weren't there. It is clear—at least to me—that she and I are talking to each other, Skye merely a microphone into which we are speaking.

"He has children. Three. Typical Indian man, very committed to his children," I say.

"Ugandan," Skye corrects.

I laugh, and quickly add, "Very good. But enough. I want to know what you and Liz will be doing. You'll have to come for dinner. Right, Alex?" Alex doesn't respond, which seems rude to me, but I guess she has only one thing on her mind today.

After a few minutes of inconsequential chatter, Skye is ready to be driven back to her house. I have no choice. If only Alex had learned to drive. It's a sore point between us, as I must always be at her beck and call. And in an instance like this, help from her would have been most welcome.

I go to the bedroom to ready myself, hurrying. I don't want to leave Skye and Alex out there together too long. And, just as I feared, as I reach the living room again, I see them standing close to each other. Their voices are low. They don't see me. I retreat a couple steps as Alex says, "There's something she hasn't told me. Something doesn't feel right."

"Yes, but that isn't news. You've known this all along. And what does it matter, anyway?"

"I don't like having been made a fool of. I feel as if I don't know her."

"Okay, but what is there to do about it? Especially now?"

"Nothing. But it's not so easy, Skye. To simply shrug it off and get on with life. I feel I need to understand what I've been dealing with here."

Skye says, somewhat flatly, "You need to let it go, Al. Let them do their thing. You're doing what's best for you, right?" There's a pause, and I wonder if they know I am listening. Sky asks again, "I'm right, aren't I, Alex?" I don't hear Alex's response, and I wonder what it is that she's doing that must be best for her.

Skye, I suddenly realize, acted this morning as if she were learning about Prakash for the first time. But now it seems that Alex had long ago told her about our thorny situation. If so, then I was lied to today by both of them.

I'm about to step into the room when Skye continues, and I pull back again. "I have to say it really worries me that this bothers you so much. Just get to the end of today and I'm sure tomorrow you'll feel a lot better."

Thank God for Skye. I suppose it's good to have a friend we can each confide in, even if it's the same friend. If she can calm Alex, that's just great. Later, at the end of today, or better yet, tomorrow after he's gone, I'll begin anew with Alex and she'll see that all's well between us. She'll suffer through this next day and a half, and perhaps that's just the way it has to be. Just until tomorrow, and then I'm sure everything will be all right. Yes, Skye, reassure her, thank you.

Skye's hand is on Alex's shoulder, comforting her as I enter the room. Her thumb rests caringly on Alex's neck. Alex hears my approach and steps back and, so parted, Skye angles her body to include me. Alex looks oddly as if she's been caught; she knows I like my privacy, I am not in favour of us discussing with friends any troubles we might be having. It's easy to lose friends when they feel they have to sympathize with one or the other. But Skye is different. She has broad enough shoulders to carry us both. Conceding that she knows more than I had realized, I say, "Hey, the weekend will fly by. In no time we'll have our lives back and our home to ourselves again." I wink at Alex. She looks away.

"That'll be a good thing," Skye says. Is she being sarcastic? I feel chastised. But if her intention is to encourage Alex, I suppose I can tolerate it. With her palm open flat, she taps Alex's cheek, two quick gentle claps, affectionately, as if rousing Alex from a hypnotic slumber. Best to hurry and take her back home, I think, before this deteriorates into a full-blown mess, with her playing counsellor, therapist, and judge.

We're about to exit the front door, Skye ahead of me, but I step back and ask Alex if she'd mind just giving the front stoop a quick sweep. Skye turns as I say this, and as I had intended, she witnesses me kiss Alex on her lips and say, "Love you. Won't be long." Alex pulls back, surprised perhaps, which makes sense as we haven't been close all day, but she seems a touch embarrassed. Nothing to be done, I think. By the end of the weekend, this will all have passed.

Turning out of the driveway, I announce that Prakash will arrive any time. I laugh and say I can't imagine him and Alex spending half an hour alone together.

Skye doesn't respond. She isn't even smiling. It feels awkward, and I'm compelled to carry on. I feel she wants to say something, but she must know there's a point where her interventions might feel like meddling. It's a fine line.

"He's like a brother," I say. I'm sure that sounded as if I were apologizing, or making some sort of excuse. But why should I have to defend myself to her? We've known her for less than five years. I've known Prakash for decades longer. Who is she to reproach me? I tell myself to breathe, relax.

Just before the turnoff into the town of Macaulay, we approach the little white clapboard house of new residents, Syrian refugees recently sponsored by a local group. I seize the chance to change the subject, remove my foot from the accelerator to slow, and point out the house to her. She says, "Yes, I know. Everyone in town seems to know." Three kids, perhaps between the ages of six and nine, dressed in winter jackets and toques, are riding bicycles, given to them by a business in the town, around a blue van parked on the grass in the front yard. I tell her that every time I pass this house I look for them and want to pull into their driveway and tell them I'm pleased they've come to live here. But after that, then what? I don't want to initiate a friendship. We might well find we don't share the same values and don't actually like each other.

She says just about everyone she knows has done just that with them, dropped in on them, taken them food and clothing and house items. Apparently they have more winter clothing than they may ever use. They themselves made a donation to the Cerebral Palsy Foundation, a handover that was photographed and written up in the local papers.

"What a gift," I say, "and what a burden. Imagine having—on top of being in dire need—to constantly smile and be grateful to everyone you meet. There'll be many of us they likely won't care for, or approve of, if they got to know us. Nevertheless, they'll have to show gratitude. Seems to me there's something demeaning about that."

Skye says, "Yup, very likely. They're dependent on us right now, and we get to feel noble and good and righteous. They won't always be in need, but they'll forever be beholden. At least the first generation of them. But that's a better problem to have than the one that got them here, I suppose."

I recall Prakash's experience and, without mentioning his name, I paraphrase and contemporize what he'd long ago told me: "They're not blind or deaf. They'll eventually feel the envy from people right here in the town who see themselves as also in dire need but who were never given a free house or car. They'll see that Canadians aren't necessarily all as warm and cuddly as we're currently making ourselves out to be. And still, they'll forever have to be expressing how grateful they are to us."

Despite the good weather, there's hardly any traffic this Saturday. I'm pleased; I'll make it back in no time. Around and behind the houses that line the road walls of lilac, sumac bushes and maple trees are all bare of leaves, and fields and roads that are usually hidden are visible through the naked skeletal branches. The land stretches into the distance and undulates. I say that at this time of year it always seems as if there's more countryside than town around here. At the beginning of the season, as it is now, the landscape appears disorientingly unfamiliar, and there is a bleak beauty about it—it looks spent and forlorn and vulnerable. Skye answers that snow actually warms up the look of the bare land. She looks forward, she says, to a proper snowfall soon so she can go snowshoeing. Winter without snowshoeing isn't winter.

We pull up outside her white-and-green two-storey house, but she doesn't immediately unfasten her seat belt. She sits staring at the road ahead. There are no cars parked on it. Everyone keeps waiting for snow, and here in town the residents have already begun parking their cars in their driveways to make it easier for the snowplows. I'm about to point this out, when, to my chagrin, she brings up Prakash again.

"Is he still with his wife?" she asks.

"Of course he is," I say. Taken aback, I can't hide my defensiveness. I don't actually know, but I'm not about to admit this—nor that in the last day or two I've found myself perversely hoping that he isn't. There is no glee in the thought of his marriage having failed, but rather an illogical churlishness: I might not have wanted him, but I hadn't ever wanted anyone else to have him either.

"Were she and you friends? Did the three of you hang out together?" Skye is usually obliging and indulgent, so why such prickly insistence? She is no longer being helpful. What does she want to know? It's as if she wants to catch me out. As irritating as this is, I keep an appearance of calm. Ever since Alex and I arrived here and met Skye and Liz—amongst the first people we connected with—we have considered them our closest friends.

I answer as calmly as I can. "She and I weren't friends. He'd told her I was lesbian. She couldn't understand this, nor why he'd befriended someone like me. I suspect she never knew Prakash and I met occasionally for tea." There is relief in this admission. He'd sit at the dining table across from me nursing a cup of tea between his hands, refilling it from the teapot on the table, as he confided his disappointment in a marriage that had turned out to be as traditional as he had feared—but there's no need to run my mouth.

Skye looks at me and begins speaking swiftly. "He was a big part of your life. Whether he was explicit or not, I would guess you're the one he wanted to live his life with. Perhaps still does. Thwarted desire doesn't easily dissipate. Culturally, you have more in common with him."

I spin my head around and look directly at her. "Than with whom? He's straight. He and I grew up in different countries, oceans apart. We might look like we do, but we *don't* share the same culture. His first language isn't English. That's my only language. I am an artist. We might have gone to the same university, but he was in business and I went to art school." The incredulity in my voice is unhidden.

I want to ask her if she thinks skin colour is enough to make him and me the same, but I still don't know with whom she is suggesting I have less in common than with him. His wife? Alex? Her? Her and Alex and the rest of our friends, all of whom are white in this rural area? I don't know if she means to be talking about race but is mistakenly using the word *culture*. I suddenly feel a rift between her and me that I've never felt before. But I don't want to be defensive, or to insult her, or have her think I'm getting very close to saying she's making a racist connection. She isn't racist. I know this. But something is being revealed here, and it scares me. It saddens me. She's our good friend. I don't want to fall out with her.

"He has more in common with his wife than he has with me," I say flatly.

"That would be true, too. But you don't actually know if they're still together, do you?" she says under her breath.

I need to be careful. "Alex might be from here," I say slowly, trying to glean what her concern is really all about, and to find some kernel with which to quell this line of thinking. "She might be white. But she and I have way more in common than he and I." I'm fumbling, but I carry on, an inexplicable panic suddenly gripping the muscles of my stomach. "In fact, culturally, she and I share a great deal of the same interests. Did you know that long before we met we'd both been involved as activists in the same kinds of social causes and had gone out on the streets in public demonstrations—that we may even have stood feet away from one another in marches against one kind of oppression or another? Do you know that long before we met we'd gone to several of the same plays—imagine that, the same plays in the same theatres. We'd listened to the same music, frequented the same galleries, on this and other continents? We both come from and know Western traditions, Western styles. Prakash knows the basics—Leonardo, Michelangelo—but he doesn't share my interests." Billowing anger is stunting my ability to quickly make a more intelligent analysis. She wants to say something but I don't let her; I carry on, more pertinently: "He may not even know the arts of his own culture, because he simply isn't interested in art or literature. Look, there are ways in which Alex and I have many more interests and experiences in common than even you—you from here—and she. And because I grew up in a Westernized family from day one, I have more in common with you than with him. Look, I don't know what you're getting at." I know I am prevaricating, not wanting to offend, discerning something but unsure of what it is exactly, unable to formulate what's troubling me about her interventions. The muscles of my stomach have clenched so tightly I feel dizzy. I must try to approach more straightforwardly the impression baffling me. "Do you think I'm interested in him? Are you trying to set me up with him?" I say, the words tumbling from my mouth, uncensored now. Out of the silence that follows I find clarity. "Look, I feel as if you're trying to get me to admit to something. I don't understand your agenda here, Skye. Are you intentionally creating something between him and me, pushing me toward him? What are you doing? There's nothing there, Skye. Nothing."

Her face has turned red.

From my skin, all through my body and up my face, radiates a terrible heat, my brain engulfed in a raging fire. I am not thinking coherently. I try to speak with more reason. "I don't think," I manage wearily, "that once he and Alex meet, we'll see much of him after." But in the next moment, with some urgency I blurt, "And just to be clear: I have everything I need or want in Alex, in my home here, in my life here. And same with her. There isn't anything she wants or needs."

"Alex isn't happy. I care about her. About you both."

She's really persistent, and out of line telling me about Alex. It's none of her business. Her edginess says she knows it, too. I want to tell her to fuck off. Can a friendship like ours handle that?

I am baffled that she carries on: "Look, there's more going on here. You and Alex need to come clean with each other. This may end up not really being about Prakash at all."

I really have to bite my tongue. What the hell does she know about our private lives? Clearly nothing. Such nonsense. Is she trying to play therapist? This is the point at which friends need to know their place and back off. I tap the digital clock on the dashboard's radio. I put my hand on the key in the ignition. "Nothing—no one—will come between Alex and me. Alex knows I love her. And vice versa. I will not jeopardize what I have with her. Neither of us is up for grabs," I tell her, and, looking at the road straight ahead, I add with finality, "He's probably already at the house."

She undoes her seat belt and opens the door. She does not say goodbye, except by knocking the roof, two taps with her knuckles, as she pushes in the door.

Twenty kilometres over the speed limit, I pass the house of the refugees again. The children are gone. The van is gone. Fuck Skye. Fuck her. Just fuck her. What is she trying to do? I'm not going to let her spoil this day.

Perhaps he's just arriving. Or maybe he arrived a minute after we left the house. Fucking Skye. What did Alex tell her? I feel exposed. A bit of a fool. But I mustn't be too annoyed with Alex. If she needed someone to confide in, Skye is perhaps the best person.

If Prakash is at the house, I wonder what they're talking about. I can just hear him boasting to Alex, *Did you know this or that about Priya, Priya used to do this, Priya and I once did that.* I can't bear that they'd discuss me in my absence. I can't get back fast enough.

I round the bend, and from a few houses away, I see a car parked in our driveway, a silverish, two-door convertible BMW.

3
THE VISITOR

. . .

I hoped Priya would return from taking Skye home before her friend arrived. I didn't want to have to spend time alone with him. I stood in our bedroom, at the foot of the bed, looking around the room. Had she, while she was in here, heard my conversation with Skye?

Clothing, hers and mine, was jumbled on an armchair in the bay window. Her pyjamas lay across the bed, and on her bedside table were her e-book and a pile of regular books, the same ones that have been there, unread, for the last year or so. On my side of the bed, I sat on the rumpled sheets and contemplated how the day would unfold. I picked up Priya's pillow and set it on my lap. From it rose a scent I'd fallen in love with years ago. I brought the pillow to my face and breathed in the familiar alluring aroma. I hugged the pillow tight.

Things that had once intrigued me about my lover of the last six years now confounded me. I used to be able to take it in stride that I couldn't guess Priya's next move. It frustrated me now.

I saw early what she was like; there shouldn't have been any surprises. Take, for instance, the time just after we met and began seeing each other. Before she moved in with me, we shuffled from her apartment to my house, spending hardly a night apart. But after any period of wonderful intensity, she would always pull far away. If we were at my house, she'd suddenly get up and run, as if she'd just remembered a pot on the fire at her apartment. When eventually we spoke on the phone, she'd say she just needed a little space, that she felt claustropho-bic and thought we shouldn't see one another for a few days. It used to distress me; I believed we were on the verge of breaking up. Then, later that same day, she'd call, sheepish. She missed me; she couldn't bear to be away a second longer, so let's forget that nonsense about space and meet up right away. And a night of fierce lovemaking would ensue, fuelled for me by the torture of uncertainty and then relief. Such a push and pull, but I went along, knowing, or rather hoping, that on her own she'd eventually come around. I used to wish I could pin her down, hold and calm her. I thought at the time that that was my job. *My* task. Waiting, the act itself, was my way of saying to her, *I'm here. You're safe with me. I won't run.* It is why I said yes when she proposed marriage. I thought that would reassure her that I was here to stay. To this day she insists—in jest, I think—that she did not actually propose, but rather simply suggested we get married. She sees some meaningful distinction in this. I don't. To me it was *her* way of proposing. Her usual obtuse way. I expected that with time she'd have become more open with me. I look back and see that not much changed—even when she professed love, I intuited a certain distance.

Time came and went, and if anything changed it was my heart. It toughened. An enormous amount of energy is required for a heart to toughen, and in the end it's draining.

I quickly pulled the bed together and went into the main part of the house, fluffing the pillows in the living room, tidying a bit. In the kitchen I washed the cups we'd used when Skye was here and began to gather the ingredients for the pasta and sauce I said I'd make for dinner. As I did so, I contemplated how Priya was capable of being as kind and magnanimous as possible, and then, without cause it sometimes seemed, cool and hurtful. She wasn't mean, but her self-protectiveness made her almost cruel.

That said, the attention she is capable of paying seems like a contradiction. I will never forget my first birthday with her: I awoke to a streamer strung across the door to the kitchen of my old house in Toronto, and little silly presents hidden in places she knew I'd look throughout the day. Then, at dinner at that restaurant she'd made reservations at, she presented me with a particular out-of-print book I'd wanted and couldn't find locally but which she'd managed to track down through a British second-hand bookseller. I'd had no idea she was doing any of this. And it's been the same, more or less, every year, no matter what is happening between us at the time. I can contort myself wondering if such magnanimous gestures were really about her love for me, her desire to make the day a truly special one for me, or if they were a project that allowed her to see for herself what a good partner she could be. But what's the point of trying to figure any of this out now?

I hadn't realized it before, but difference as an attraction only lasts while it's new. A life with someone is different than a courtship.

After Priya announced this man would spend a night in our house, I naturally asked about him, about the nature of their friendship. Not because I was jealous—I was not. At least, not at first. I simply wanted to know who this visitor was, this person she said she was once close with. It was a way of finding out more about the person I was living with. But her defensiveness and skittishness made me wary. I began to wonder what she was hiding. Unable to extract answers from her, I took the opportunity several days ago, the instant she left the house for a haircut in town, to take a peek in her studio for a photo album she'd long ago shown me. The studio was pristine, everything in its place. I usually enjoyed going in, but only did so when she was there. I did not want to turn on the long fluorescent tube lights in case she returned to get something she might have forgotten, and moved through her space keeping my ears peeled to the driveway. Large canvasses dwarfed the room. There was enough light from the large windows on one side so I could clearly see images of shimmering lake water, reflections in them of holiday cottages, white pines and birds, canoeists and water skiers—all northern landscapes and activities but painted in her vibrant, carnival-like tropical palette. She is a good painter. A room comes alive, dances with her palette. I can admire that honestly, despite how we've drifted apart.

There were a few labelled boxes on shelves—*Ends*, *Reviews*, *Sequins/Ribbon/Fabric Paint*—and an unlabelled one under the table in the studio. It had been pushed so far to the back that I was naturally drawn to it. But I'd have had to untape it, an act that might eventually have been discovered. I began my search, then, in the office area, a room at the back of the studio. My hands shook as I rifled among books on a shelf. I was disappointed not to find the album I had come for. I quickly scanned through her filing cabinet and a cupboard in which she kept printer paper and office supplies. Then I noticed a large suitcase-like cardboard box atop that cupboard. I pulled up a chair and took down the dusty box, behind which was a row of shoeboxes. I brought those down, too. None were taped, and in them were albums and what must have been hundreds of loose photos of people and places I did not recognize. If you're going to snoop, I thought, you better be prepared to come across something you'd rather not have found. Something which you will *not* be able to pretend to not have found. My heart thundered. My limbs were ticklish with guilt. I calculated that she was likely at that time just having her hair washed before the cut.

I didn't think Priya was a liar exactly, but rather that she was secretive, and I wanted, this late in our relationship, to know what those secrets were. What I saw were old discoloured photos of her parents—at least, I thought that was who they were, for the young woman resembled Priya—and photos of their marriage, then ones of each of them with groups of people who might have been relatives or close friends. They appeared to be fun-loving people. Groups of them in front of landmarks I didn't recognize, at house parties, in gardens. So many group photos. And several of an older couple. In one of them that couple is standing on the front step of a house, waving to a young woman as she is about to get into a car. Was the couple her grandparents, the woman her mother? It seemed terribly unfair that I was seeing these without Priya there to tell me who was who, and how she was related. Why wouldn't she have shared her family photos with me, I wondered. Did she not trust me? Or did she simply not think I might be interested? There was lots of smiling for the camera; you could almost hear the laughter of the people sitting around food and drink, and in the frothy, frilly water's edges of what I imagined were Caribbean beaches. Jealousy that she'd so guarded these photos made me want to scatter them all across the floor of her office and later confront her. But, of course, considering how I learned of them, I wouldn't have done that. There were a handful of her as a baby—her name scribbled in a flowery hand on the back—her as a toddler, and then in her various school uniforms. I wanted to stay with each and examine them all, but there wasn't time. Sharing the contents of those boxes could have been a kind of gift given to me by her, a glimpse into parts of her life or her mind. My sense that she kept things from me was validated. This was the real problem—not that she had an old friend coming to visit, but that she kept things from me.

I shuffled the photos as I continued to search, and then in one of the boxes was the album she'd shown me once, years before. I looked through it quickly, stopping at one photo I recalled of a table-tennis team she'd belonged to. There was her first love, a woman named Fiona, and there, in that same photo, was Prakash. There were no more of him or Fiona. But in an envelope at the back of the album I found a stack of loose pictures, all of which were of Prakash, some of Priya with him. I could not help but note that this stack did not include any other people, and it was this—this isolated but specific grouping—that weighed on my mind. What did it mean that she'd gathered these together? There's madness in such scrutiny and questioning. I knew this, but I couldn't help myself.

He was an unremarkable presence. He was thin, and there was in almost all the photos what I remembered Priya calling years ago "the trademark V sign" made with his fingers. The photos were likely taken by her; I recognized her signature in the manner of framing the subject. If I am correct that it was she who took these photos, they must have travelled together to various places across the province and perhaps even across Canada—I recognized landmarks in Toronto: the zoo, the Islands, Kensington Market, as well as the landscape of Tobermory—

and there were photos of him posing on large rocks at the seashore, and from the vegetation and colour of the rocks I guessed the location was the east coast. There were two photos, both taken on the same occasion, of the two of them standing side by side. A body of water was behind them, an ocean or perhaps it was a lake, with no sign of land save for the bare rock on which they stood, both of them thin and young, and though their feet were planted wide apart to steady them, they looked as if they would topple forward. They seemed happy, laughing or with large smiles spread on their faces, but there appeared to be no obvious closeness between them, and it might even be said the distance between them had been intentional. I wouldn't know whose intention that was, but given that he was supposed to have been enamoured of her, I would say it was likely she who initiated the apartness. There was an odd resemblance between them—not their Indian appearance, but perhaps the shyness, the hesitation in their stance, both seeming unsure of themselves, each other, the world in which they were caught.

I found nothing that day to suggest she and Prakash had been involved in an intimate relationship. An envelope of photos of no one else but him and her proved nothing. But since then I've wanted to tell her that I found evidence of something graver—of how closed she was with me. But I would have had to admit I'd searched through her office. Secrecy and snooping seemed like different sides of a single coin.

Priya had not yet returned when, from the kitchen, I heard an unfamiliar car pull into the driveway. I went to the front of the house and pulled down a slat of the blinds to have a look. He'd arrived in a grey convertible BMW with a blue soft top.

I suppose I had expected a simply ordinary person to arrive at our door, perhaps fattened by age and of no remarkable uniqueness. So I was quite surprised to find a medium-build man, fairer in colour than I'd imagined. He was a year younger than Priya, but he looked older than she. He had the kind of almost-handsome face that is cast in Bollywood films as the good-natured supporting character. Too soft, too fleshy for the hero, but sensible enough looking to be confided in.

It wasn't as awkward as I'd expected. I explained that Priya had had to run an errand and would be back in no time. He was unfazed by her absence and immediately talkative: "I've been down this way before, you know. Just for the day. Just once. The dunes, we spent the day there, some guys from work and I." In the foyer, as he slowly removed his shoes, he said, "I'll never forget, at sundown just before we left the beach, we heard what we thought was a pack of dogs yipping as if they'd just been let loose from a cage, but they weren't dogs."

"Coyotes," I said.

He nodded. "Yep. Three of them, but they sounded like they were half a dozen or so. At the edge of the water, tugging at the carcass of a large animal. I remember the vultures silently circling overhead." He'd taken pictures with a film camera using a telephoto lens, he said, but couldn't bear to look at the photos once they were developed.

It took him an eternity to stuff a plaid scarf into the sleeve of his grey-green coat before he handed it to me. He had an immediate kindness about him and a credible effervescence, and I had the impression he must have grown up pampered by his mother, sisters, aunts, and female cousins. His hair was grey and cut close to his head. From the coat emanated the hot scent of leather and lime.

I said something inane, along the lines of there's neither kindness nor malice in nature, and he chuckled as if what I'd said was terribly funny or astute. I was not immune to the flattery in such a response, but as intrigued as I'd instantly become by his appearance and manner, and this talkativeness I hadn't expected, I still didn't want to have to entertain him on my own for any length of time.

I took him up to the guest room, where he plunked down his overnight bag, and suggested he could rest or freshen up if he wanted, but he followed me back down the stairs. Intending to excuse myself and return to the kitchen, where before he arrived I'd been chopping onions, garlic, and herbs for a marinara sauce for their dinner, I thought I'd set him up in the living room with a magazine or two to browse while we awaited Priya's return. But he herded me through the living room, and we both ended up in the kitchen. I put on the kettle for a pot of tea for him and tried not to look at the clock. He wasn't short of chatter—I asked questions—he asked me nothing—and he answered at length. We could just as well have been strangers seated next to one another for hours on a flight, our bodies pinched into our seats to minimize the possibility of encroaching on the other's space, our immediate fates bound inextricably, and yet, like horses wearing blinders, our eyes locked straight ahead, not a neigh between us until just before landing, when one of us thought it too weird not to know a thing about who it was she'd sat next to so almost-intimately for endless unstable hours, and, with only minutes left before the end of the journey, decided it was imperative—and finally safe—to utter a word or two to the other: *Are you going home or on holiday? Oh, business. What kind of work do you do? Your first visit here/there?* But in this case, it was me asking the questions. How was the drive? From where was he coming? How long was it?

The drive was fine. He enjoyed cross-country driving. He'd once driven to Vancouver and once to San Diego to a friend's wedding, so the drive here was nothing at all. He has lived in the same house for almost twenty-five years. His was the first built in what had previously been a barren area, about an hour northwest of Toronto, he told me. Today it's a city with its own mayor. There was a mall with a Winners, a Starbucks, a food court, and behind it a Cineplex. There were numerous game arcades, one of which one of his sons frequented—plenty to do in his neck of the woods, he said.

He might have asked what it was like to live down here, on an island, in the countryside, or in a tourist town, but he didn't, and I didn't bother to offer an opening for such an exchange. He hadn't been to Uganda in more than four decades, I learned, but was planning a trip there soon. He wasn't worried all that much about flying and planes exploding in mid-air—what is to be will be—there was so much to be afraid of in the world, he said, that you couldn't live your life in fear, otherwise you wouldn't ever leave your house or open your windows or doors.

Nothing personal.

Then, as if seizing on an opportunity he had been looking for, he said, "When Priya left her island in the Caribbean, it was a peaceful place, but it's become like Uganda. Daily murders that by the end of a year make up mass-murder kinds of totals. Aren't we all glad to be living here?" It was rhetorical, and elicited from him laughter. I didn't know if he was serious or being ironic. "You know, I've known her almost as long as I've been in this country. But it's been years since we've seen each other. Is she still painting these days?" I pointed to two paintings on a far wall in answer. He glanced over at them. From where we were, he would not have seen the details, the surface of green lake water, fanciful weeds waving beneath, all rendered in thick paint with knives. I suggested he go and have a closer look. He said, "There's time. I'll see them later," and he turned back to me.

"You lost touch with her?" I asked. "When was the last time you saw each other?"

"Oh, maybe six years ago. But then she just kind of disappeared. She's always been hard to pin down." I might have agreed, but I wasn't about to let him in on the private details of my relationship with Priya. He looked around the kitchen and said, "But finally she's found a home. Looks like a lovely home, too."

"What made you decide, after all these years, to come down?" I asked. They'd last seen each other "maybe" six years ago. She and I had met and begun living together six years ago. Was it during that time, then, when he and she last saw one another? If so, she had never mentioned it.

"I saw she was active on Twitter and I wrote and told her to write me at once. I wasn't going to let her disappear from me again. That's how we reconnected."

He laughed at everything he said.

Trying to sound as casual as possible, I said, "And you decided to come down and, well, here you are. Let me get you a drink." I didn't want to press. It seemed too obvious that I was fishing.

But then he offered, "So, yes, when she invited me, how could I not jump at the chance? Priya was my closest friend, but, you know, she used to come and go—appear and disappear—but never had there been such a long period of silence between us. And, of course, I accepted the invitation because I also wanted to meet the new partner with whom she was so happy that she'd forgotten all about her old friend." At this last he opened his palm to take me in, and I smiled, and again he laughed heartily.

So she *did* invite him. I turned away so he wouldn't see my lips purse and wiped the granite counter with the edge of my hand. This crossed a line, because this very thing, how he came to be visiting us, had been contentious from the start. Everything, it seems, always comes out one way or the other in the wash.

Other than that, I didn't ask questions or comment more than a nod to indicate I was still with him. I let him speak, which he was clearly happy to do.

He said she was the first friend he'd made in this country. The reiteration wasn't lost on me. She'd known him before he'd properly learned to use a knife and fork, he told me with what seemed oddly like pride, and he remembered her smacking his hand once when he used the fork incorrectly. This was, I imagine, meant to be evidence of something—trust perhaps, or intimacy—and I could have added, *Ah, yes, so she's always been particular, has she?* and confided that this trait of always wanting to get things "right" had been the frequent cause of arguments between us, but I kept quiet.

He persisted, though. He opened his arms and held his palms out in front of him as if to hold or behold all that was before him, and said, rather paternalistically, "So she's landed on her feet. I can't tell you how happy I am to see this myself."

I did not want to know what he meant. Any substantive response would have been to discuss her life as he once knew it and as I know it today, and such scrutiny behind her back and with someone I was only just meeting seemed unfair, regardless of what was transpiring between her and me. You can, I know, feel alienated from your lover and still not want to disrespect her.

As he spoke, I continued with my task, dunking tomatoes into a pot of boiling water and scooping them up a minute or so later. I dropped them in a bowl and covered it with plastic wrap. When he saw no response was forthcoming, he added, "When you're young, it's inconceivable you'd ever reach your parents' age, and when you do arrive at the age at which they had once seemed so ancient, the world has changed so much and you realize they were not role models for the changed world you're living in. There's triumph and disappointment at once. It's a miracle we survived our youth and evolved in the ways we have."

If I were younger, more tarted up, would he have been more curious about me? I could have told him my parents did not live to the age I currently am—I have, in fact, survived well beyond the ages to which they'd lived, dying one soon after the other when I was in my early thirties—so sometimes I feel as if I am coasting on borrowed time, as the saying goes. They were not role models; I had to figure it all out on my own.

When finally we heard the front door open, he swivelled to face Priya as she entered the house but remained planted where he was, and from him erupted ebullient laughter. He outstretched his arms and, addressing both of us, exclaimed, "Look at her. Just look at you. Long time no see." Still he stayed where he was. I gathered he wanted to share the reunion with me, so I leaned against the stove on my side of the counter and watched. Priya didn't take off her jacket and boots, but came through the house directly to him. The warmth of his greeting was touching—he clearly wanted to hold on to her longer than she wanted. Priya was less effusive. She seemed less delighted than I'd imagined she'd be. I hoped this was not for my benefit.

She said to him, "You're entirely grey."

"I'm not grey," he returned, his voice seeming to feign a peevishness belied by the irrepressible grin he wore. He looked at me—an appeal, it seemed—and I gathered this elaborate show of offence was a way of creating complicity among the three of us. He wore thin, gold wire-rimmed glasses, and behind them his eyes had turned misty. I thought I should turn away, leave them for a while, but I was more curious than ever about some obfuscated truth about their connection and did not want to miss any of this, so I continued with the task of removing skin from the blanched tomatoes as I looked on.

After inane banter about what time had and hadn't done to them both—Priya commenting that he'd come to resemble his father, at which he beamed—he reached for and held on to both Priya's hands and attempted to pull her toward him. That was a bit much, a bit theatrical, I thought. Perhaps she did, too, as she stepped in toward him for barely a second, and then, rather oddly, pulled a hand away and, although it seemed—mostly because of the smile she wore—as if it were meant to be playful, gently slapped his cheek. There was an intimacy to that odd gesture that I admit made my heart skip a beat, but I didn't want to succumb to petty jealousies. I needed, I'd earlier decided, to remain strong and focused.

I couldn't have known for sure, but I thought hurt flashed on his face—despite the ensuing chortling, which I took to be a manner of defence. Priya removed her jacket and threw it around one of the chair stools at the island counter. She made her way around the counter as I slid the skinned and chopped tomatoes into the skillet with the softened onions. And with more warmth than there had been between us earlier in the day, she wrapped her arms around me and kissed my cheek. She had taken on the scent of his lime-and-leather cologne, and this was like a fist tightening around my heart. To an onlooker there would, I'm sure, have been no hint, in the swift and almost ordinary gesture for two people who live together, of the distress that hung like a heavy curtain between us. It is possible such warmth was an indication, a display, either to him or to me, perhaps to him *and* to me, of where her allegiance lay. It is possible, too, that in front of a third person, dispensing affection was less complicated, required less of us both, than when we were alone. Her kiss on leaving the house with Skye earlier is a case in point.

I couldn't bring myself to respond in kind, and she shifted away to inspect the pot on the stove, the awkwardness she felt as a result noticeable only to me, I believe. She stirred the sauce, the sweetness of the onions and garlic, the tartness of the as yet uncooked tomatoes rising from the skillet, and under her breath asked if I was sure there was enough for us all. I nudged her aside and told her I knew what I was doing, to let me do my job. It has been a long-standing irritation between us that she is forever telling me what I've done wrong or how this or that should be, or should have been done, and so this back and forth between us is rote, and could just then have easily been construed as a kind of usual play.

"It's your pot," she conceded. "Carry on, then. I'm sure it'll be good."

Prakash laughed and said he's just like me, that when he is in the kitchen he doesn't like anyone telling him what to do.

Being with the two of them in the same room, seeing them together, suddenly had a new effect on me. I felt, for the first time, that it was good that he was here at this particular time. What was to be would be, and his presence here was probably, in the end, all for the good.

Forever conscious of what others are thinking and feeling, Priya announced in a suddenly bold voice that the aroma of the sauce was the most pleasant we'd had in the kitchen in weeks, a preamble to asking her friend if he'd as yet gotten a whiff of the dead mouse. He brushed off the question, saying that while he was not colour-blind, he had no sense of smell. On the heels of that, pointing to my pot, he exclaimed, "She's cooking for me."

He appeared to be an affectionate man, and when Priya responded, "Fancy that!" she seemed to me, in contrast and despite the attempt to keep smiling, churlish, and I couldn't tell if this had something to do with him, or if it was about her and me.

He engaged me, saying, "No, really, she said so. She told me she doesn't usually cook. So this one's for me, and it's vegetarian, too."

And I found myself pulled along—against my will or not, I couldn't tell—or should I say *siding*?—with him, this man I'd only just met. "Yes, that's right. It's for him," I chimed in.

I had not been able to confidently hold my own earlier when Skye was in the kitchen here with us. I'd felt as if I were struggling to be myself in the face of too many lies, and resorted to speaking at unusual length about Lorenzo Valla's motives for debunking the veracity of the Donation of Constantine I. But— here, now—I was less agitated in front of this man. He was a buffer between Priya and me, slowing our tearing at each other.

Unaware of the role he'd played in our lives these past weeks, and more so now, he followed Priya with his eyes watery, a pleased broad smile on his face.

My reserve irked Priya. I could tell her mind was more on me than on him. She turned her back to us with a hand on each of the handles of the fridge and pulled open both French doors. For many seconds she stood there, the interior light brightening her face and torso. Whatever had happened to us? Perhaps it is more common than not that things break down in slow motion rather than with a single grand gesture, and you can get so inured by the slow demise, even as it happens and happens and happens right before your eyes, that you don't notice the approach of the point of no return.

As if her reason for having gone to the fridge suddenly occurred to her, she asked if either of us needed a drink or something to nibble on, and her friend pointed to the cup of tea on the counter and said, "I've already been well taken care of."

He wouldn't take his eyes off Priya, nor for a long time did the smile on his lips fade. I can't say if my reading of him was accurate, but his expression wasn't simple delight at being in the same room with her. It was more as if he were a parent looking with amazement at what had become of the child he'd brought up. This was ridiculous, of course, because they were only a year apart in age, and I've never known Priya to accept being treated by anyone—including her parents—like a child.

Removing her jacket from the stool, she excused herself to go hang it up and change into house shoes. But she was gone for longer than these little tasks would have taken. Prakash was saying something about being a vegetarian, but my mind was on Priya. I wondered how long it would be before she left with him to show him around the area. I needed time alone but I didn't want to show agitation over not knowing when they'd leave.

"They amaze me," he said, and I realized he was speaking of his children. "When they were very young—five, six, seven years of age—they knew all their friends from school went to fast-food restaurants at the mall and they used to be invited to other kids' birthday parties where there'd be hot dogs and that sort of thing. I didn't have to tell them they couldn't eat this or that, they just saw what we did and didn't ourselves do, and on their own they put two and two together and acted accordingly. As far as I know, they never gave in to any temptations."

I nodded, but I had to wonder, what kind of young kid wouldn't want to try a hot dog—especially if everyone around was having one and their own parents weren't watching? Did they really not take even a tiny taste, or was he a doting father, a gullible man who believed his children were infallible when, here and there, now and then, they were in fact nibbling forbidden fruit behind his back? There are probably things about his children he doesn't know. I was about to put the idea in his head, but thought quickly better of it, as a small incivility could unnecessarily escalate out of control.

There was a bit of a ruckus coming from the front of the house—sounded like Priya was cleaning up the foyer, sorting through shoes and boots—and from the clanging of the hangers in the cupboard, I guessed she was rearranging coats and jackets.

"And then, one day—and I don't know what precipitated it, but it was out of the blue—they were asking: why do other people eat those kinds of things and we don't?"

With a finger held up in the air, I interrupted him and called out, asking Priya what she was doing. She said, in a voice I know well, that she was making room for her jacket and Prakash's. She was telling me, I suppose, that I could have hung his jacket instead of throwing it on the couch in the living room. I called back to her to leave those things and come and hang out with us—my own wording to suggest to her and to him, in a semi-playful way, that she was not being hospitable. He didn't seem to notice her admonishing tone or my playful snarkiness; he just carried on.

"I explained to them about different cultures," he said, "about how a person's culture makes him or her special. In our culture, I explained, there are things we do and don't do that make us who we are. They understood at once and have never asked again to go to a burger joint, or for any kind of meat."

I continued, of course, to be tempted to challenge this noble picture he had of himself and of his children, but I asked instead if he'd ever, even once, succumbed to temptation or pressure to compromise his beliefs. He was only too eager to be asked.

"When I was in high school, just after we arrived in Canada," he related, "one of the guys in my class invited me along with some other classmates to a formal dinner given by his parents. I didn't really know these boys, but I was the new kid in town and I appreciated the gesture."

Priya returned. She pulled out two of the stools on that side of the counter, seating herself and pointing out the other to him. He interrupted himself to say he'd been in the car for several hours and was happy to stand, then carried on with the same story. Priya nodded, and under her breath said, *Yes, yes.* He mumbled in response that he knew she'd heard this before, but he wanted to tell me. Priya lifted her palm, a gesture to say, *Of course, go ahead.*

"The dinner was held in a large banquet hall—long tables formally set, and servers bringing out dishes, pouring drinks. I was in awe of everything then, having only just arrived in this country. Everything was brought and put on your plate for you. Suddenly a plate with a steak was dropped down in front of me. In those days you weren't asked about dietary restrictions, allergies, or anything like that."

I broke in, expressing an idea that was out of my mouth before I could stop it. "Yes, but nowadays it's not just vegetarian or not—everybody has some damn thing they can't or won't eat. We're all so fragile and don't mind imposing on others to show concern for us. The other day we had to cater to someone who, besides being vegan, couldn't eat fruit or vegetables with red skin."

As if some affinity between us had been cemented earlier on when we were alone, he broke into laughter. One would have thought it was the funniest thing he'd ever heard. I am shallow; I was flattered.

While I was speaking, Priya looked up at the glass shade that encased the ceiling light in which a plump food moth lazily circled. Her face was blank. So intentionally non-judgmental did she look that I felt she was in fact critical of my comment. "So? What did you do? Tell her," she encouraged, still following with her eyes the erratic movements of the trapped moth.

"So there in front of me was this big, sizzling, glossy slab of meat. I'd never had an experience like that before."

He was enjoying being the storyteller, unaware that Priya and I were really only half listening. I know her well enough; she wasn't as rapt as he might have thought. She was, no doubt, dying to get out of the house with him. She had no idea how much I, too, wanted them to leave.

"I'd never eaten meat. I mean, really, I didn't know what to do," he said, pausing to sip his tea and no doubt to prolong his moment onstage. "And on top of that, there was all that cutlery surrounding the plate. You see, at home in those days, if we weren't eating with our hand, Indian-style, we'd most likely use a spoon. It was in my university days that I grew more used to eating with a knife and fork, but even today, I and my family eat using our hand when we are at home. It is more natural for us. The food tastes better this way." He laughed at his own humour and pointed to the pot on the stove, saying, "Don't worry, I eat spaghetti with a fork."

I smiled, and nodded to suggest I was grateful for this.

"Anyway," he carried on, "that was the least of my problems. Here was this big pinkish-brown thing lying on my plate, and in that moment it came to me that meat and meat-eating was a kind of emblem of Canada and of Canadianness, and I wanted there and then to be Canadian like the guys at the table cutting so confidently into all parts of their meal, those guys so completely oblivious to what was going on with me. I had to make a decision. I didn't say anything. I just stared at the slab. I kept staring at it and it stared back at me. And we remained like that for an eternity."

Okay, Prakash, we get the picture, I wanted to say. I wondered if Priya and I would get a chance to chat privately before she left with him for the afternoon. I needed to tell her, at least for a start, that I wasn't going to eat supper with them. I didn't look forward to doing that.

"I was thinking: what would it mean if I put even a small piece of that meat in my mouth? It was my first big test in this new country. You know, I felt so much appreciation for my parents and me being able to come to this country, but looking around me I knew, too, I didn't want to lose my culture. We were despised back home, thrown out of the country for being Indian, but that's what I was, an Indian. And I couldn't afford not to be proud of this. I didn't know what I would become, who I'd be, if I let even a drop of that bloodlike juice pooled on the plate around the slab touch my lips. And so, just like that, contemplating a plate of meat, I made the decision that that was not the way to become Canadian. I didn't know how I could accomplish that very desirable identity in a single stroke, but I understood that it would have to include who I was at my core."

Ever since beginning this relationship, this partnership with Priya, I had often been reminded that *I* had not had to apply for or be granted citizenship to this country. And after living in this predominantly Caucasian countryside for so many years, I was experiencing in our kitchen what Priya experienced constantly amongst our friends: the revealing fact of difference, this time them—Priya and Prakash—from *me*. He and she could have passed for each other's family. But people who didn't know us as a couple and saw us standing side by side might never have assumed she and I, who were indeed family, were at all so. It is not enough to know you're family with another person. The relationship takes on true meaning only when outsiders also agree upon and recognize it. Their recognition is an ingredient in the complex medium that gives the relationship a chance to grow and thrive.

Still, *I* was born here. Priya and Prakash had to declare an oath of loyalty to this country when they became citizens. That fact is enough for them to have more in common with each other than either has with me. Thirty-something years later,

Priya admits to still being moved when she sings the Canadian anthem. I have never had such an experience. Rather, I am critical of it. Sometimes I can't bring myself to sing it. In fact, I want several of its words changed.

Prakash took his eyes and his attention off Priya and spoke to us both. "You didn't tell her how we met," he said.

I wanted to answer that the topic hadn't come up between him and me, and his assumption was incorrect. But there was an agenda, I realized, in the statement. I let it play itself out.

"Yes," Priya responded, looking at me for corroboration and rising from her chair, ready, I thought, to escape with him. "I did. You know we met at university. Don't you?"

"But did you tell her *how* we actually met?" he insisted.

Priya said something about table tennis, the club room in the basement of the McKinnon Science Building.

"Yes, yes. Technically that's true, but how did we start talking?" He sounded impatient. He wanted her, I imagined, to have cherished the memory as he had. "Well, let me tell you. I'll tell you. Just a sec, you'll see," he said.

While we waited, he drained his cup of tea and poured himself another.

"When I arrived at the university, I knew no one," he began. Priya rested her bum on the edge of her stool again. "I wasn't into drinking and I didn't have a girlfriend. So I didn't have anything in common with the other students in my courses. I was staying at the YMCA, and I didn't like it there. I was lonely. I wanted to meet people. So how do you meet people?"

Apparently, the question wasn't rhetorical, and he waited expectantly for an answer. I shrugged. Priya shook her head to say she didn't know—he should get on with his story. Such liberties between them revealed their old closeness. But his eyebrows were raised, and he still waited. The two of them knew how they had met, and although my knowing it wasn't going to enrich my life in any way, this story was clearly for my benefit.

"How?" I acquiesced.

"No, you tell me," he said.

Priya rolled her eyes theatrically and motioned with her hands for him to get on with it. And he did.

"Well, you join a club."

"Of course," I muttered.

He carried on, "So I thought about it, and, since I used to be one of the top table-tennis players at my high school in Kampala, I decided to join the university's table-tennis club. I saw you there the first night. Do you remember?" Priya nodded weakly. "And then a few days later I was in the Student Centre, and you were there, too. Isn't that right? You saw me and you came and said hello. That was the very first time we talked. I'd never met a Trinidadian before. I'd always assumed Trinidadians, and all Caribbean people, were black, and I was surprised that an Indian-looking person could be Trinidadian. You asked if I wanted to get something to eat with you, and you pointed in the direction of the cafeteria. I told you I'd accompany you but that I'd been in the cafeteria and it was difficult for me to find things to eat there because I was vegetarian. Do you remember that? You told me to come to your apartment and you'd make dinner for me. That night, you and Fiona—" he paused, looked at me, and clarified "—Priya's roommate—"

To which I responded, perhaps noticeably defensively, "I know."

And he carried on, "—made curried potatoes, cauliflower, and rice. I remember that meal to this day. It was the first time you'd cooked for me, but not the last. The three of us became close friends after that night."

I was not sure what the minutiae of their meeting was supposed to mean to me, but I felt as if the tip of a knife were being pressed against my skin. Was he informing me of how much they had in common, the length of their friendship, that there were people they knew in common who were unknown to me—of the primacy of his place in her life?

I watched, but, truthfully, couldn't see evidence of even a patina of an old love or fling between them. Why had she been so cagey about him, then? I don't think I would have minded an ongoing friendship between them. He's not my type, but he didn't have to be. A presence like his in her life down here might have eased things for her, and by extension for me, for us. How often over the five years here had I had to bear the brunt of her hurt when a local thinks they're complimenting her when they assure her they don't think of her as "of colour," that they think of her as one of them, as white? His presence in her life might have been enough to temper that pattern of behaviour she had when we were, say, at a dinner, chatting perhaps about what was on the family Christmas table when we were children. Everyone except Priya would have had what one might call "the usual"—turkey, cranberry sauce, Christmas pudding, parsnips, and turnips. She would remain silent, at least at first, as if waiting to see if anyone would think to ask her what was on *her* family table, the question being for her their acknowledgement of her difference from us and the possibility of hearing about interesting fare—like the pigeon pea soup, pastelles, ponch-de-crème, and sorrel drink I came to know from being with her—or customs they didn't know about. It would be unfair to say there wasn't interest, but her background was so foreign that our friends had trouble imagining it, and with the pace of conversation, everyone wanting to tell their own story, there really wasn't usually the appetite to have details described and explained, she the star suddenly, being interviewed. What in those times we all wanted was not so much new knowledge as validation through having had common experiences: *Yeah, that's right, you too? No kidding. And what about this or that, wasn't that hilarious?* She was outnumbered. Those gatherings were about our similarities, not about our differences, and often what she interjected was amicably nodded at but not engaged with—poor things, I could see our friends didn't even know what questions they could have asked of her—and so we'd return to what bonded the rest of us, like our hippie days—most of us having just clipped the end of the era, but enamoured of it because nothing had yet replaced it. Those days were a topic we loved, the drugs we experimented with, the so-called free love that was freer in reality for the guys we knew, but not for us women. Some of us took off and went to live for a minute or two in the bush and didn't shave our legs, and chopped wood and bathed naked in the lakes. And all that awful food we used to eat so righteously—this grain and that lentil. We'd reminisce and howl with laughter, marvel at our inventiveness or resilience, or cringe at our tastes or activities back then. At some point Priya would break in, and knowing full well that her own experience of that time would fall flat at the feet of our friends, she'd still relate what "hippie" meant to a Trinidadian in those days, and I'd admire her for her courage and insistence on being part of the conversation. Hippie life in Trinidad, she'd say, was about what was being worn on Carnaby Street in England—bell-bottom pants, oversized colourful watches, flowered jeans, braided hair and bandanas, bare feet and toe rings, ankle bracelets. It was fashion and consumption. I knew our friends were thinking, *Yeah, yeah—really, eh. But that's not hippie life,* and her version, sounding a little naive and thin, would land under the rug, and we'd turn back fast to recalling this sit-in, that love-in, that music festival, that demonstration. I'd feel for her; I'd feel her aloneness, and I'd try to fill in things I knew about her world, try to help her flesh out her stories so they'd understand. But in the end, I'd do it to her, too, I'd be right there with them, bonding over what they and I had in common. I did feel for her. It was tiring, though, to have, once we were back home in our private space, to commiserate with her against our friends. It made me have to acknowledge their failings, too, and this was isolating for me. When you live with a person of colour, never-ending problems that centre on how the world treats one and not the other enter your house, and these differences can alienate you from one another. And your house becomes not a haven in which harmony can be sought, but a refuge in which to hide. It gets unbearable when you're hiding not together from the world, but from each other.

Suddenly Priya stood. "Come, let me show you my studio," she said, already walking past him toward the back of the house. He turned to watch her but did not move. He had stretched his hand out along the counter toward her, tapping it as if to call her back. She stopped and said, awkwardly, "Don't you want to come? I'd like to show you what I've been doing."

He said, again, as he had said to me earlier, when I pointed out her two works in the house, "There's time." Priya did not hide her disappointment well, and he quickly added, "We can't leave her here all by herself slaving at the stove. Later, we'll go later. There's lots of time."

I began to protest. I was fine alone, I said, wishing they would leave, but Priya had quickly started gathering plates from one cupboard, napkins from a drawer, and glasses from another cupboard, with which to set the table for the night's dinner.

He got up and followed her into the dining room. While they remained in there for some minutes chatting, I noted to myself that while he wanted to regale me with the story of how they met, he didn't seem in the least curious about how she and I had met.

I often felt guilt that we were here. Countryside on the mainland would have been one thing, but an island is psychologically more isolating. But it doesn't make sense that I felt guilt, for it was she who had been rather more gung-ho about the move to an island. She was born on an island, she'd say, and she plans to die on an island. The idea was that we'd be here forever.

They returned just as I turned the stove off, and I was about to retreat to my office when Prakash addressed me: "I'm a refugee. Did you know that?"

Priya had told me he was sensitive about having come here as a refugee, that he didn't like talking about it, and that I should be careful about bringing it up. But here he was announcing it. I could not walk away.

"When my family came to this country, it was a very different time than it is today, you know," he said, and laughed. "People didn't want us back then. Today everyone wants the Syrians."

"Well, that's not exactly true," Priya said. "There are communities and individuals sponsoring families, but there're a lot of people, too, who don't want them here."

"*No one,*" he stressed, "wanted the Ugandans." He took a sip from his drink, hiding the seriousness his face suddenly took on.

"Canada did," I said.

He didn't respond.

I asked, "Am I not remembering correctly?"

Still he didn't answer. I'd clearly gotten something wrong, but I couldn't imagine what that might have been. I shrugged my shoulders and raised my eyebrows to let him know I welcomed being corrected.

"Put it this way," he said. "No other place wanted us. We didn't necessarily all want to come to Canada, but this was the only country that would take a handful of us. Beggars can't be choosers."

"How many of you did Canada let in?" I caught my choice of words only after they'd left my mouth: *you*, and *let in*, and was grateful I'd said Canada and not *we*.

"It depends on who you ask. Some sources say 40,000 Indians were expelled. Some say there were 30,000 of us, others say 90,000. And then every site you consult on the internet gives a different number of how many Canada let in." He didn't look at me to suggest any complicity in those words I regretted using. "Some say," he carried on, "under 6,000. Others say precisely 6,675." His voice had changed; he seemed suddenly crestfallen. I suppose a nerve had been hit.

My instinct was that we should move on from this topic. I picked up my phone, my pack of cigarettes, and my reader from the end of the counter, slapped my hand on the counter in a gesture of finality, and addressed Priya. "Where are you two headed?"

There was more, it turned out, that he wanted to say. He did not let Priya answer my question but cut in to add, "There was a time, before the actual expulsion, when we used to talk about where we'd like to go to live once we left. My mother's first choice was Britain, where she had family. She was a British citizen, having been born in British India, and after the expulsion she was accepted there, and I, her son, too. But not Pa. You see, in 1962, when Uganda got independence from Britain, Pa, in a flurry of national pride, gave up his Indian citizenship to become a citizen of the place he lived in and loved," Prakash said. "Pa was like that, you know. But this meant he was no longer British or Indian, and so his application as a refugee was turned down by England."

Priya and I exclaimed at once, "What?"

He nodded his head to agree with our shock. "And we wouldn't leave without him, naturally," he carried on. "And no other country—not even India—would take us. So when Canada opened up, we had no option other than to come here, and here we were accepted as a family. On the flight over, I remember my mother announcing with determination in her voice that she'd made the decision to find happiness in Toronto, where she knew other Ugandans had landed and stayed. But she never saw Toronto until decades later. We ended up going instead to a place we'd never heard of: New Brunswick."

In New Brunswick, they'd been placed in a small town called Salt Island, which wasn't an island at all, far north of St. John.

"Do you remember Salt Island?" he asked Priya. "Do you remember that long and winding road we took from the airport to my parents' house? It's now a highway cutting the length of time it used to take by half."

I had thought they'd soon leave, but Priya jumped up, reached for and noisily opened a bag of bagels. She asked how his mother was, and while she sliced the bagels and popped them one by one in the toaster, he answered.

She hadn't ever told me she'd visited him at his parents' in New Brunswick. I realized the photos I'd dug up in her studio, of the two of them with a body of water behind them and no identifiable landmarks, must have been from that time.

I took my phone and cigarettes, excused myself, and left for the sunroom. The sun was bright, and the room had warmed up. I opened the door to the outside while I smoked my cigarette. A female downy woodpecker, trying desperately to hack at a tiny morsel of fat in the suet cage, took off in fright. I stepped away into the garden, texted Skye, and told her all was well, better than I'd hoped—although everyone was a bit testy because there was a lot of conversation about race, and I was, truth be told, an outsider in this reunion. She texted back that she was on Skype with Liz. I replied I'd be alone in an hour or so and I'd try her again.

Back in the sunroom, I looked up Idi Amin and Canada on my phone's internet. One post said 80,000 Asian Ugandans were expelled. One said more than 8,000 Ugandans entered Canada between 1972 and 1974. Ten per cent. Asians, one site said, escaped by and large with their lives, but under Amin black Ugandans *paid* with their lives. Everyone was a loser, it seemed. There were all kinds of things happening in those days. I would have been twenty-one then. I participated in many organized protests on the street, and felt rather good about myself for standing up, waving placards, shouting slogans of protest, my fist held high. But in the light of someone being forced to leave their country of birth and seek refuge from it elsewhere, I couldn't imagine my version of a proximity to history would interest them.

When I returned to the kitchen, the bagels were set on three plates, and a container of hummus was open, a paté knife dissecting its swirl. Priya watched me as she asked Prakash, "Were you able to bring anything with you? Your mother must have had gold jewellery. Was she able to get it out?"

"She was lucky. She got most of her jewellery out," he answered. "We didn't have time to pack anything. We'd had just a few hours' notice." He looked at her, somewhat blankly, I thought, and said, "You know the story. You've heard it before."

Priya jutted her chin at me and said, "Yes, but I don't remember all the details, and besides, she hasn't." I had thought this was a topic that was not to be broached. Had she imagined his story of escape would warm me to him, or had she become so insensitive that his trauma was for her some way of entertaining me?

He jumped at her cue. "Okay, I'll tell you." He turned to me.

When a person decides to tell the story of the flight for his life, you can't just walk off. I had to stay and listen.

"Indians had to leave Uganda by November 8," he began. "People who had means and connections left well before that, but there were many, too, who for various reasons waited until the last minute. My father, and therefore our family, was always going to be amongst the last to leave because of his job at the bank where he worked. But one day, two weeks before the deadline date, my father didn't come home from work. He'd been arrested. He hadn't done anything wrong, but that's how it was in those days. When finally he came home, he said we had to leave right away. We'd always been more or less ready to go at a moment's notice. So the next morning, we were on a plane full of fleeing Indians. If we hadn't left right then, he would have been dead in days."

With that, he'd concluded, it seemed, the story Priya wanted him to relate. It wasn't much of a story, but some response was needed, so I offered, "I imagine there's a difference, isn't there, between how the Asians in Uganda had to leave, and the seemingly endless, daily flow of Syrians out of a land that their ancestors lived on for millennia?"

"Yep. That's right," he said, and nothing more.

After some long seconds I was about to say, *Well, there's time for this later,* and attempt to shoo them out of the house, when he said, "He'd just confiscated a lorry of goods. He was taking it to the warehouse. That's when they arrested him."

I must have looked puzzled, because Priya said, "Alex doesn't know any of this. You have to explain why he was taking the goods, and where."

The confident, jovial man of minutes before became pensive. "My father was the bank worker tasked with removing goods from clients' warehouses," he said. "He and the driver of the lorry were transporting such goods to the bank's warehouse. That's when they took him." As if to hide his face, he lifted his cup and took a long sip of his tea. In the discomforting quiet, he added, "He came home so late. His clothes were dirty and smelly. He knew we didn't have a lot of time."

Priya put her hand on his for a moment and, rubbing it gently, said to him, "Prakash, slow down. I've never really understood what happened. You never told me about this. Why did they take him?"

Witnessing her affection toward him brought out a sadness in me. I did not feel jealousy. Just overwhelming regret. It had been a long time since there'd been any such tenderness between us.

Prakash's eyes glazed. He looked suddenly older. "You know, there are Asian Ugandans here in this country who, so many years later, still won't befriend other Asian Ugandans? We all went through the same things, but none of us wants to be reminded of what happened. It's like we're all ashamed of what was done to our families, to mothers, sisters, wives—to our women. We carry a collective shame, you know? It's why we work so hard. My generation still feels we must show that there's worth in us Indian Ugandans. We smile and smile and smile. We're good people—we want everyone to know this. We won't allow ourselves, or our children, to show anger about what had been done to us in our own country. Anger would be an admission that we'd been wronged, and none of us can bear having been a victim. You know, those of us who came in '72, we've always been quiet. I was fourteen when we arrived here, and I learned from then that we Ugandans don't make trouble, we keep our heads down, work hard, and just try to get ahead so that people will respect us. Above all, we all learned that we must be respectful of others. We've never publicly expressed anger about how we'd been treated—whether that was regarding our expulsion from our own homeland, or by the international community."

Under all that laughter earlier, that bonhomie, a subterranean hurt, some tempered rage, had just been revealed. He looked away. He'd exposed himself. Priya kept her eyes soft and on him. There was probably more anger in him than even he realized. The more I contemplated it, the more I saw it. This realization had the exact effect I didn't need right then. I felt myself drawn to him, and into Priya and the unknown parts of her life that at another time in our relationship I would have longed for but couldn't afford to be seduced by today. I needed to maintain my distance. But I was seeing—rather, she seemed to be making every effort, after all, to show me—who this mystery friend from her past was. Who she was, by extension. And I oscillated between feeling like an outsider and wanting to be drawn into the corners of her life, as I had once hoped would happen.

Despite my discomfort, I actually didn't mind, at this point, hearing more of what he had to say. I had no investment in him, nor am I attracted to stories of trauma and escape, but he was willing to be open and weak in front of me, and wished, I thought, to be seen as good and brave. He would not be a friend—that didn't interest me—but he was, as far as I could see from this short time with him, a fragile and frightened man who wanted to be seen to be a good man.

"I've wanted to talk about it lately, you know, with the Syrians being in the news, and all of that, but I didn't know to whom, or how," he said.

I wanted to go around and stand next to him. To touch his shoulder. Or pour some more tea. But despite these unexpected kinder feelings toward him, I stayed where I was.

He looked at me and said, "I'll try and explain. You see, my father worked at the bank, but he wasn't in banking exactly. What I mean is that my father was not a career banker. He'd been a teacher. A math teacher. Well, he was not just a math teacher, but also the principal of one of the best high schools in Kampala. He was well-known, and well thought of. Indians and Africans of the higher classes all wanted their children to go to his school."

As he spoke, Priya pulled the tray that sat on the counter closer. It held onions, garlic, ginger, root vegetables, and fruit, and although she began to clean the dish of old bits of vegetables, dried-up garlic scapes that had been there since last spring, and fragments of hard-curled onion and garlic skins and dust, she did it as quietly as if a sleeping baby were in the room.

"One day," Prakash said, having caught his breath again, and seeming now to have found his stride, "Idi Amin fired most of the Asian teachers without notice. My father was replaced by a friend of his, an African teacher. Because of my father's math skills, the father of one of the students in his old school, a bank manager, offered him a job. But Pa didn't deal with tellers or actually handle money. He was more of an accountant, not a qualified accountant, but it was his job to deal with the unpaid loans of Indian traders ordered to leave the country."

He looked at us, and from what he said after, it was clear he must have been calculating how much backstory and history he should relate to make this personal tale clear.

"You see," he said, "the majority of traders in the country were Indians. We hadn't been given much warning or time to leave. Shops, like almost every business, depended on loans from banks. Almost everyone got the loans they asked for, because business in general was very good, and loans to the Indians were usually paid back on time. When the announcement came, ordering us to leave the country and to take nothing with us, it was clear that business owners would have to abandon their businesses and all those goods that had been bought and paid for with the loans. The banks immediately became concerned. If everyone just left the country owing money to the banks, the banks would fold, the economy of the country would collapse. So my father was one of many bank workers whose job it was to go with a bank lorry to the deportee's store to confiscate unsold goods. He had to watch and make notes on everything as merchandise was loaded onto the lorry. He had to make sure nothing was left behind, nothing pocketed. Pa would then accompany the lorry and the storekeeper to a warehouse owned by the bank, and he'd supervise the unloading there.

"On the morning of October 25, he was carrying out one of these—these, these"—he couldn't find the word, so I offered the word *repossessions*, but Prakash adamantly said, "No, I won't call them that. That implies that the owners were unable to meet their financial obligations and the bank was taking the goods in lieu of payment, but that's different than what was happening." For him there was no word for it.

Priya and I both indicated we understood what he meant, and he carried on.

"The lorry had just been packed up at a furniture and household goods store, and Pa, the store owner, and the driver were in it, on the way to the bank's warehouse, when it was stopped by army hooligans. They made them come down from the lorry and asked for everyone's ID. But some days earlier, at a roadblock, soldiers had asked for Pa's ID, and when he gave it to them and they saw he was a Ugandan citizen, they laughed and said that it was not real ID, that no Asians were Ugandans. They made him get out of his car, tore up his ID right there, pushed him about, and ripped his shirt. They told him to walk. They kept the car."

Priya said, sharp surprise in her voice, "Prakash, you never told me any of this."

He stopped short, perhaps as confused as I, and for a moment it was as if she were accusing him of telling a lie, of having taken— rather than of having kept—something from her. I thought of the photos in her office and bit my tongue. She was clearly affected by what had happened to his father. I supposed this might have been because she had actually once—perhaps more than once, how would I know?—met him.

In response Prakash said, "It was common. It happened regularly to Asians who'd taken out citizenship after Uganda's independence. I don't remember what details I told you and what I didn't. These days, as I listen to the stories of Syrian refugees, I am piecing together my own. It's taken me a long time to remember, but I'm remembering more lately." He took her hand and held it. "Let me tell you. I'm trying to tell you."

I walked around the counter to the cupboard with the glasses, took three out, went to the fridge, and poured us all club sodas. The noise caused by my scooping ice from the freezer seemed like an affront, but I carried on, and splashed Angostura bitters on top. I handed one glass to Prakash and one to Priya. He still held her hand. I stood next to her, pressed my body lightly against her, and put my hand on her back. I felt the knots of her spine, and ran my hand down slightly into the curve of her back and rested it there. She took her hand from his and leaned against me. How much easier it was to be affectionate in a third person's presence. In that brief connection, the desire I once felt so immediately for Priya filled me. I felt ill and a weight descended on me. This was not going to be helpful to either of us in the long run, and so I backed away and returned to my side of the counter.

"I still feel sorry for my father. He had always tried to be a responsible citizen in Uganda, taking part in community events, et cetera. It didn't matter if the events were for Indians or Africans or for both. But after Amin's expulsion order, the army went wild and we were on our own. There was no one to look out for Asians.

"So, on that day when the lorry was stopped and he was asked for his identification, he explained that it had been taken from him by other soldiers some days before. But the hooligans"—Prakash's voice was filled with emotion—"they wouldn't accept his answer. They began to rough him up. Without ID, my father was considered a stateless person, and stateless persons had no rights. They accused him of smuggling the goods that were in the lorry. He was pushed around, hit, kicked, and taken away by the soldiers in a jitney. They threw him in a prison that was packed with other Indians who, he later told me, had been treated much worse than him. When he didn't return to work that afternoon, the bank manager did some calling around and heard what had happened. Furious that one of his workers—not to mention the bank's lorry and all the goods—had been taken, he called the Minister of Defence and implored him to release his worker. The minister said he'd see what he could do. At three the next morning, Pa was released."

As Prakash spoke, I realized that, forty-three years later, in telling this part of his life, he used words that were of a different time and place. *Lorry. Jitney. Traders. Hooligans.* Words, I thought, likely exchanged among people here who'd survived the same experiences, those people he'd told us about whose only bond was this singularly profound and defining experience. I asked him if he had been scared.

"Yes, yes. I'm coming to all of that," he said.

I watched and listened, and it dawned on me that his experience *in Uganda itself* was not only a story about his family or about the history of Uganda, but it was part of Canada's history, too, as are the conditions in the Middle East that have led to the arrival of the Syrians today.

"I don't think people ever really cared then, or today, about Uganda," he said. "But Idi Amin was so bizarre and unpredictable, he was such a clown as a statesman, that it was *he* who made the news. People in the rest of the world knew more about Amin than they did about the Asians who had to leave, or about the state of Ugandan Africans once we'd left." Without further prompting, he recounted details, and where he heard them muddled, he stopped himself, gathered his thoughts, and made his way around again. It was interesting to watch him, as he seemed, at least in my opinion, to be figuring out how to create a narrative out of his family's experience.

"My mother was seriously ill in bed with typhoid," he said. "Her mind was so confused she couldn't keep track of time. When I came home from school that day, I did my homework and waited for my father to return from work so we could eat the dinner my ayah had left under a cloth on the table for us. For the last couple of days, Pa had taken my mother her meal and fed her before he and I sat down at the table. When Pa didn't come home at the usual time, I thought nothing of it, because I knew it was a busy time at the bank, with so many traders leaving the warehousing of their goods until the very last minute before they left the country. But when my mother called out for some food, I realized that Pa was much later than usual. By this time, he would normally have telephoned to explain why he wasn't home yet and to say when to expect him. I dished out my mother's food and took it to her room. She had enough presence of mind to ask where he was. I was beginning to worry but didn't let on about this to my mother. I told her he'd telephoned and said it was busy at work, and he'd come as soon as he could, so not to worry. She accepted this, and I fed her each morsel by hand, like Pa would have done. I helped her to the washroom, and back into bed. I sat in a chair in the room and watched her. I fell asleep, and when I awoke saw it was almost ten at night. I went out into the dining room and looked out the window. In the distance I could hear small explosions, but this was usual. Sometimes it was fireworks and sometimes it was gunfire. Everyone had learned soon enough to differentiate between the two. It was known that Indians were being picked up on the streets, or taken from their homes with no explanation given. Ninety per cent of such people were not heard from again."

This man was a stranger to me, but I was being drawn into him by this story he was revealing in minute detail, and a party I'd attended in the late eighties flashed through my mind. There was a man there, I recalled, Ricardo, an exile from Argentina's Dirty War. He was surrounded by women and his shirt was drawn up, his stomach exposed. There was a long wide scar across his chest and ragged, discoloured patches of skin on his stomach. He was describing how he'd been tortured by the military. Then, later that night, I came upon him on the back porch of the house, holding the face of one of the women who'd been listening. His mouth was pressed against hers and his tongue was clearly working its way around inside her mouth. She seemed to be a willing receptacle for his trauma, and I guessed he'd expected this would happen with one or the other of the women he'd been regaling. A man came up behind me and laughed. He said, "Ah, Ricardo. Every time. He shows his wounds and never fails to score."

Prakash carried on over my thoughts. He was saying that he went into the kitchen and checked that the back door was locked, then walked around the house making sure all the windows, too, were locked. Back in the kitchen he took the rolling pin from a drawer. He held it in the air and swung it.

At this, Priya put her hand to her mouth and barely held back a chuckle. "Are you serious? A rolling pin?" He stopped, and the two of them burst into laughter. I did, too.

He said, "I was a skinny fourteen-year-old kid. What was I to do?" Tears welled in his eyes. He took off his glasses, and Priya threw him a kitchen towel. He caught it but reached in his back pocket for a white handkerchief and wiped his eyes, all the while laughing and moaning playfully with the embarrassment of having wielded that particular weapon.

"I turned off all the lights in the house and, with only enough cast weakly from a street lamp across the road to guide me, went back and forth between crouching in the corner of the sofa, a throw pulled over to hide me, and standing at the side of the window peeping at the yard in front. I scanned the neighbours' yards, trying to see into shadowy areas behind trees and parked cars. Every so often I tiptoed into my mother's room and checked on her. I grew exhausted with worry, then almost sick with fear. I didn't want to sleep, but I lay on the couch and dozed, and eventually fell into deep sleep. Suddenly I awoke: the front door lock was being fiddled with. My heart raced so fast it felt as if it had stopped beating. I glanced at the clock and saw it was 4:00 a.m. I pulled the throw over my head and tried to sink into the couch and stop shaking. The door opened quietly, and I heard someone enter. The person was coughing into something that muffled the sound, but in a few seconds I recognized it as my father's cough. I drew the throw back hesitantly and saw it was indeed him. Pa was barefoot and seemed to limp. He smelled of urine. I eventually stood, shakily, and was about to switch on a side lamp. Pa said, in a calm but quiet and sharp voice, 'No. Leave it off.' In the weak light coming in from outside, I saw his shirt was ripped, the buttons missing. There was a cut above one eye, and blood and dirt streaked the rest of his face and his arms. I began to shake and weep. Pa did not hug me but held one of my shoulders with one hand and shook me. 'Stop it, Prakash. I am fine. No time for any of this.' He spoke in our Gujarati rather than the Swahili he enjoyed speaking, even at home. He pushed me toward my bedroom and shut the door behind us. In a low, controlled voice, he gave me a five-minute account of the day's happenings, and said there was a bus hired by the Canadian government leaving one of the hotels for the airport at 7:00 a.m. We had to leave on the very first flight that morning. If we stayed even a day longer, we risked not only his being killed the instant they found him, but my mother and me as well."

From everything I'd ever read of these kinds of situations, according to documentaries I'd seen, films, news clips, I knew that an expelled person, or one running from mass persecutions in a country in turmoil, doesn't simply get on a bus that happens to be going to the airport and then get on a plane and leave. Perhaps, I thought, details that people like Priya and I—people who weren't there—wanted, and for whom such stories were a history lesson or even entertainment, were irrelevant to him. But he got to them, after breaking off a piece of bagel and putting it in his mouth. He chewed slowly and we waited.

"From the phone in the dark kitchen, Pa made some calls," he continued. "The first three, he dialled ready to press the switch hook, and the instant he heard the line ringing he cut the call. On the fourth, in Gujarati, he said, 'It's me. Cricket match. I'm calling about the cricket match.' He was quiet as the person on the other end spoke, then he said, 'Yes. Thank you, my friend.' That was how we all lived," Prakash explained, "with codes for the various situations, which someone you could trust would know how to decipher. The man on the phone was a friend who planned to leave the country two days later. He would come and pick us up.

It was risky for him, but every day had become risky for Ugandans, regardless of whether they were African or Asian. We kept the lights in the house turned off, and Pa showered and put on clean daytime clothing. Many days before, we had decided what was to be worn out of the country when the time came, so he and I collected and laid out the clothing for the three of us. In time, we woke my mother, and Pa helped her to wash and dress. It would be many hours before she'd understand what had happened to him, learning of it only when he explained to the Canadian officers why he was a special case and had to leave the country that morning. But we'd all been aware that a day like this one could very well come, and so, despite her illness, my mother was prepared, at least mentally, for it. The friend arrived at about 6:00 a.m., and without carrying any luggage with us that might alert the soldiers at any roadblocks we were sure to encounter, we drove to the bus-meeting spot."

Although one might have imagined the answer to her question and therefore not asked it, Priya asked, "What's a bus-meeting spot?"

He looked at her as if everyone knew what a bus-meeting spot was. Then he said, "Oh, right. That's what we called it. The bus-meeting spot. The place where people gathered to meet the bus that would take them to the airport. It was in the parking lot of a hotel in which Canada had set up a temporary office to register applicants, process emergency visas, and hand out boarding passes."

I wanted to ask then about the Canadian government's involvement. Was it a covert operation? What were the politics of their operating on Ugandan soil? But it didn't seem like the time for an interrogation of logistics, facts, or details. By way of understanding what was being left out, I thought of the current photos that showed towns and villages in Syria being bombed and destroyed, lifeboats limping through the seas, crammed with people, people on larger ships trying to pull refugees out of the water, pictures of bodies floating in the sea—some alive, some already drowned, and the tragic little boy whose body had been washed ashore from a capsized boat. I tried to recall footage of Ugandans at the time, of the deportees, but I could only remember images from the newspapers and TV of Idi Amin in his military uniform, the red band in his green cap.

"There were hundreds of people there," Prakash was saying, "all wanting to be handed their boarding passes for the flights that would leave the country that very day. It took what seemed like an eternity, but we were processed and were on the first bus of the day heading for the airport.

"Our bus," he said, "was stopped eight times. The soldiers combed through, making sure that the very people they wanted out of the country had boarding passes for the flights, and that no one was trying to leave with currency of any kind, including gold. The guards frisked passengers, laughing as they touched women and girls on their private parts, and if they found any gold hidden on anybody, they roughed up that person and then pocketed the jewellery. In the days just before my mother fell ill, she had begun the process of hiding her jewellery. She didn't have much to begin with, but into the bands and hems of the pants my father and I were to wear out of the country, she had stitched light necklaces, earrings, the stud she wore in her nose, and rings with sapphires and rubies, pearls, emeralds, and zircons, not big or expensive gems but little ones that were of astrological and religious significance, and heirlooms passed down from ancestors, and pieces that might fetch a little money if needed wherever we landed. She had two studs for wearing in her nose: a gold bead and a diamond, both of which she'd stitched into the hem of her sari. They were so light and small they would not give the sari a telltale unevenly weighted hemline. She knew, too, however, that if she, an Indian woman clearly of some means, was seen to be wearing no jewellery whatsoever, it would be a sure sign that she was hiding it, and this would invite a search. So she wore a few pieces she'd decided to sacrifice if necessary. When she was told to remove them at the first stop, she remained calm but did so slowly, giving the impression that she was giving up everything she owned. My father wore a watch of no great value that had been given to him some years before for service in education. On that first stop he was made to hand it over."

My mouth was brimming with the kinds of simplistic questions journalists and anchors on TV ask as their camera person closes in on the face of the interviewee to catch the frightened whisper, or the tears the questions—like instructions—are meant to provoke. He seemed moved, a little shaken by all he'd been recalling for us. I wondered if, like the Argentinian at the party, he expected something in return. Not something physical, but sympathy or admiration for having gone through such trauma. I'm not being harsh, just wondering. I was moved, but it's what researchers do, they look at all angles. I couldn't hold back. Wasn't he frightened? Even as I asked, I saw what a silly question it was.

There was a slight tremor in his voice as he said, "You know, the plane we got on was totally packed. Not a seat was empty. Men, women, children. Babies, old people. I can see their faces. If I saw any of them today I would recognize them, as aged as they would be. As the plane filled up with passengers, no one uttered a single word. There was only the sound of people's clothing brushing against the seats in the aisles, filing into their seats, the clicks of seat belts. You know, it was quiet, it was a kind of silence, yet I still hear it, very clearly. We imagined that at any minute soldiers could enter the cabin and remove any number of us off the flight. My father, for one. It seemed to take forever for us to leave the ground. When the plane finally lifted into the air, still no one spoke. For an entire hour no one seemed to breathe. All you heard was the hum and drone of the plane's engines and of the air-conditioning system inside. Then the public address system crackled and the pilot's voice, faint but clear, announced that we had just crossed the Ugandan border and were now in Sudanese airspace. It took us a few seconds to believe what he'd said, and suddenly a loud cheer erupted. People burst into tears and began finally to speak, everyone, all at once. So yes, I was frightened, but I didn't know it until that moment, until we were properly out of Uganda."

Some kind of response was needed to break the silence in the kitchen that followed. But what does one say to a man like him? *Well, I'm glad you made it out? So sorry you experienced this? Wow, were you ever brave?*

I hesitantly offered, "At university I knew an Asian man from Uganda. He'd come as a refugee, too. His name was Karim. He was on the students' committee with me. He was a real play-boy. Once we asked him what he missed most about Uganda. He said, his ball boy."

The two of them looked puzzled, and Prakash said, "Ball boy?"

"He played tennis," I explained. "The person who fetched the balls around the court."

Prakash said, "Ah, one of those. Well, there you go. No one was spared."

Priya caught my eye and I could see her displeasure with my story. Before she could finish the disapproving twisting of her mouth at me, I turned away, not appreciating being policed. With my story I'd intended to hear from Prakash more about the fact that no one, meaning not even those with money to employ ball boys, was spared. His personal story was interesting, yes, but I wanted us to talk, too, about the larger situation. Priya's censure made the room feel small and tight and provincial.

Prakash jumped off his seat and excused himself to go to—as he called it while winking at me—the little boys' room. Priya pointed in the direction of the washroom.

In a quick conciliatory gesture, I whispered to Priya, "I guess we've lived a happily boring existence, eh?"

She didn't answer. I added that he was interesting but I seemed not to have made an impression on him. "He tells a good story, but he isn't even curious about me," I said. "He hasn't asked me a single question about myself. He's not even curious about how you and I met. And he isn't interested in the larger picture."

She asked what I meant by this last. I whispered, "The situation in Uganda back then affected every person there; it is interesting along political lines, and geographically and racially, and it would have been interesting to have had—after he'd finished with his own story, of course—some conversation that included us all. Don't you think? It is not as if you and I know nothing of Uganda."

"But the story wasn't academic. It was real, personal, and traumatic," she said. "You veered off into the topic of class."

She was right, of course, but I responded, "Nevertheless, he's in my house, he could at least have asked me something about myself, or engaged with an angle I took up." I spoke in what I hoped was a measured tone, but I surprised myself. I'm not the type to be affected by something like this. And in all truth I had been finding him fairly tolerable, yet suddenly, in talking to Priya I was being critical of him. I couldn't stop myself. "You'd think he'd show some interest. Does he know I'm a writer? Did you tell him?"

She said no, she hadn't, and reminded me that she hadn't had any real conversations with him before he arrived. There was no point asking if I was to believe this, as I'd have had to reveal that I knew she had invited him here, and that they had perhaps met with each other after she and I got together. There was no time for such a conversation. Then she said, "But you're taking it way too personally. It's not that he's not interested in you—he doesn't like prying. He's always been like that. But I know it comes across as if he's not interested in anyone but himself."

Under my breath I said, "You can be so naive," and began clearing the dishes.

She ignored that and said, "But seriously, that was quite an experience, don't you think? Can't you be a little more compassionate?"

I walked back to her and said harshly, "Priya, all that happened over forty years ago. He's been in Canada ever since. It was a terrible thing he went through, and he took on more than a young boy should have had to. I'm not at all unsympathetic, but it's not the first or the second or the third time he's told that story. It was in perfect chronological order. He may not know he's doing it, but this is how he gets attention."

"He has earned the right to tell such a story as many times as he likes," she said sharply.

She intended to say more, but I cut her off. "Look, he just told us a story of very difficult events; there was no affect, it's as if it were just a story. He hasn't mentioned a thing about how he or his parents fared since. Does he even know how he *feels*? Being a refugee is no reason for thoughtlessness."

An odd smile pulled at Priya's lips. She shook her head at me and said, "I can't believe this is your response. You can be so cold sometimes. You're the one being selfish. You just want him to have paid you attention."

"And what's wrong with that? As I said, he's in my house," I responded coldly. We were fighting.

"It's my house, too. He's a guest in my house, too, and I'll ask you to please be a little kinder," she snapped.

Every interaction, no matter how unrelated, was an opportunity to underline how things were falling apart between us. I cleared the counter and put things away in the fridge. My harshness was not meant for him. I wasn't being selfish, not entirely. I could see a closeness between her and this man, and it felt like a slap to my face. If she was capable of such closeness, why had she not been so with me? I thought of the envelope of photos of the two of them. I was seeing, and feeling, an intensity between them that predated my appearance in her life. Irrationally, I wanted to blame her, and him, for all that had gone wrong between us.

When he returned, Priya said it was time they headed out to see some of the area, but he'd just received a text about a work project, he said, and needed to go online for a few minutes. I gave him the password for the internet, and he went up to the guest room.

She asked me to come into our bedroom and speak with her. They were going to leave soon, so I knew this would be short, and I followed her.

She slipped off her shoes and lay on her back on her side of the bed. She patted my side for me to join her. I lay down. She said nothing, and I wondered why she'd asked me in. Then she reached over and took my hand. For a few minutes we lay awkwardly like that.

"I want to apologize," she whispered.

"For what?" I asked.

"For everything. I'm sorry I let him come here."

"Don't be. He's not the problem."

She turned and looked at me. "What is?"

The guest room is above our room, and although we don't hear our guests conversing, nor have any said they hear us from up there, we continued to whisper.

I shook my head to say that I didn't know. Or that I couldn't say. Or that it was way too much to elaborate with a guest in the house. I eventually said, "I am sorry, too. I'm really sorry, Priya."

She squeezed my hand and said, "It's okay. It'll all be okay. We'll get through this."

I lost my breath. I didn't let her see, but I'd begun to cry, albeit without sound.

"He seems happier than I've ever known him to be," she said.

Some moments passed before I could ask, "Are you pleased he's here?"

"I've known him for such a long time. Forever, actually. It's good to see him. But we don't really have much in common, do we?"

"Doesn't seem so. But he's an okay person."

"He's very ordinary, I know. But he's also extraordinary. He's known that I'm lesbian for decades. He's a straight, conventional, Indian family man. And yet we've remained friends. He's never abandoned me. Yes, I can use that word, abandon. He's never abandoned me."

"We're all victims of our pasts, aren't we?" I said.

"I guess it's the excuse for our present selves. But you're right. He isn't a bad person," she said wearily. "He's not cruel or mean or malicious. I've never known him to hurt anyone. I told you that people at the university used to tease him about how he pronounced English words, interchanging v's for w's and vice versa. But I was ashamed to tell you that Fiona and I—his closest friends—also teased him mercilessly. In those days, no one thought that imitating someone's accent or teasing them about it was a form of racism. We thought we were being funny and affectionate. It never occurred to us to consider how he might have felt about it. He always laughed and played along. What else was he to do? I wouldn't tease him anymore about that sort of thing, of course. But have you noticed: he no longer mixes up his v's and w's. Is that a good thing or a bad thing?"

The conversation was revealing—she clearly had affection, and even admiration, for him. "He's very straight," I said.

There was quiet upstairs. I wondered what he was doing. I didn't want this conversation with Priya to end. It had been a while since there had been any connection between us. I felt grateful, and at the same time terribly sad. If I could have right then, I would have put my face in her chest and bawled.

"Are you being a bigot?" she responded, and chuckled softly at her own words. "But so what? We have tons of straight friends. How different is he from any of them?"

"Come on, you know what I mean. I don't mean heterosexual. I mean he's ordinary, a member of the card-carrying mainstream. Years ago, I knew a guy, Rao, a Brahmin from Calcutta," I told her, whispering. "He grew up here in Canada. He was studying English—a theory guy. He once told me he tried living with what he called women like me—intellectual, opinionated—and he'd had one long relationship with such a woman but they fought a lot, and when they broke up he agreed to a marriage arranged by family members to a nice woman from India who was not likely to challenge him. I guess that's what he wanted in the end. Did Prakash ever really imagine he could be with a woman like you?"

"Like me? What am I like?"

We heard him come down the stairs, and Priya got up.

She stood and came to my side of the bed and looked at me for some long seconds, waiting perhaps for an answer. I said nothing. Then she asked, tenderly, if I wanted to come with them.

For the first time, I think she really did want me to come. "No. We're already on a path here. You go. In any case, I'm a third wheel."

"It's inevitable with old friendships," she said.

I asked what time she thought they'd be back.

"We'll be a few hours, but definitely in time for dinner," she said, adding with a soft, heartbreaking smile, "I can't wait to eat a meal prepared by you."

I told her I was going to rest in bed for a while, and to tell him goodbye for me. She stood at the door watching me. I couldn't read her mind. Then she briskly walked back, bent down, and kissed me on my lips. The scent of his cologne was still on her.

"How do I look?" she asked.

"Handsome. As usual," I answered.

She rolled her eyes and, smiling, said, "I don't look like a flaming lesbian, do I?"

"Not 'flaming,'" I said. "But you can't hide what you are. Why do you care, anyway?"

"I just don't want to be *flaming*."

I did not say anything about dinner. "Take your time. Be careful." I reached my hand out to brush her as she walked away.

When the door to the bedroom shut behind her, the tears came. I couldn't stop crying. I heard them walk to the back of the house. Their voices faded, and then several minutes later they returned and I listened to them put on coats and boots. They were taking their time, Priya pointing out the paintings she'd made. I waited until I heard the main door close behind them. Then the screen door. Then the car doors. I got up from the bed and looked through the blinds on the bedroom window and saw the car pull out.

I went into the living room and sat on the sofa. I don't know how long I sat there, but eventually I called Skye. Her answering message came on. I left a message telling her I was alone and she could call as soon as she liked.

4

A DRIVE IN THE COUNTRY

. . .

She's gone in for a rest, I tell him, and prefers to stay to work on her book. In any case, I say, he and I need time to catch up, and there are things I want to speak with him about. He doesn't ask what those might be, he just says, "Uh-huh. I know."

As I walk past the mirror in the dining room, I check myself. Not flaming, but definitely not straight.

I go into the kitchen to make sure the stove is off and the fridge door properly closed, then into the storage room behind the kitchen to fetch two bottles of water. He follows me into the room. He's blocking the door, and stands there as I face him on the way out. I can feel the heat off his body. He holds me by my shoulders and says, "Come on. Give me a proper hug."

I've heard those words before, and wonder if he remembers saying them.

"It's been a long while since I've seen you," he says. "I'm glad to be here."

We're not alone in the house, but in the storage room we are. We are enough alone. A warmer hug than when he arrived can't hurt. I am not averse to it. He has seen my little world and my place in it. He will surely respect this. And so will I. It's possible, of course, that Alex might come out to tell me something she's just remembered she needs to say. I wouldn't want her to see him and me in the storage room like this, let alone embracing. I do the hug-and-release thing, gentle in the hug, insistent in the release. But he continues to stand firm and to pull me toward him. A lime-scented heat rises from his neck and face, I smell him, the scent of his thoughts, the scent of desire. My pelvis suddenly aches, and memories of the morning's dream wash in waves up and down my body. But this feeling of desire flooding me is not for him. This I know well. Of course it is not. It is purely a trick of a body that's alive and has feeling. We have been here before, but so very long ago. I take a breath, put my hands to his chest, and push against him slightly. I lean my head back and look at him. "It's great you've come all this way for a visit," I say. My smile quivers, my body begins to betray me; I need to separate from him immediately. "And in December, too!" I add. "Everything's closed in the area. Except for Madame Bovary's. We can have tea or an ice cream. Let's go." I push him back and step away, whispering, "But don't tell Alex. I shouldn't be eating ice cream." And I throw in a pretense of complicity, an ounce of mischievousness, to reset things. "She doesn't stop me, but it'll weaken my position when I harass her about smoking."

He chuckles, but I know that look of his, when he feels slighted but doesn't want to show it—the sound of laughter, but a smile that is forced, behind it eyes that know better. He holds his head up high and says brightly, pleasantness still managed in his voice, "Your secret's safe with me." I'd wanted to take him to the studio, but I don't want a repeat of this while alone in there with him. He follows me to the front of the house. He points toward the bedroom and says, "She's nice."

I want to tell him that she's very smart, but this will sound foolish. Or defensive. I want to say she isn't always so quiet or reserved or cool and she reveals herself slowly, that he should ask her questions about herself and listen. I love her and she loves me, I want to tell him. I want to announce that she and I irritate the hell out of each other, but in the end we will always love each other. But I stop myself.

He assumes we'll go in his car, that he'll drive. I don't mind. It's a treat not to have to drive. The car is new, I can tell from the boozy, tobacco-like smell of the leather upholstery. His circumstances have changed. I won't ask. He'll tell me, no doubt. I direct him to turn right. I am alone with him in his car. It's been many years. I've changed a great deal in that time, but I feel myself softening, my muscles giving way. It is immediately as it used to be when I was with him in the past—I relax, I let him take charge. I know my hair is short. I whisper every time I go to the hairdresser, *Remember, not girlish, nor like a man's—but a little boyish.* And yet I feel as if my hair is parted in the middle and long, down my back.

I think of my mother, as she would have been at the age I am now, being driven down the road by my father in his car. If Prakash and I had married after university, that's how we'd be now. Like them. We'd stay at one of the bed and breakfasts, tour this quaint town, me hanging his clothes on the towel rack to air at the end of our drive, finding his toothbrush for him from the little carry-on bag I'd have packed for both of us. I'd smell like him. He'd open the door for me. Put his hand on my back when we stepped through. I am the one who has always held doors open, for girlfriends BA and for Alex, too. I am the one with the hand firm on a woman's back, gently ushering her forward. It has always been an unspoken expectation of me. How is it that I never expect a woman to reciprocate, that I never mind this one-sidedness, and yet, in Prakash's presence, I don't mind being the one catered to? Not only do I not mind it, but I find myself falling into it easily.

White wicker furniture that will stay out all winter long to furnish an ambiance of colonial leisure is displayed on some of the curved front porches of the red-brick bed and breakfasts we pass as we drive through the village. Imposing wide concrete stairs are hemmed in by elaborate white-painted concrete banisters. Like ours, many of these houses were built in the last half of the nineteenth century. Red-and-blue banners announce the presence of a glass artist's studio or a painter's, a ceramicist's, a forged-iron worker, the arts and crafts store, the French grocery, a secondhand and antique shop, and that they are open for business. I imagine I am Prakash driving through this neighbourhood and seeing its appeal, and I see it myself as if for the first time. I feel pride in having chosen to move to such a picturesque place. I am pleased to be showing it off to him.

"Last year at this time," I say, "it was minus nineteen degrees Celsius and everything was under ice. Look at it now, it could just as well be spring." The sky is less cerulean than when I'd come out earlier to drive Skye to her house, but it is still bright, and bulbous milk-white clouds fringe the horizon. From shrubs and trees dangle a few stubborn, dried-out orange-coloured leaves, and their long pale bones draw fanned-out fingers against the sky. As beautiful as it is, it is a discordant winter scene because the lawns around the homes have recently been mowed and remain vibrant green. Prakash doesn't answer. He's texting something on his cellphone. I want to ask him not to text while he's driving, but I don't want to sound bossy, or timid.

Our village's Christmas parade will take place the following weekend, I tell him. He should have come next week instead of this week. It's a quaint affair, I say, with Santas driving tractors and elves in carts drawn by donkeys dressed up as reindeer. He glances at the road and then back to his phone repeatedly, muttering to me *um-hm*. His hair has indeed greyed. I imagine I must look to him as aged as he looks to me. But he's aged well. Doors and verandah posts are garlanded with boughs of dark green fir that hang in arched loops, each section anchored by oversized red bows, and shiny gold, red, and blue baubles and long white candy canes are propped in the nest of bare limbs atop mulberry trees. Iridescent bluebird ornaments dot deciduous trees and glisten in this winter light. We pass a house on whose lawn is parked a life-size sleigh overflowing with large wrapped boxes tied elaborately with ribbon. It all looks out of place without any snow on the ground. I want him to see this place in which we live, but he is not paying attention. In the main part of the village I count three plastic snowmen, all exactly the same, with black-gloved hands raised in greeting. We must slow down in the area of a handful of boutiques and restaurants, some of which are open. In this commercial hub, where a sudden profusion of cars lines both sides of the street, pedestrians cross as leisurely as if they own the road. I want to point out our local pasta joint, and our favourite place to buy hostess gifts, and the new oddity—a Japanese-style coffee shop that recently opened—but Prakash uses the slowdown of the traffic to find a file on the cellphone with pictures of his children. He hands it to me and tells me to scroll through them, and as I do so he glances to see which I am looking at. I have never met them, but I'd seen photographs of them before. They are no longer children. I don't recognize them. One of the boys has a moustache. I think the girl resembles her mother.

"Varuna is sixteen," he says. "I've spoiled her. She thinks she's a princess. I've always made her feel that way. When she isn't treated like that at her school, it shocks her." He laughs. He is a proud father. I scroll and there are the two boys. "Vikram on the left, Arjun on the right." I ask what they are up to these days. "They're on holiday from school," he says, "and are currently in India with their mother."

"Why haven't you gone with them?" I ask, hoping for more understanding of his life today.

"Don't worry," he tells me, "there's time enough for all of that later."

His response irritates me, but it is in keeping with his usual manner. The mysteries and intrigues that aren't at all mysteries or intrigues, but rather his need to control the moment, and when and how stories are told and information is let out. "So for the time being you're a free man," I say.

He responds rather seriously, "Actually, I *am* a free man; the secret is that I've always been a free man. Don't you know that?"

Outside of the village, where the residential houses thin out and the road widens, the speed jumps from fifty kilometres to eighty. The car lurches forward. We pass farmhouses, acres apart from one another. As we climb a small hill that a bicyclist in light cool-weather gear struggles to mount, he turns to face me, and asks, "So?"

I watch the car veer across the centre line as he waits for an answer. "So what?" I answer. A vehicle approaches and he pulls us back onto our side.

"Tell me."

"Well, what do you want to know?" I suspect he means for me to tell him what I meant when I said minutes before that I had things about which I wanted to speak with him. But the urgency I'd felt earlier has faded.

"I want to know everything," he says.

Weak words dribble from my mouth. "I've taken myself out of the centre," I say.

"Um-hm," he says encouragingly, but I regret my vague words. They sound like a plea, and it shocks me that it takes nothing more than being alone with him for just a few minutes before I revert to my old role with him, the one in need, appealing to him for help or sympathy. I suddenly don't remember anything I'd begun the morning wanting to say to him. My mind has gone blank.

I fumble and try to hold on to the last words spoken, and I open my palms out, gesturing for him to look around on either side of the highway—fields, a farmhouse here, one there, silos, barns, more fields. "Last year this time," I say, "these fields were under a heavy cover of ice and snow, and then more ice and more snow. I can't get over the difference this year. Last winter, any of us living down here could have been felled by the elements, but this winter, cyclists are still out riding. There is so much uncertainty living in the countryside."

As we near the roundabout, the home of the Syrian refugees comes into view. The house remains closed up, the van still not there. "That's where the island's first Syrian refugees live."

He glances at the house and says, "Um-hm."

I wait, and he offers nothing more. I ask, as we pass the closed-up roadside farmer's market next door, "Do you think about them much, about the Syrians?"

He says, "Of course. I think about them all the time." But he offers no more.

I don't pursue it. I wonder if pointing out their home irks him, if I've played into some stereotype he knows only too well.

I look at his arm, I want to touch his wool jacket and apologize. I don't. If I do, I won't be able to stop apologizing. If I reach out and touch him, I'm not sure what I'll be encouraging.

We pass more bare fields, a large spread of a hardware store surrounded by a big asphalt parking lot in which there are a few cars and trucks. More farmland. A couple more farmhouses. An auto-repair garage and a garden centre. A home for seniors. A vineyard and an optometrist next to each other on the local highway.

"So, carry on. You were saying," he says eventually.

"This is not the centre," I say again, a little deflated, and not quite sure what I mean.

He says, "Um-hm."

"There's nothing going on here," I say, aware—but unable to stop myself—that I am talking as if the move here was a mistake. I don't want him to think I am in bliss. Now that he's back, I am not sure I want him to disappear again. Perhaps he will if he thinks I don't need him. "I miss the city. I sometimes feel as if I've removed myself from the hustle and bustle, the diversity and the unexpected, wonderfully crazy flow of life. It can be lonely down here."

"I thought so. I can see that. You're not the country type. Tell me more," he says.

He's ready to sympathize. I am speaking as if I want him to think I regret what I've done, that I'm as broken as ever. That I'm not benefitting from this relocation. It's a pattern, this dance with him, and how compelling it is. But it wasn't hours ago that I so strongly felt I no longer want his pity. I want him to see that I am strong, that I can fend for myself. With Alex at my side, I can.

I've begun to perspire. My ears feel as if they're on fire. I remove my jacket. I press the control to lower the window an inch. He turns down the heat. I sip water from one of the bottles.

I say, "Yes, I'm not a country person, but neither am I a city person," and, having come to a stoplight, I point in the direction we must go.

He looks over at me and asks, "I can tell you're lonely. Are you happy?"

The car veers, and as there are vehicles passing us constantly, I want to point this out, but before I do he has pulled back to our side again. I guess he knows he has this tendency to veer whenever he takes his eyes off the road.

Is this the entitlement of an old friend who thinks that because they've known you longer than your lover has, they are free to speak their mind? It irritates me that he watches me so closely, that he thinks he knows how I am. I say, "Of course," and leave it there. We are quiet for a few minutes. Then, to soften the abruptness of my response, I add, "But is there anyone who's really happy? Are you?"

He says, "Good point. It's possible, but you have to be willing to be blind, to be deaf, to not think too much. To not feel. To not feel sadness *or* happiness, for that matter. That's happiness. But your brain, Priya, works overtime. You'll forever be searching for happiness, and it's that search that makes people unhappy."

This used to be one of his pastimes—analyzing me, and the philosophizing, as if he is the voice of Brahma or Buddha. I tolerated it in the past. I will again now.

But I'm caught off-guard when he says, "Do you realize I've met several of your girlfriends?"

He waits for a response; I'm annoyed but I don't want to show this.

"Hmm? How many people can say that?" he continues. "I probably have known more of your girlfriends than anyone else who knows you. We've known one another for a long time."

I wonder where this might be leading. He rephrases: "What I meant was, are you happy with Alex?"

What does he really want to know? Was he suggesting that Alex is simply one among the several girlfriends he's met? What should I tell him? Was this drive a bad idea?

"Yes," I say. "She's amazing. She's different. She's not like other people."

He says, "Yes, not like the others—not like the ones before. She's not young like the others were."

"They are no longer young either. We're all older," I say. Alex would be horrified if she knew we were discussing her in this manner. "She's good for me. I'm probably less good for her. I brood a lot. But I really do love her. I love being with her."

"Um-hm," he says. "But can she accept that unstoppable brain of yours? I've always thought you needed to be with someone who will let you ruminate and then catch you before you fall because of that very rumination."

"Well, in that way, she and I *are* alike," I tell him. "We catch each other. We entered this relationship late. Late in life, so to speak." Everything I say to him will be an explanation. I will unreel before him like a tossed ball of twine. "We were already formed when we met. We didn't grow together to become the people we are today. I wouldn't make the same choices, nor the same mistakes—at least, I hope not—that I did back then."

"Um-hm," he says again.

He doesn't like her. I can tell. She's too strong for him. I'd wanted them to like one another. Was I daft, or what?

We come to Madame Bovary's and I tell him to turn off the main road, we can park in their lot at the back, but he says, "No, let's drive. Do you know a pretty route?"

And, in fact, I do, an unusual one on which I enjoy taking visitors. "Shall we get a cup of tea to go?" I ask.

He says he's already had enough tea at the house, and he laughs as he adds, "You know what that means."

I tell him, "Let's take the free ferry across the bay. It is an event—a small event—in itself. We could head in the direction of Kingston along the coastal road and turn back whenever we're ready. Yield at the Y intersection," I say, "and then take the arm on the right."

"So how long has it been?" he asks.

I don't know if he means how long since he and I last saw one another, or how long since we moved here. Before I can check myself, I am saying, "Alex and me? Six years. I've learned it takes about that amount of time to only just begin to see your partner. You should know. How long has it been for you?"

"Let's not talk about my marriage. I've come here for a break. You're my break." I don't respond, and he asks, "Are you willing to be my break?"

I don't know what he means, but I say, "Sure. You don't have to talk about anything you don't want to."

"You don't appear to be close, the two of you," he says.

"What do you mean?" I ask. I don't like this insinuation into my life. This is what he used to do, and I used to allow it, but this can't carry on. I must let him know that.

"Alex," he says. "As I said, she's not like the other women you've dated. She's not very warm. Is it because of me, or is she always like that?"

"She *is* a warm person," I say defensively. "The ones you knew, you met years ago. I am nothing like I was in those days. Alex doesn't wear her emotions on her sleeve. She's as warm as she needs to be."

In response to my obvious defensiveness, he answers, "Yeah. I know, I know. I didn't mean anything. I just worry about you."

I want to tell him he doesn't have to worry about me and put an end to this talk about Alex. At the same time, perhaps I *can* commiserate with him. I can't speak with my friends here about difficulties with Alex because they are all her friends, too. Perhaps I can be open about my unhappiness. But I'm not really unhappy; it is he who says I am. I don't think I really am. But in some ways it's true: Alex isn't as warm as one might wish in a partner; she doesn't rush to carry me nor want to be carried herself; she will be there if I need her, but she doesn't swoop in under me unasked; her independence is often a source of conflict between us. It is true: she is so self-sufficient and expects me to be so, too, that it's clear we are two separate people, not bound up in each other. For this reason there might not appear to be much passion or chemistry between us. Perhaps that's what he's talking about. I guess he saw something back there at home.

"I was just thinking of your Ismaili girlfriend. Yasmin," he says, pulling me back onto the road with him with a jolt—I hadn't thought of Yasmin in a very long time, and had forgotten he'd met her. That was almost twenty years ago. "She didn't like me," he says, "but my God, she had a beautiful body." He puts his hand on my knee and says, "Do you remember her? Her breasts?"

Oh God, I can't let him do this. I must stop this at once. "Oh, come on, Prakash, that's crude," I tell him. "I don't want to talk about past girlfriends. Nor about women's bodies."

"But I do," he says.

Such firmness from him is new to me. He's never contradicted me before. I decide I can at least try to change the subject. I return to something he was clearly pleased to speak about—his refugee story. "Hey, that story you were telling us in the kitchen—you'd told me some of it, but we've known each other for a long time, and that was the first time I ever heard the details."

"It's not a story." I think he instantly regrets the firmness in these words, for he quickly adds, with a show of peevishness in his tone, "And besides, you never asked. In any case, back then it wasn't something I could talk about. I would have tried if you'd asked—if *you'd* asked—but not otherwise. I can speak about it nowadays as if it happened to someone else, but back then I couldn't remember any details. They've only just been coming back to me. But it's not a story. It's all true."

"You can talk about it now because of the Syrians, do you think?" I ask, still trying to sort out in my mind why he mentioned Yasmin.

"Yes. There's so much sympathy for them here, coast to coast. In my day, people were curious, but not so sympathetic. I bet they don't get teased about their accents and clothing and manners the way we did. It brings up a lot of stuff for me. I'm thinking of going back, you know. Lots of people are going back, reclaiming their land and trying to restart their businesses. I'm thinking of checking it out."

We are nearing the ferry terminal. I am no longer sure that leaving this side of the island is the best thing to do. It seems as if going to the other side is taking me much farther away from Alex than I want to be.

He says, "I wasn't being flippant when I mentioned Yasmin, you know. I have thought of her because an Ismaili woman has come into my life."

There's such a jolt inside of me, I feel he must surely have felt it. I turn quickly to face him and ask, "Aren't you and Aruna still together?" as if that is what has surprised me.

"Well, that is one of the things I wanted to tell you. She and I parted ways four years ago. She went back to her parents in India. We have not divorced yet, though that will come eventually. Hence the new car. Do you like it? I could not have made such a purchase with her here. She would have had a fit. Not because of money. There's plenty of that these days—business is booming. And you know, I've always wanted a Beemer. But she doesn't like flair or, as she calls it, ostentation. Yes, her word. It's the kids, they made her learn to speak English perfectly."

"What about the kids?" I ask, trying to take in this major change in his life. It amuses and horrifies me at once that I feel a twinge of what I cannot but call jealousy that he has met someone he wants to tell me about. "Are they permanently with her?"

"No, they had a choice and wanted to stay in Canada, but they're with her for the holidays. They left for India a week ago and will stay until the first week of the New Year."

He's free, he'd said. Free for *what*?

"So did I ever tell you," he says, "about my Ismaili babysitter?"

"Tell me about the Ismaili woman you've recently met," I say.

"That's what I'm trying to do. In Uganda she lived in the house opposite ours. Her parents and mine got along. She began babysitting me when I was about ten and she was sixteen. She was very beautiful. Like Yasmin." When he says "Yasmin" he looks at me. "I've been in touch with her—the babysitter, I mean."

I pull the neck of my sweater up over my mouth and blow air through my pursed lips, trying to cool myself. I drink again from the bottle of water.

"She's married and lives in Vancouver. But we've been in touch and—"

"Am I going to have to hear about her body, too?" I ask, one third smiling, one third chiding, one third worried about where this, too, is headed.

He doesn't answer, but says, "It's one of the things I want to tell you. She and her husband are returning to Uganda. His family had cacao and cashew land there and they're trying to reclaim it. She and I reconnected on Facebook, and they've asked me to return and help set up a central commercial production for the country."

"So you're going?" I ask.

"For a while. I'm going because of her. She used to love having her breasts fondled."

It takes a few seconds, and then I realize what he's telling me. I exclaim, "What? When you were ten? Do I want to hear this? I'd rather not."

I am not sure if the twist of his mouth is a smirk or a grin. "It started when I was ten. And luckily my parents thought I needed babysitting right up until we left Uganda, when I was fourteen. Oh, don't look at me like that. I'm joking—by the time I became a teenager they stopped calling her my babysitter. But she'd still come over and keep me company the moment she saw them leave the house in the evening. Sometimes I'd suggest to them that they go out, to a movie or to dinner, or for a drive, and when they left I'd go into the yard and kick my football against the chain-link fence at the front of our house so she'd hear the noise and look out. Of course, I'd be glancing over at her house waiting for her. I'd signal to her and she'd come over. We were almost caught a few times. But how she loved having them—her breasts, I mean—how she loved having them fondled. Can you imagine?" Is he boasting? Is he relating this detail to seduce me? "I can remember it as if it were happening right this moment. She would tuck her hands under them, under her breasts, and offer them to me—me, six years younger than her—to lick and suck."

That image, the fact of us being alone in his car, the windows up enough so not even the wind can hear us, of Alex's absence, sends my mind and my body tumbling. I feel fear, but the direction this conversation is taking is tantalizing, too. I should know better. I should know better. But I want to know where this will take us. Should I let it play itself out, or should I stop it right away? No one need ever know of this conversation. But after this, then what? Wouldn't he expect more? Would he want to come down regularly? Would I have to dodge Alex to speak with him on the phone? Can what happens, if I let this go on, stay here and go no further? Or will I be courting future trouble? The blood that has rushed to my brain makes me dizzy.

"But there was one thing that was very interesting," he continues. "I could never kiss her on her mouth. I suppose she thought she'd catch my Brahmin germs. I wanted to, but she wouldn't let me. I could touch her breasts, I could put them in my mouth, but I couldn't kiss her on her mouth."

He laughs uncontrollably. Is he attempting, I wonder, to draw some parallel between her and me, between how far she would allow him to go with her, and how far I let him into my life before I pushed him out? The spell that was being cast on me is broken. I need to be firm and strong.

"That would all be called abuse over here, wouldn't it?" I say soberly.

He doesn't answer but gets right back on his horse. "I used to stand at the front windows and look for her. I got very excited when I knew my parents were going out. Anyway, I've been to Vancouver to meet with her husband and, well, she and I met again. He knows she used to babysit me, but nothing else. I haven't been able to get her out of my mind ever since. We write to each other."

I try to calm myself. I can't get it out of my head that he was ten. I am horrified, and at the same time there is something titillating about this. He knows it and that's why he told me. He wants me to be turned on. He wants to wreck what I have with Alex.

But perhaps there was nothing wrong with what happened between him and that babysitter. Perhaps because today he remembers it fondly—so to speak—there's nothing wrong with what happened then. But isn't his talk of it to me problematic? It is meant to be provocative. Sexually provocative. He was ten years old. Why does he still carry a torch for her? What does that say about him, and her carrying on with him now? And, really, why tell me these details?

"You know, when we were thrown out," he says, seeming to segue, "people who didn't have British nationality, those without British passports, had nowhere to go. I was serious when I said no country would take us in. Including India. Do you know why Canada has the most Ugandan Ismailis?"

I shrug my shoulders. I am pleased he's stopped the nonsense about breasts.

"When Uganda got independence," he explains, "their leader, the Aga Khan, told his followers that they should be citizens of the country in which they lived. It's exactly as my own father thought when he took Ugandan citizenship. So the Ismailis in Uganda became citizens of that country. And when Amin took away citizenship status from Asian Ugandans, they, too, ended up stateless. The Aga Khan and our new prime minister Justin's father were apparently good friends, and the Aga Khan called up Pierre and pleaded with him and he agreed to take the Ismailis in. That was how the conversation regarding Ugandan refugees in Canada was begun. They had their leader, the Aga Khan, looking out for them. There was no one to help the rest of us. To Ismaili Ugandans the rest of us are beholden. They look down on us."

"So if this Ismaili woman kissed you, would you forget about her?" Why I say this, why I refer to his babysitting adventure, surprises me. But I've done it purposefully. I've fallen for his talk. I do want him to tell me more. If he reaches his hand to my knee again, I will place mine on it. But then what? I must remain still. I must stop this pull toward him.

"Well, apparently she isn't afraid of Brahmin germs anymore, and here's one non-Ismaili Ugandan she doesn't look down on. And so, no, I can't forget her." He chuckles at his cleverness. But again my mind burns with the idea that he was ten and therefore this babysitting gig allowed her to abuse him, even if he had enjoyed the activity then.

"But you were ten," I insist. "Do you feel what she did was wrong?"

"She was so beautiful, and she wasn't supposed to be doing this to me, and I knew it, and it felt as if I had all the power over her. It wasn't abuse. At least, not for me. I have not suffered because of it. And, apparently, neither has she."

I've known him for so many years, and, in some ways, we'd been so intimate. But clearly, I don't know much about him. It has begun to seem to me that no matter how long you know someone, or how intimately, you can't really fully know them. What then does *intimate* mean?

When we get to the terminal, I want to ask him to turn back, but we've arrived precisely at the boarding time and ours is the only car. We are waved on by the ferryman and, without stopping, Prakash complies. The boat pulls out of the dock and we get out of the car into the cold wind. My hair is whipped in every direction. I clutch the railing and watch the water like black oil slide fast behind the ferry. Last year this time, the ferry had to traverse a straight path that had been cut through deep ice. Dead ducks and gulls lay on the frozen edges of the path. It was a strange, sad sight. Looking over the edge of the ferry, you could see how thick the ice was then. There were layers of it, like shelves, in varying shades of turquoise. The vast sheet that covered the rest of the lake was as smooth as glass, parts of it cloudy like menthol candy, with hairline cracks weaving across the surface. It was eerie moving through that narrow channel of black water. Every few metres lay an upturned dead bird, its wings splayed and stuck to the ice, the rest of its body rigid, facing the sky. Brilliant red blood had smeared the ice around most of the birds. And overhead, a few seagulls followed our path. In some places you saw birds frozen just below the surface. They'd likely used the passage cut for the boats to dive below the water to fish, but were killed by the boats themselves, and eventually washed up onto the ice in the boats' wakes. There had been swans in the channel, too, hugging the edges of the ice shelf. It seemed dangerous. Cruel. There was nothing you could do. It's different today. Now, gulls sail overhead, ducks bob on the water at a safe distance. The water, billowing like taut plastic, is so densely black it appears nothing could exist beneath its surface.

Prakash walks about the deck, from side to side, taking photos with his phone. He hands it to me and I take a picture of him, behind him the Mill House on the shore from which we just sailed. I expect him to suggest we take one of us together, but he takes the phone from me and pockets it.

Back in the car, as we cross the bay, he says to me, "Do you ever think about the times you and I slept together?"

Slept together? Is he mad, I wonder. Times—plural? Perhaps he is simply confirming my supposition that if you dream of someone, they too surely have dreamt in the same manner of you. I've never told him I dream of him—him and me about to have sex. I wouldn't talk with him about such a thing. Imagine if I were to tell him that this very morning I'd had such a dream—it would be an invitation. So why is he asking me this now? It's an opening, of course. But to what? This is not a conversation we should be having.

"The first time. Do you remember the first time?" He turns to face me. He is not smiling, but for some odd reason, it is a smile, a nervous smile, that breaks on my face. I fidget in the seat and grab the seat belt across my chest. I hold on to it tightly.

"Slept together. It's a euphemism, right?" I ask. Is he trying engage in some kind of seduction?

"You don't remember, do you?"

But he is not flirting, he seems serious. Stern. There's an edge to his voice. I've been caught off guard. My smile dissolves.

"I'll remind you from the beginning," he says. "Fiona had gone away for the weekend with that guy she was seeing, Stan."

That was decades ago. My breath catches at the mention of Stan's name. Why has he remembered Stan? Did he know Stan? What does he know about him?

"She and you suddenly weren't as close as you thought. I had a suspicion about you, but I didn't even know the language to use back then. And I also, somehow, didn't really want to know. Anyway, you were down, very depressed. I called and asked you out, but you declined. You told me to leave you alone. I wanted to help you, but you wouldn't let me. By midweek you were not answering your phone. I was desperately worried about you and I asked the superintendent of your building to let me into your apartment. She'd seen me often enough so she agreed."

Yes, I remember this, but we didn't sleep together. What is he talking about?

"You had lost weight, and acne had broken out all over your face. I sat with you all that afternoon, until you made me leave. How much I wanted to hold you through that night. But I left, as you asked."

Exactly. So what is he getting at?

"I'd already told my mother all about you, so I called and asked her what to do. She said to bring you home to her in New Brunswick."

Oh God. New Brunswick. I want him to stop the car. I feel ill, but I can't bring myself to ask him.

"You didn't agree to go, but neither did you protest, so I bought us tickets and presented them to you. You asked me, in that weak voice I remember well, 'What will I need to take with me?' Do you remember?" He looks ahead and doesn't wait for an answer. "I told you I'd take you to see lighthouses and we'd go for a hike on the coast, and you cheered up. It was what I wanted, and it worked. So we went to Salt Island for a few days."

He'd rented a car at the airport. I remember us pulling up in front of the house, yellow clapboard with green trim. The memory of the smell of curry in the house comes to mind. I say nothing. "How can you not remember?" he asks, frustration in his voice. "That first night, the Boses and the Gokools had come for dinner. We chatted until late with them and my parents. After the guests left, my parents eventually went to bed and left us alone in the living room. We stayed there for a while and then you helped me turn off the lights in the house. Then you came into my bedroom with me. Shall I remind you of it all?"

He's replayed this, perhaps many times, I realize. And he's reciting it to me as if he has intended all along to do so. But now, yes, I do recall. I had sifted the incident, put most of it out of my mind, but I am remembering. *Just stay with me for a while. Don't worry. They're sleeping. Just lie here with me,* he'd said, patting the bed. I half-alighted on the twin bed that was pushed against the wall. He made room for me, but I propped myself sitting against the headboard, my legs on the bed, yes, but my slippered feet hung off the edge.

He's watching me, and as if he reads my mind, he says, as if he's just won a prize, "So you remember. Of course you do." The smell of him here in the car reminds me. Yes, I remember. Of course I do. I close my eyes and wish away that memory—and this moment. I wish away not just the memory, but the truth of it.

I don't answer him. It was such a long time ago. Why is he bringing this up now? I can recall in enough detail the dinner party with those two couples, driving with him along the coast, the white-and-red lighthouses—beacons themselves for land dwellers, reddish-brown cliffs, pillars of red rock filed by the relentless pounding of the wild ocean into angular shapes towering out of the sea, their tops crowned by sudden bursts of evergreens. But I'd put—what can I call it, the incident?—I'd put the specific details of the night he wants to talk about in a box and tucked it out of sight, recalling of the incident my own brief moments of courage rather than why that courage was needed. And yet here it is playing out in my mind, with him sitting beside me, as if it had happened just the other day. He was lying on his side, his head propped in his hand and his back against the wall. I do remember. The pale yellow flowers on the thin, balled flannel sheet, and his bare feet. His toes were long and finger-like, his toenails pink and shiny.

He lay like that, and I was half sitting up for some moments, an awkwardness that hadn't been between us before, silencing us. I remember he put his hand on my leg, barely touching me. When he got no protest, he let his hand down and rested it there. What came immediately to mind, then, was Fiona. Stan's hand on her thigh, just like that. I had felt like crying. I slid down and moved toward Prakash, and he lay back to allow me to stretch out and lie next to him. I put my head on his shoulder. Fiona, I was thinking, was probably with Stan right at that moment, and the thought of this made me weak. I adjusted myself and buried my face in his shoulder. I don't think he knew I was crying, or perhaps he did because he drew me closer and angled himself to hug me tight with both arms.

Yes, I do remember. Perhaps it's possible to successfully shelve the full memory of such a situation, but not to erase it. He began to kiss my hair, and after some moments he slid down so his face met mine. He held my face by my chin, and when I looked at him, he began to kiss my temple, and I remember I held my breath and he kissed my cheeks. He brought his lips to my mouth, but I turned away and pressed my face into his neck, and at once he moved back and asked me if he could remove his clothing. I remember saying, feebly, *Yeah*. He watched my face as he undressed. The tears had ceased. I remained clothed, and watched, and I remember wondering, *At what point is harm done?* Be calm, I told myself, this is what women do. This is what women at the university are doing right now. This is normal. His skin was pale, his chest flat, caved in slightly. His nipples were dark purplish brown, like Thomson raisins. A sparse bank of curled black hairs accentuated the paleness of his skin and ran from just below his neck down his breastbone. He continued watching me, but his eyes seemed glazed, and I felt he no longer saw me. He undid the button of his trousers and pulled the zipper down. He lifted his buttocks off the bed enough to slide off his pants and at once revealed his high-waisted underpants, white as if they were brand new, stretching to contain the rise of an arrow-like penis. The muscles in his thighs and lower legs were long, like a runner's, and every fibre of his pale body seemed as if it were concentrating. My only knowledge of sex had been with a woman. She had moved on. She *wanted* to move on. And here I was, with my opportunity, too, to metamorphize. This is your chance, I urged myself. Life could be simple. Family. Children. A normal life. You can love him. You will learn. I thought these things, but it was as if there were two of me. One was aware, watching, trying to work out what was happening, what to do, while the other was across the room, frozen, and neither moved because of the other. He knelt on the bed beside me and began to undress me. I let him, helping only when it had become awkward not to do so. From the distance to which my mind had gone, I watched him touch my stomach, bend, and hesitantly put his lips to my hip bone. He pulled down his underpants and, I remember, yes I do remember, I looked with fear. I was looking at the body part Fiona must have desired. I felt confused. I wanted in that moment to know what it was she felt when she lay like this with a man, with Stan, what it was she knew that I didn't. Prakash stretched out on his side beside me. His penis touched my skin and he at once lifted himself to lie on me—I watched him—again, from across the room—as he lowered himself, and the instant his penis made contact with my pelvis, he convulsed, and I felt a warm wetness on my thigh, and it was all over. He jumped out of the bed, grabbed his shirt, and went over to his desk. I could not look at him. I wiped my leg repeatedly with the top sheet, the wetness to my horror smearing along me further rather than being easily absorbed by the sheet. I was overwhelmed by the bleachlike smell and by its stickiness.

I pulled on my clothing quickly, as if someone were about to enter the room, and, taking my slippers in my hand, I opened his door and hurried to the washroom. I soaped my leg and rubbed it with the wet corner of a towel and, without brushing my teeth or washing my face, I tiptoed to the room I'd been given.

"It was a very long time ago," I say firmly. "It has nothing to do with today. And nothing really happened, did it?"

The ferry docks. He starts the engine and drives onto the road.

"There isn't much to see farther on. The ferry ride is the main event around here. We can turn back," I say.

He ignores me and drives on. "I suppose you can say, it's true, nothing really happened. Nothing and a lot, at the same time," he says. "You've always kept me close, close enough for your needs, but just out of reach for mine."

Whatever has happened to the jovial man who was just in our kitchen entertaining Alex and me, I wanted to know. Why is he now talking to me about the past—not the past, but this particular past? Is this why he has come to visit, to remind me of that time, to tell me how I had been with him? A fire rages in my mind, my face burning. I want to tell him that we both have things for which we must apologize. I want to tell him that he always came when I called. That he could have declined. Was I to blame for the choices he himself made, and continued again and again to make? He comes to a fork in the road and looks down the roads on either side. I say those are residential areas, we should go back and wait for the next ferry. He says, "No. We're taking a little drive. Relax."

I find myself looking around, wondering why no cars are coming toward us and why there were no others on the ferry with us.

"And do you remember the second time?" he asks.

I shake my head to say I don't know what he's talking about. I am ready to return home. I say to him, "Why don't we turn back? Alex will be waiting for us for dinner."

He says, "No, let's carry on. It's early still. Surely she's not expecting us back this soon."

"I think we should turn around and go back to the house, Prakash," I say firmly, but he ignores this plea. I cannot tell if my car door is locked, and if I myself have control of the lock.

"Both those times, I remember well. I no longer dwell on them. But for a long while, even after Aruna and I were married, I would think about one or the other and I would crumble. They had quite an impact on me."

Two times. Could he possibly be counting his attempt to kiss me in San Francisco? Other than that, a far cry from any real intimacy, I can't think of a second. What more does he need to get off his chest? I suppose I will hear about this supposed second time whether I want to or not. Before he arrived today, I had imagined telling him why I had cut him out of the picture when I came down here, and I wanted to explain how much I had appreciated all his attentions, and how little he'd asked for in return. I don't have the courage to tell him at this time that it was his very persistence that made me cut him out of my life, and I see now that he is in fact angry that he got little from me in the way of the physical relationship he clearly wanted. I look away from him, through my window. I turn back as if to watch the horses that are in a field, two of them with blankets over them, and I note that the door is locked. I hadn't myself locked it and realize it must be an automatic system that locks when the car is in motion. I focus on the knobby limbs of apple trees in an orchard. A stand of maple trees knee-deep in a pond of water. Banks of sumac bare of leaves, their burgundy seed tufts like fat solstice candles that have curved in the warmth of the sun.

He carries on. "I came to tell you I was going to India to get married to a woman I didn't know. You asked me if I loved her. I told you I didn't know her well enough to know that, but if I married her, I would, in time, learn to love her, but that my heart was at the moment with someone else, and I wanted to know if that someone else"—here he points to me—"would consider having me. That night we walked down Yonge Street, from Bloor all the way to the lake. You wouldn't give me an answer, but we held hands. You kept close to me, but you were quiet. I felt that you were considering, and I didn't want to push you, so I let you think. When we got back to your apartment, you went to your bed, and I went onto the fold-out bed in the living room. I was restless. I couldn't sleep. You heard me moving about and you came to me. You sat on the fold-out bed and you stroked my hair. I didn't touch you. But you took my hand and led me to your room. Do you remember?"

The car veers once more and I am startled. I instinctively reach for the steering wheel, and he looks ahead for a second and then back at me.

It's not how I remember it. I thought it was on a phone call that he told me about the upcoming marriage. I don't remember walking with him on Yonge Street. I don't remember him in my bed. But as he tells me, there is a vague sense of his account having happened, except that I am still unable to say I remember it. It is a sense, not a memory. And I don't know that I had this sense before he put the idea of it in my head.

"Do you remember how we made love?" His voice, almost a whisper, seems to crack a bit. "I'd never felt anything like that in my life. Before or since."

He brings his open palm over my knee, but he does not immediately bring it down to touch me. It hovers there, and then his fingers curl as if readying to play a piano, and then he slowly drops his hand and lets the tips of his fingers alight on my knees. Nothing more than the fingertips. They remain there for about five seconds, the rest of his hand hovering, and then he slowly withdraws it, places it back on the steering wheel. It is hot inside the car. The scent of his cologne is more powerful than it was when we left the house. And there is the smell behind it of his body.

I say—my voice, too, cracking—that this conversation is making me uncomfortable, and that he should turn the car around, that it is time to return home, but he drives on slowly up the coastal road. He says, "We slept hugging the whole night, but in the morning you were, as usual, distant. I wanted to take you out for breakfast, but you sent me on my way, saying you had an appointment, you had to go. Did you really have an appointment? Don't tell me, I think I know the answer. Do you remember where you took me the following night when I came over unannounced?"

I don't.

"You don't remember anything." On the word *anything* he hits the steering wheel with his fist. My heart seems to have stopped beating.

"You took me to a lesbian bar. We stood drinking at a table, and I was terribly uncomfortable, but I didn't say I was. You acted as if going there with me was the most ordinary thing, and I went along with it. Then a woman came and asked you to dance, and you went with her. You weren't close on the dance floor. She tried to be close to you, but you held back a little. She kept talking to you, you to her. I watched you. You never took your eyes off her. I watched the woman as she watched you, too, and as she was drawn into mimicking your moves. You were kind of cool, and it was as if I hadn't seen you before. You were so attractive. But I knew right then that I would marry Aruna. I decided I would try to be the best I could be for her."

He had accompanied me more than once to a lesbian bar. The occasion he speaks of left no impression on me.

We pass a sign marking the turnoff toward the lake for a provincial park. He stops on the highway and, as no cars are ahead or behind, he reverses. At the turnoff for the park, he turns down onto the unpaved road. I tell him the park might be closed, we should go back, go to Madame Bovary's and have hot chocolate or ice cream and talk some more. He shakes his head, says, "No, let's see where this takes us." The car bounces along and we remain quiet. I think of Alex, what she'd say if anything were to happen to us.

The park has not closed. We come to a parking lot and he pulls into a space between a van and a motorcycle. When he stops the car, he presses the button for the lock on the doors and mine pops up. I follow reluctantly when he gets out, putting on my jacket and zipping it. I am tired and it has become cold. Exhausted and dizzy, and yet I am wide awake, buzzing with apprehension. Vultures circle overhead and squirrels run up the trunks of the pines, along the branches. Through the trees the black water of the lake glistens. We walk along a short dirt path wide enough to see that the sky is fast losing its blue tinge and taking on a cool yellowish white. From the dogwood at the edge of the path, small birds rise and take off as we approach. If I were to take off, to turn around and run, would I make a fool of myself? I would have to ask for help from some stranger, to help get me home. The police might be called. Would I then get him in trouble unnecessarily? Would I end up having to explain to Alex why I felt I needed to run? What would it say about me? And where would I run to, anyway? He has the car. The keys.

I walk beside him, and the path opens onto a narrow strip of pebbled beach and the lake. Rippling waves roll in and split apart weakly onto the beach. On either side of the strip are massive slabs of grey-and-brown-pocked limestone arranged in steplike formations that invite climbing, and so we climb and hop over slim crevices, from one slab to the next, until we are a couple of metres above the beach. A flock of late-migrating Canada geese flies overhead in perfect V formation, honking and squawking one after the other. I stare out at the water that is not quite as black as it was on the ferry ride, but a deep, dark green. Farther out, it moves swiftly, flows like a river. Wisps of grey cirrus clouds move fast across the sky. In the distance there's a man and a woman and it looks as if there's a baby's carriage, or some kind of wheeled vehicle parked on the beach near them. They go to the water, bend and remain bending, and then move purposefully back toward the trees. The man is wearing red pants. They appear again, return to the water's edge, then back into the trees. Perhaps they're collecting fossils. Then they stand on the beach together. Suddenly the man runs and the woman runs behind him; they're chasing each other, it seems, running in ragged circles on the beach. I can hear them laughing.

Prakash stands next to me on the rock. He is not taking in the view. Neither am I simply taking in the view.

"I want to ask you something," he says. "It's been on my mind all these years. I want you to answer me truthfully."

I shrug.

"After we returned from Salt Island, I didn't see you for a while. Then one day I came to your apartment. There'd been a blizzard the day before. I came to check on you. But you weren't in the apartment during the blizzard. I waited in the foyer for you to return from wherever you'd gone. Then a car rolled in to the parking lot. At first I couldn't see the occupants, but then I realized you were in that car. And the driver was that man, Stan, whom Fiona had been seeing. It seemed to me that he was hugging you. I pulled the hood of my jacket over my head, and dashed across the road to the foyer of the apartment building opposite and watched. He didn't get out of the car, but when you did, you had an overnight bag with you."

He stops there, and I try to firm myself on the rock, but I feel myself sway in the slight wind.

Then he says, "What was that about? Why were you with him? That seemed strange. Had you spent the night with him?"

What right has he to ask these questions? The air has seeped out of my lungs, and I don't have the strength to challenge him.

I want to see where we are. I want to know where I am. I want to be my own witness.

The man and woman are still in view. They're sitting now, lying down more likely, only their heads visible behind a log. There is a wind here, a cold wind. I pull up the zipper of my jacket. I will stand tall and wait where I am. I'll look at everything. I'll be able to name everything I see. Every detail. There are rust-coloured lines in these rocks. Pockmarks, some of them full of water. There is moss, lime-green moss on the rocks near the edge of the water. The pebbles on the shore can fit like misshapen oranges in one's hand. But I need a defining landmark. There, on the far shore, on the other side of this body of water, directly across from where I stand, among the pines I see an H-type hydro pole.

"Don't be ridiculous," I say so softly he asks me to repeat myself. I tell him I'd gone to the gym with Stan that morning and what he saw was Stan giving me a lift back home. Fiona had dumped him, I say, and add that I don't know why Stan came to me, but he did. The words, once I begin, come fast. Stan knew

Fiona and I were no longer together, I say. We went to the gym and for coffee a few times. But we didn't remain friends.

"Why was he hugging you? Or you him?" he asks flatly, like an interrogator.

"I don't remember that. You must have been mistaken. Why is this important, anyway? If he was dropping me off, it might just have been a friendly goodbye hug or something. I don't know. Whatever it was, it didn't make as much of an impression on me as it did on you."

He does not respond. We stand there in silence. He turns and begins to walk away, calling to me that he needs to clear his head. I try to breathe deeply, but my lungs seem to have shrunk. I think to walk toward the couple, but to get to them from the rock I must be prepared either to get my feet wet or go back onto the path on which we came, back toward the parking lot, and find another opening through the trees on the other side of the rock on which I am standing.

The beach curves in and out and, as Prakash walks on it, hopping up on slabs of sandstone and down again onto the beach, he disappears and reappears. I remain standing so I can see all around me. So much has happened that I am confused.

A broken heart can make a person go mad. Do uncharacteristic things.

I had gone mad. And, back then, I did uncharacteristic things. Yes, one could say I had gone mad. How angry has he been? How mad is he now?

There he is, stooping, looking, no doubt, at the shale and rock. In these parts you find fossils in almost every bit of rock. He is more like a Jain than he is Hindu. He would not hurt an ant in his path. He has never before shown anger. I think he has a right to be angry with me, but this thought confuses me. I was confused then, and I am now, too. I hadn't made him stay at my side—he stayed because he wanted to, isn't that right?

He'd phoned one night late. Stan, that is. I was awakened from sleep by a telephone call from a man asking for Fiona. She was no longer sleeping in the apartment, although most of her belongings were still there. I told the man she wasn't there and I had no idea when I'd see her. It was best, therefore, not to bother to leave a message for her with me. The following day another call came, the same voice asking for her. And then later that evening, again. I heard distress in his voice. It could only have been Stan, and I was shaken—for if this was indeed Stan trying to find her, she was, then, clearly not with him. She was, I immediately understood, with someone else. So yes, Stan had been dumped, too.

The man shouted on the phone, "She's there, isn't she? Why won't you let me speak to her?" I told him wearily that I didn't care if he spoke to her or not, but that she wasn't there, and I hung up the phone.

When she finally turned up, I told her, as if indeed I didn't care, a man had been calling for her. She said, yes, she'd been expecting him to call—he was a musician who needed a pianist to accompany him for his recital, and he'd been trying to get her to work with him. *Bullshit,* I thought, but I didn't challenge her. She'd take care of it, she said.

The calling stopped. Then, some days later, there was a knock on the door. I opened it and a handsome black man, dressed in a smart dark blue suit and a beautiful white shirt opened at the neck, was at the door. I thought he was a Jehovah's Witness, but he was alone. Perhaps he was selling something, I thought, and I was ready to shut the door. But when his disappointment upon seeing me registered, I realized this was Stan. He tersely asked if Fiona was there. I told him she wasn't but that he could come in and wait for her. I knew she wouldn't come home that day, but I wanted to see who this man was. He refused my invitation. I said to him, "If she cheated on me, didn't you think she might one day cheat on you, too?" He came in.

He slumped in the corner of our armchair—a chair I knew he must have sat in before—his body twisted to hug the arm, his head on his forearm. He hit the arm of the chair again and again, unabashedly. He must have muttered, out of clenched teeth, "Fuck," a dozen times. I felt embarrassed for him. And pity. But it was as if I were invisible to him. Of no consequence. Had I been a beautiful woman, a straight woman, he would not, I was willing to bet, have so shamelessly emoted. Time passed and he began to groan that he loved her more than he'd ever loved anyone. I was tempted to mutter loud enough that *she'd* told *me* she loved me more than she'd ever loved anyone, but it seemed petty, childish. He wailed and I watched. We "waited" for what seemed like hours like that, hardly a word spoken between us.

And so there we were, accompanying each other into the night.

Then, in the middle of the night—he'd long become quiet and had curled up on the sofa—he bolted up, straightened himself, and looked directly at me sitting awake in the chair opposite, watching him. He said, "She needs to be taught a lesson. She can't do this to people. Why can't she at least say where she's spending her nights so we don't worry about her? Why is it that she gets to have so much fun, and people like you and I, who really love and care, sit and wait and get hurt? Why can't we have fun, too? Why don't we go out and enjoy ourselves?"

I heard myself respond, "Let's. Let's go out. Let's go to a restaurant. Or go and have a drink. But I don't think anything's open at this time of night."

He stood up, saying it was exactly what we should do. He dangled his keys. I started pulling on shoes and my jacket, and he stopped me and said, "I have an idea. Just a minute." Without looking for it, he walked directly to the phone, and I noted his familiarity with where it was. He dialled, and there seemed to be no answer. He said, "Have you ever been to Bracebridge?" I had no idea where that was. He had an ex-girlfriend whose family owned a cottage up there, he said. He used to go there with them. The cottage wasn't winterized, so no one would be there. We should go.

It was a crazy idea. I didn't know him. I didn't know where this place was. It was not his place. He was crazed by rejection. He didn't really know if I was currently a threat to his relationship with Fiona.

"Surely," I said, "you have to ask if you can use the cottage. Wouldn't she or they mind? You have to get the key from her." I imagined this would be a plan then for another day, by which time he would have calmed down, and I wouldn't be involved in his drama.

He said she wouldn't care. He knew where the key was hidden.

What if something happened to us, and we got killed on the road, or he killed me, or we were caught and arrested and thrown in jail for breaking and entering? I remember I thought about Prakash. What would he have thought, I had wondered, but in the moment I didn't care. There was a kind of freedom necessary in that moment in going far away with someone who wanted nothing from me. But then I thought about my parents. They knew Fiona was my roommate, not my lover, and that in itself was another enormous pain. I didn't care if I died or ended up imprisoned. I felt I was going mad.

I turn and look behind me, stare into the trees and up and down the beach, but I don't see Prakash. I move to a higher part of the rock so that I can see farther. He still isn't in view. On the other side, the two people are still visible. I hope they don't leave.

An hour north of the city, it had begun to snow hard and fast, and I learned first-hand that night what a blizzard was and what a whiteout was. Stan drove slowly. The road signs we passed were whited out in blown snow. I couldn't tell at any point where we were. We hardly spoke. My heart was breaking, and in the dark, in the constant torrent of snow rushing at us in the headlights, in the wordlessness between him and me, I wanted to let myself go mad and bawl, but when I realized Stan was stifling his own crying, I stiffened. I listened to his occasional sobs, and when suddenly he slammed his open palm violently against the steering wheel, my breath caught. I put my hand on his shoulder and gave a squeeze of understanding. He took his hand off the wheel, grabbed my hand, and flung it off, shouting at me, "Don't touch me." It didn't frighten me. I understood.

The man and woman on the beach are up and running again, chasing each other in circles. One of them catches up to the other, hits that one with what looks like a fluorescent green foam noodle, and then the one who's been hit turns and grabs the noodle and chases the other. Their screams and laughter are brought to me on breezes pushed along the shoreline. Prakash is nowhere to be seen. I lower myself and sit, and the cold of the rock quickly penetrates my jeans. I stare in the direction of the bend. The light is changing fast. A hint of pink creeps into the sky at the horizon, already reflected on the crests of the billowing water. I keep my eyes open for Prakash and recall that long unpaved road off the main road to Stan's friend's cottage. It had not been plowed. On the drive in, the wheels of the car caught again and again in the high snow and spun, the car lowering into it fast, and several times Stan had to try to reverse, and in frustration he'd accelerate hard and send us further into the ground. He got out of the car and pushed while I sat in the driver's seat and he shouted frantically, *"Go. Go. Go, damn it."* I prayed that on acceleration I wouldn't send the car flying, spinning, skidding into the gulley or into trees. I had never been in those conditions, that kind of snow. Eventually the car would go no further. We had to get out and walk. I had never before experienced anything like this; my ankle-high winter boots could not keep the snow out, and my feet became wet and numbed fast, and the wool scarf I had wrapped to cover my face grew horribly wet and icy around my nose and mouth. Wet wooly hairs entered my mouth and I felt as if I'd choke. I was sure I'd stumble and freeze where I fell and wouldn't be found until the spring, when the snow thawed. As my heart sank further at the thought of my parents' disappointment in me, the cottage came into sight. Stan left me at the back door, while he went to fetch a spare key that was kept in a shed on the property. In the dark, I hugged and rocked myself, my teeth chattering uncontrollably. I fully expected some dangerous animal or person to appear out of nowhere. I stomped my feet and wiggled my toes to keep the blood flowing. Stan returned, not soon enough, with a key, let me inside, and left again to look for wood to make a fire. The house was freezing, but thankfully dry. I sat on one of the several couches and blew into my hands to warm them every few seconds while I removed my boots and the wet socks. My feet were a frightful pink. I wanted to cry. Stan returned, cradling a few logs in his arms. He muttered that was all the dry wood in the shed. He lit a fire, and he too removed his shoes and socks and placed them, with mine, before the fire. He rummaged through a large wicker basket and drew out oversized knitted socks, and we pulled them on. It took almost an hour for the area in front of the fire to warm up, and about that length of time for my feet to begin to thaw. I can still recall the sense that they were on fire and, at the same time, were being pricked by thousands of needles. I hobbled through the five small bedrooms, trying to figure out where I might spend the night, and was disheartened to find that the heat of the fire had not reached them in the least. Stan grumbled that he hadn't properly thought through driving up to the cottage; in the past, when he'd come with his girlfriend in the winter, they'd bring heaters and duvets and big sweaters. I slumped on a bed, cold and shivering and near tears. He came into the room with several blankets, which he piled on the bed for me, and he went to another room. After a while I heard him piling more logs on the fire. Where he found them, I have no idea.

The fire went out in the middle of the night, and I clasped my hands between my knees, rubbing my feet hard on the bottom sheet, hoping that friction would warm them, and tucked my head under the covers. At one point I heard him shifting about and I called out softly to ask if the fire had gone out. He answered that it had, and to start it again he'd have to dress to go out to the shed and dig around for more dry wood, and he didn't want to do that. He said the best thing for us to do was to make a bed on the floor in front of the embers and lie together, with as many blankets on top of us as possible. I said I couldn't do that. He said, "Suit yourself," and I remained in the frigid room, listening as he dragged a mattress out and fixed a bed for himself. After about half an hour or more, I got under the covers with him. It was warm under there. We kept our distance, our backs to one another. I slid further down, pulling the blankets over my head. It eventually got too hot, and I had to come back up. In no time, I was cold again. He spoke. "Are you awake? Are you cold?" His voice had softened.

"It's cold," I mumbled, my teeth chattering.

"When the fire is going, this place is like a furnace. But yeah, it's cold. I love this cottage." He was whispering as if there were others in the cottage whom he didn't want to awaken.

I didn't respond. He didn't seem to be the same angry, hurt person I'd travelled there with.

He continued, "Susie and I were together since we were in high school. When I got my licence, we would come up here almost every weekend."

"On your own?" I asked.

"Yeah, her parents were liberal hippie types. They treated me like I was their son. Well, son-in-law, I guess. But we were kids, really."

I asked what happened to her, to them. They outgrew each other. They were still friends, but he was no longer as close to the family as he had once been. He asked if I'd ever been to a cottage in Ontario before. He told me that when it snowed like this, outside looked in daytime like a black-and-white photograph.

We were talking. The hostility between us had evaporated. We talked for a long while. I told him about my family back home. I realized he must have grown up in Canada because he had a Canadian accent. But I thought his family was from one of the Caribbean islands. I learned that they were from Nova Scotia. That they'd been there since the eighteenth century, freemen who'd come up from the American colonies. Neither of us mentioned Fiona. The room was getting colder. My feet were painfully cold. I told him I wished I had heavier socks. He turned and lay on his back. I too lay on my back. He placed his foot over mine. He rubbed it back and forth. After some moments he stopped, but left his foot touching mine. We lay like that in silence. I whispered thanks, and he moved a little nearer, one of my hands next to one of his. He locked fingers and said, "Why were we fighting? We're both hurting. Let's not hurt one another." I began to sob, and he turned and held me. I wept, and he kept saying, *Shhh, shhh,* and then he lay on top of me to try to hold me still. I held on to him. I'd never lain with a man like that and it felt good. I felt safe with him. It wasn't until the light broke outside and showed us that it had stopped snowing, and our eyes were heavy and sore with crying and with tiredness, that we both fell asleep, almost together. We awoke clinging to one another. I didn't want to part from him. Was it because he, unlike Prakash, didn't seem to want anything from me? Or was it because lying with Fiona's lover was a way of lying with her? It was as if, having both been spurned by her, we had become a kind of unit. Eventually he dressed and left the cottage. I curled into the warmth he'd left and fell asleep again, awakening only when he returned carrying a box of wood that he said he'd found in a neighbour's covered pile. I sat on the mattress on the floor, the blankets wrapped around me, and watched as he poked and prodded at a slow-forming fire. In time, the room became warm enough to remove the blankets from around me. He filled a bucket with snow and put it on the fire and found tea-bags and cups in the kitchen. We washed our faces and had tea. He took me down to the dock, and it was as if we were walking on a cloud of soft whiteness. We walked through the woods in the deep snow, holding hands in the black-and-white landscape. The only sound was the powdery slip and slide of snow beneath our feet. Could I ever admit to anyone this strange adventure, I wondered. At one point Stan held me back and said, "Stop. Listen."

"I don't hear anything," I whispered, looking questioningly at him.

"Exactly," he said, a smile broad on his face. "Not even the hum of a car in the distance," he added. He was a good-looking man.

Later that day, he dropped me off at my apartment. In the car we'd hugged. A long tender hug. It was easy being held by him. I'd felt something for him.

It was Fiona. That's what I felt for him. Fiona. And yes, it was Stan I'd wanted—not Prakash.

In the car, sitting there, he said he didn't want to see Fiona again. He said he'd like to see more of me. Was I interested in getting together with him again?

If we were to spend one more day together, we would, I knew, pass that day in bed. And this time we'd do so without a stitch of clothing on. That was, of course, what he was suggesting. Sitting next to him, I could feel it. I wanted to reach over and put my hand on his face, but if I did, he would have felt my desire. I kept still and allowed myself to feel my body opening up for him. I debated asking him to come up to my apartment. I saw myself tearing my jeans off and pulling him into me, him fucking me and me fucking him at once. I felt dizzy. But I knew it was not love I was feeling. It was a hurting and an aching. I thought of Prakash, of half-sitting, half-lying next to him in his childhood bed in New Brunswick, and although that had occurred only weeks before, I felt as if I'd grown up, as if I understood myself better. My mind returned to the past night spent in the cottage, and I saw that what I really wanted was Stan's full weight pressing down on me, our individual and separate grief meeting in sympathetic resonance at the seam between us.

How long could any kind of closeness between this gentle man and me, then, have lasted? Weeks? A day? Until he and I had had sex, and both of us relieved by orgasms of hurt, would one immediately want the other to disappear without a word? Until Fiona's rejection no longer had such a hold on him that he would ask a lesbian out? Until a woman walked by and looked me directly in my eyes? And because I had had the mind to understand the genesis of his question—was I interested in getting together with him again?—I knew I wouldn't see him again.

That was three and a half decades ago, but I can still recall that day outside of my apartment, in his car. The snow had been cleared from the parking lot and pushed to the side. What I remember is the mountains of whiteness, a wall that had been erected daily. And I remember standing inside the lobby of my apartment, the door open so that I could wave, and watching as his car slowly pulled out over the crunching snow, the tail light blinking as he waited to turn out of the driveway. As I watched, a sadness washed over me, followed in an instant by a lightness that travelled over my body. Fiona's hold on me, I felt, had loosened.

I certainly had not seen Prakash, and don't remember seeing anyone else that day, actually.

There is suddenly a rustling behind me, and the scent of his cologne on the wind, and then there is Prakash climbing onto the rock on which I sit. I stand quickly. He must have returned along the road, or on a path through the trees. His face is red, his nose running, no doubt from the wind, which is strong here by the water, and the chill that it brings. He swipes a gloved hand at it repeatedly. He looks younger, more like the man I used to know years ago. But he's not smiling, he won't look at me. He walks to the edge of the rock and lowers himself. He sits with his legs hanging down, facing the water that laps at the base of the rock. He sits and I remain standing. After ten minutes, or perhaps it is half an hour, or maybe it is five minutes, I lower myself and sit a little way behind him. For several minutes we sit like this, him in front, I well back. Eventually he turns his head toward me, but he still won't look at me, and he pats the rock at his side. To not move forward to sit next to him seems like an accusation. Unsure of myself, I nevertheless slide my bum down toward the waiting spot, and I, too, hang my feet over the rock.

Behind our quiet, carried on the wind, is the occasional sound of the two people up the beach talking. Their words are not distinguishable, but the man's voice is deep and pleasant. Hers is not heard as much, except when she laughs loudly.

"Prakash," I say, and stop. I must choose my words carefully. I must choose the order in which I tell him what I think needs to be said, what, perhaps, he needs to hear. He does not encourage me with even a grunt. I am on my own.

But where do I begin? It is a long friendship, more than half of our lives so far, but there can only be a few words with which to explain myself. I want to say, *I am lesbian, Prakash,* and hope that that explains everything. But I know it doesn't. He will then say, *But then why...?*

I could tell him we'd both have been miserable. And again he'd say, *But then why...?*

I could tell him I did love him, and I did think and wonder and imagine, and I tried. And what would he do if I said this to him? If he were then to push me off this rock, he'd almost have a right.

"Prakash," I say again. And I stumble through as I tell him: "I've never had a better friend than you. I already knew when I met you that I would not be with a man." I correct myself and say, "*I would not be happy with a man.* And that a man therefore wouldn't be happy with me." And I continue, "But in those days, a life with another woman was not easy. We could not be out and open with each other in the world. And by the time it became easier in public, it was ingrained in me—and I see it still in my generation of queer people—that we needed to be careful and to be fearful. These were not conditions conducive to healthy, happy relationships, even between women who loved one another deeply.

"In all my years in this country, you were my stability and my constant. You were always there for me. I never had to beg you to be there. You showed up in an instant. You paid for my meals when I had no money. You paid my rent. I never asked you, but you listened and you saw and you didn't hesitate to help, and you didn't then ask for repayment. You seemed to give freely and willingly.

"You knew. You knew about me. You could have walked, but you didn't. And when I saw you staying, and staying, and staying, I had to ask myself if I was mad not to try to be with you. You were good. You were kind to me. You were loving. You never forced yourself on me, not really. In many ways, I fell in love with you. I made myself imagine what a life with you could be. Sometimes I'd dream we were together, you and me, and I suppose my dreaming—even after you were married—was a trace of those times you spoke earlier about. When I was at your house, your parents' house, in your bed with you, I was conflicted. I watched you on the bed and I said to myself, *This is your chance. He comes with family. His parents will be my family. He and I can have children. We'll have celebrations with his parents and with mine, and they'll love us because we've given them grandchildren, and he and I will be loved by our children.* I wanted all of that so very much. The whole circle of family.

"But as I came to know myself, I realized I would never have been happy with you, no matter how much I might have loved you in other ways. And yes, you in the end would not have been happy with me. It would have been wrong. I felt shame for not knowing that sooner and I think I made myself forget those times with you."

As I try to explain and excuse myself, I think of the dream I awoke to this morning. Mere hours ago, in the bed I share with my lover, this treacherous body on fire and rocked with passion. Not five minutes passes after I've awakened to those kinds of dreams about him, and whatever desire so controlled me dissipates like a drop of water on the surface of a hot skillet. I am here with him on this rock, trying to apologize, and I feel an old and familiar tenderness, I want to take care of him in this moment, but there is not an iota of physical attraction to him. Why the dream? Will it ever stop?

"When I met Alex," I say, "I dared not carry on this conflicted affair with you. It *was* an affair. Even after you were married, we carried on like this, but I couldn't maintain it once I decided to be with her. I knew she was my best bet at happiness. I didn't want to ruin whatever chance of love and companionship I had with her. I had to end it with you, to move away from your grip. It would have been unfaithful to her just being friends with you. You see, I loved you. I've always loved you. But not the way you've wanted—even after you were married. I still love you, Prakash, but…"

There are no more words with which to end that thought. I want to say *I love you* to him a thousand more times, but what I mean really is that I am sorry. *I am sorry that I pulled you and then pushed you, you my dear friend, again and again. I'm sorry that I let go of you only after I saw I could stand on my own without you. I don't want to stop explaining, apologizing, but short of repeating myself, there is nothing more to say. Except that we should go now, it's getting very late.* I am about to say this when, with a short but violent gesture he throws his arms around me and holds me tightly. It's not what I want, but I can't now push him away. I won't respond, I mustn't encourage anything at all, but I mustn't push him away. He presses his face into my neck, his cologne stronger than it was before, suffocating. Hot. So tight is this grip. A forceful pulling. I feel myself being shifted from where I sit. Is he trying to pull me closer to him? But I'm too close to the edge of the rock, his grip hurts, I want to tell him he's hurting me but I'm not sure what's in his mind, I make myself rigid, I must push him back, I should, but if he needs me to hold him, I'm not sure. But no, no. Yes, this is *pushing*. He's shoving me. I hear him groan with the force of his attempt, and I say sharply, "Stop, you're hurting me," but I don't know if he can hear or understand what I'm saying because my voice is dark and thick and even I can't hear my words. My fists are like rocks and

I'm trying to pound his shoulders but can't get enough leverage, I'm pounding and I can't form words, I'm growling—

Suddenly there's the man's voice from on the beach, closer, shouting. I try to see, but Prakash still holds me. He is rocking me hard, side to side. Perhaps he is just rocking me, or rocking himself while he holds me. This is so very confusing. The man's shouting is closer. And I am also shouting, but my voice doesn't sound like mine. *Prakash, let me go. Let go.* I shove him hard, and as if stunned he lets go and I almost lose my balance. He pulls his knees up onto the rock and hugs them, buries his head in his lap. I shimmy away from the edge and jump up. I step well away, trembling, and face the man on the beach at the ready, but I'm not sure what for, and Prakash remains rocking in place and the other man is still yelling, two unhinged men, and the woman is far back, standing straight up like an arrow and watching, and the man is yelling and pointing beneath the place we've been sitting, and I am hugging myself and trembling. I think I am crying.

A raccoon, I think he is saying. A raccoon. And I think so what—it's their land, it's a beach, so what? It'll move away. Why should we? He's frantic. He's stopped approaching, but he's still waving his hand, attempting, it seems, to shoo us off the rock.

Then I understand. He's yelling that just below the rock on which we sit is a sick raccoon, possibly rabid, unpredictable, he shouts, and we shouldn't stay there. I step well away from Prakash and then closer to the edge, and peering over I see the thing inches from the water, curled and shivering. It looks harmless.

I relay what the man is saying and repeat that we have to leave right away, but Prakash is curled into himself. I reach down and thump him on his back: *Get up, let's go*. He remains where he is. I grab his shoulders hard and shake him. "Get up, we have to go!" I shout. There is no kindness in my touch or in my voice. He uncurls himself slowly and gets up. I grab his hand and pull him down the rocks, back to the path. I have to push him. I pull and then push. I grab his hand, like an ayah, like an older sister, and I try to run, but he won't come. I am pulling this man whose hatred of me is palpable. Or *is* this hatred, and if it is, is it of me? Surely it is of his actions, just as well. I need him to get me out of here and back to my home, back to Alex. Ours is now the only car in the lot. The man and woman on the beach must have parked farther up in another lot. Will sound carry from here to the beach, I wonder.

We sit inside the car for some minutes before he slowly straps himself in and starts the engine. I do not buckle my seat belt and the alarm dings incessantly. He drives well below the speed limit on the road back to the ferry. The sky has turned a pale persimmon, in some places a florid orange hue, erratically striped with clouds the colours of diesel exhaust and dirty slate. Alex is probably wondering why we haven't yet returned. Ours is the only car on the ferry again. As he drives on, rolling toward the front of the boat, I'm not confident he'll stop when he reaches the barrier. I imagine him suddenly accelerating and bursting through it. I brace myself, ready to open my door in an instant. He stops the car where the ferry man tells him to and turns off the engine. His hands are clasped on his lap and he stares down at his fingers.

To stop myself from muttering, *I'm sorry,* to stop myself from pointing out that he hasn't himself said he, too, is sorry, I engage in a mental exercise of mixing colours on an imaginary palette to emulate those in the bruised-looking yet weirdly beautiful sky, and I try to send telepathic messages to Alex that we're on our way back home. Alex and I travel well together. This mild winter weather won't last long. It'll be cold soon. I will tell her tonight that we should book a flight to Mexico, or to Costa Rica. We've dreamed of going to Costa Rica. We've always been disdainful of package holidays, but we should try one. Lie by the pool. On the beach. Snorkel together. Footballer fish. Clownfish. Brain coral. Go in search of quetzals and sloths. Sleep holding each other under mosquito nets on hot nights. Her skin is like silk. It's been a while. I can't tell her what this trip with Prakash has been like. She'll wonder why we didn't go to Madame Bovary's. I'll tell her we went, got coffees, or tea, or something, and then took a little drive, a tour. I just want to melt into her skin, become one with her.

I'd spoil everything if I told her what has just transpired. But perhaps nothing in truth happened. I must have mistaken his intentions out there on the rock. Perhaps Prakash loves me as he always has, and I've confused his sadness, his disappointment, for a violent impulse. Surely I was foolishly terrified. He was simply acting out of disappointment. No crime was committed. There was no actual violence. There are no scratches on my body. Was any harm really done?

Nothing happened and he's taking me home, back to Alex.

She'll be waiting, wondering where on earth we are.

Neither of us speaks on the twenty-minute drive back to the house.

In the village the street lamps have come on. The sky is black, an orange glow at the edges. A few stars are out. Winking.

Alex has, in her typical thoughtful way, turned on the porch light for us. Prakash stops his car behind mine—such a

274

necessary and meaningless positioning nevertheless makes me realize that I feel as if I'm suffocating.

The door is locked. I knock and at the same time pat my pockets to locate my set of keys and, successful, I unlock it. Inside I call to her. Prakash immediately goes up, in his jacket and boots, to the guest room, and I head to the back of the house to find Alex. I notice and am pleased that the dreadful smell of something dead seems to have subsided. But Alex is not in the sunroom, as I'd thought she'd be. I return to the front of the house and call up to her office. There's no answer. Where could she have gone? Everything's closed in the village. Perhaps she's down by the water. The dish of tomato sauce sits on the kitchen counter covered in plastic wrap. We will eat soon. She'll know something went wrong.

I notice that next to the dish is an envelope. My name in her writing. Inside:

Hi Priya, I've hit my stride with my writing and don't want to stop. Skye offered to let me stay the night at their place. I can write there with quiet. Enjoy yourselves. You just have to boil the pasta and make a salad.

Alex

No *Love*. Just *Alex*.

I am alone in the house with Prakash. This is not good. I hear him thumping down the stairs and I shove the note quickly back into the envelope, fold it into two, and put it in my pocket. But nothing happened. Nothing happened. I mustn't let this terror erupt. He was annoyed. Anyone would have been. But now he's going back up. I must call Alex. I don't want to be here alone with him. I'll let her know we're back, suggest she return, promise her we'll be quiet—we're both tired, and I imagine we'll go to bed early. She must return and work here. I will first see if I can get him a cup of tea or something, and I'll retreat to the bedroom, I'll lock the bedroom door and phone her from there.

At the stairs up to the guest room I call to him, and notice that he has brought his overnight bag down and parked it by the front door. He comes down the stairs again, his jacket and boots still on, and a slim square package wrapped in brown paper in his hand. He says he's decided to leave. I tell him to eat before he goes. He says no, he's not hungry. I tell him I'll make him a cheese sandwich for the car, it'll take only a couple minutes. He says, firmly and dispassionately, no thank you. He—this version of him—is unrecognizable. I move toward him and he steps back. He hands the package to me.

"This is yours. You can have it back."

I don't remember what I might have given him that he'd need to return. I pull back one edge of the taped paper and see that between two heavy sheets of cardboard is the painting he'd so very long ago exchanged for payment of my living expenses. My very first sale.

"But it's yours. You paid for it," I say, holding back my tears. He does not respond, and I'm trembling.

He picks up his bag and I move toward him again, my free hand about to touch his shoulder. He holds that hand firmly with one of his. He says, "Don't. Let me go. Just let me go. I'm leaving for Uganda in a few days. I won't contact you again." He opens the door and steps out, his back to me. I say his name. He does not even hesitate. He closes the door. I stand there for a few seconds, imagining he will surely come back. When he doesn't, I step over to the window and watch through the blinds as he gets into his car. He waits at the top of the driveway. Then he pulls out onto the road. He doesn't look back at the house. His car slowly disappears from the window's view.

I unwrap the painting. The greens of the bottles, mixtures of thalo and ultramarine blues and cadmium yellow, are heavy, coarse-looking, and the white of the light that lends them form has turned oily-looking and yellow. It is not a work to be proud of, but a feeling of sadness and tenderness comes over me. I realize it is not for the work itself, but for the young person who painted it, the one who, along the way to the present, has fumbled and stumbled, making so many mistakes. It's over. I clutch the painting to my chest. He'd brought it with him. He knew all along, then, that he'd give the painting back to me. He intended it to end this way.

It's over. It's finally over.

I feel dizzy with regret.

There's a certainty about it this time; I won't hear from him again.

I am about to dial Alex's cellphone number to tell her to come back, that he's gone, she can work here without being disturbed. But I'll have to go and pick her up, so I think, why not just get in the car and go, surprise her. She should be pleased he's gone.

It's dark as I drive into Macaulay. I've just had a dreadful experience with my oldest friend, and an unexpected parting of ways, and yet I have to say I feel as if I've won something. Light. I feel light. How is that possible?

A wave of renewed desire—a fired-up sense of commitment that I will make this relationship with Alex work—washes over me. I will not be distracted from her from now on.

God, I mustn't speed, but I simply can't get there fast enough. I want to begin anew with her, immediately. A real future with her. The road seems to lengthen before me.

The front porch lights at Skye's house are not on, but there are lights on inside. Her car is pulled far up into their drive toward their garage that is used as a storage room—with no space for a bicycle, let alone a car. There is room behind her car.

I am about to turn in, but I catch myself; I suddenly feel as if I'm doing something wrong by coming here. I can't think. What's happening? Suddenly I can't sort things out.

Perhaps I should go back home and phone them from there. It isn't good to drop in on people unannounced. People here do, but I'm not really from here.

I drive slowly past the house and two doors down I stop. I decide to park on the street. I'm no longer in the city. People call in on one another unexpectedly all the time down here. I'll have to explain why Prakash left so suddenly. They're probably having dinner. I can eat with them. I feel elated, but I also feel I'm on shaky ground here. My heart is beating too fast. I feel as if I can't control my legs. They're awfully weak. God, I can hardly breathe. What's happening?

Skye and Liz hardly ever use their front door. I go to the back of the house, toward the porch and the back door. I must move confidently. Not like a thief in the night. Confidently. Smile. Hold yourself up, Priya. Yes, smile. Relax your face, but smile.

It's dark back there, too. I am about to alight the stairs to the porch, but something holds me back. I stay at their foot, and for a moment I can't decide if I should continue up or turn and go back home. I am not thinking clearly. Okay. Let's see. Perhaps she'll think I'm weak, if I come running, looking for her the instant I'm alone. Perhaps they want an evening to themselves.

Yes, but that's the thing. Why would that be so? I'm being left out. That's the problem with the Valley Priest, the Catholic, and his donation or whatever it's called. Skye always knows more about Alex's work than I.

Those weekends. The cottage. Skye, does she go to the cottage? When Alex is there, I mean. Does she? When do they discuss her work? Has Skye read her papers? Skye can't have attended any of Alex's lectures in the city, can she? Or overseas? I can't breathe. I should go back home.

I mount the stairs, tiptoe onto the porch, and stop before I reach the sliding glass door. I can hear music. I should not have come here. The light is on inside the kitchen; I will not be seen if I look in, but is this right, should I be doing this? I hold the frame of the door and lean my head toward the glass. No one is in the kitchen. The house seems empty. Knock, get on with it, but no; there's movement, in the hallway toward the living room. Skye, her back to me. I don't see Alex.

God, what if Alex isn't actually here, and Skye sees me like this? Christ, I need to get a hold of myself. Tiptoe back down and leave.

Okay, so after what happened in the park with Prakash, I'm jittery. Naturally. Just knock. Go on.

And suddenly I realize that Skye's tall body blocks someone from view. I see feet, part of her jeans. There, standing in front of Skye. Hands reaching around Skye's neck.

Blood rushes to my ears, and the pounding in my head is unbearable. I can't hear anything, and I'm dizzy. Faint. But I mustn't make a sound. *Breathe. Calm yourself. Breathe.*

I am, oddly, somewhat aroused, but it's not sexual. It's fear. There's anger, or a terrible hurt, I don't know. I don't know what to do.

I should just bang on the glass and put a stop to all of this. But perhaps I'm wrong. What if I'm wrong? They'll think I've gone mad. We all comfort one another at times. They'll laugh at me. I'll have to live with that all my life. There's nothing wrong with friends comforting one another. *Calm down, Priya. And announce yourself.*

Just as the pounding in my head begins to subside and I am about to bang on the door, their bodies have shifted and I can see. And I see, I see. It is Alex. And. Kissing. Alex. Skye. Kissing. My Alex. Not like friends. They are kissing.

They are kissing.

I want to throw up. I hold my stomach and tiptoe down the stairs fast and run and stumble and run in the shadows of the foundation cypresses, past the house and to my car. It's terribly cold. So nauseated. Prakash. I want to call him. Prakash. Wait, Prakash. Immediately, before he gets too far away.

I can't, can I? I can't call him anymore. I'm on my own. Alone.

I sit in the car, unable to figure out the steps, the logic of driving. As if I've never driven a car before. An hour, or is it a minute— maybe more, maybe less—passes. I don't want to go back to our house. But I don't know where to go. My hands won't stop shaking, my teeth chattering now.

Oh my God, I forgot to fill the birdfeeders. That's it, isn't it? This one act of neglect. It's the reason, it's why this. An empty birdfeeder—a sign of neglect.

I need to get home right away, I need to go out and fill the birdfeeders. In the dark. Don't waste time. All six feeders, suet and seeds. That's it. That's what I need to do. And then I'll call Alex and tell her I refilled them and that I'll always keep them filled. I can't believe I didn't take care of them earlier today. We'll get a birdbath for the backyard. A heated birdbath, I'll tell her. We can go to the wild-bird store in Brighton tomorrow morning. They're open on Sundays. Yes, that's what we'll do. It'll be a nice outing. Or wherever she wants to go. Whatever she wants to do. I promise. I really do. Whatever you want, Alex.

Alex, my love. Please.

. . .

ACKNOWLEDGEMENTS

Every day I am reminded of how fortunate I am to be able to live here, within the traditional territories of the Haudenosaunee Confederacy. I am thankful, also, to the land itself—that is, to the flora in its amazing variety, all the land, water and air animals, the rivers above ground and running underground, the big lake and all the smaller ones.

And to all the farmers who feed us in this area.

I am grateful to have around me a number of people who sustain me as I insist on this writing life, and on making art. In particular, as regards the writing of this novel, I'd like to express appreciation to Jane Howard, Shelagh Hurley, Pam Joliffe, and Deborah Root for friendship, for ongoing writing conversations, and for so generously urging me forward.

Thank you to Nandish Yajnik for his enduring support of my work, and for sharing with me stories of exile.

Thank you to Sue Hierlihy for astute editorial work on early drafts—a process that helped me "see" the shape of the novel as I worked, and to Kathryn Kuitenbrouwer for reading and offering valuable feedback.

I would like to acknowledge the Canada Council for the Arts for supporting the writing of this novel.

Thank you to David and Barbara, for so often renting me a table in the backroom of Lily's Café for the price of a coffee and an excellent salad bowl.

I want to thank Samantha Haywood of Transatlantic Agency; my publishers Jay MillAr and Hazel Millar of Book*hug Press for their unwavering support of this book; copy editor Stuart Ross; my editor Meg Storey, whose philosophical, logical and lyrical mind made for a project larger than the book—which, in the end, is what is truly meaningful; and a special thank-you to book designer Ingrid Paulson for the beautiful cover creation, and her design work in general.

During the course of the writing, I was, as usual, tirelessly championed by my family—my father and siblings—and so, too, by Deborah Root, who encourages me daily to imagine I really do have something to say in my work. I can't be more grateful to have her in my life.

SHANI MOOTOO was born in Ireland, grew up in Trinidad, and lives in Canada. She holds an MA in English from the University of Guelph, writes fiction and poetry, and is a visual artist whose work has been exhibited locally and internationally. Mootoo's critically acclaimed novels include *Moving Forward Sideways Like a Crab*, *Valmiki's Daughter*, *He Drown She in the Sea*, and *Cereus Blooms at Night*. She is a recipient of the K.M. Hunter Artist Award, a Chalmers Arts Fellowship, and the James Duggins Mid-Career Novelist Award from the Lambda Literary Awards. Her work has been long- and shortlisted for the Scotiabank Giller Prize, the International Dublin Literary Award, and the Booker Prize. She lives in Prince Edward County, Ontario.

COLOPHON

Manufactured as the first edition of *Polar Vortex*
in the spring of 2020 by Book*hug Press

Edited for the press by Meg Storey
Copy edited by Stuart Ross
Type + design by Ingrid Paulson
Author photo by Ramesh Pooran

bookhugpress.ca